Han<

Producer & International Distributor
eBookPro Publishing
www.ebook-pro.com

Handle with Force
Uri Yahalom

Translation: Adi Cafri

Contact: yahalomuri@gmail.com
ISBN 9798539613266

HANDLE WITH FORCE

URI YAHALOM

1.

"It was our daughter who died, not me."

Amit gazed at her, trying to dredge up some deep-seated empathy. She looked back at him with empty, red eyes. A look both defiant and pleading.

Long, flowing hair, a narrow, pretty face. No, he paused. Not merely pretty. Beautiful. Truly beautiful. A small nose above a wide mouth that once knew the expression of joy.

She loves me, he told himself. *But what do I feel for her?* Trying to answer the question made the pit in his stomach grow. The follow-up question—*What am I even doing with her?*—he was wise enough not to ask. Not even himself.

They met in the summer, four-or-so years ago. Amit had just broken up with his girlfriend of the time, Michal.

It was at a concert of some obscure band in a Tel Aviv club. That wide mouth of hers smiled at him. Her eyes, which had been dark brown back then, did the rest. He was caught in her charms.

In front of her, she had seen a fit, six-foot-tall man with

dark-blondish hair. She never did manage to decide whether or not he was a blond or a redhead. Still, what she found most attractive was the way he spoke. Or, more accurately, the way he *didn't*. He didn't work hard at hitting on her like all the others, he simply stared at her silently with a distant gaze.

She'd recently finished her degree in speech therapy at the university, passed her finals, and had already found a clinic to work in. She was still contemplating whether or not to continue her studies for a master's degree.

Amit had recently returned from Nice, France, where he had been for a few years. He had left Israel almost straight out of his army service. There were many more like him, graduates of *Sayeret Matcal*—the Israeli elite forces—who found their way to Nice to work security. They had all been soldier-fighters, not officers. Amit had been an officer—a team commander. Officers had more attractive opportunities once they completed their service. Amit, though, had needed to leave the country. To flee. He hadn't had the mental capacity to deal with all that had happened back then.

In his final year in Nice, he had met Michelle—Michal—a daughter of former Israelis who worked in Monaco at options trading, or something of the sort. Amit had never understood, exactly. Perhaps if he had, he would have managed to avoid the comment that had made Michal kick him to the curb after a passionate year together.

Amit returned to Israel and met her a month later.

"You're looking straight through me," she pulled him out

of his musings to the here and now. "I'm right here—say something!"

Amit wanted to. But he didn't know what. All he could think of seemed completely inappropriate. It would all lead to a discussion regarding his shortcomings. Or it would start yet another fight.

He knew what she was thinking. The things she didn't say. She didn't accuse him of thinking of Michal—not because she thought he wasn't, but because she was worried he would affirm her suspicions.

Those two months after they met each other, they had been inseparable. Two months of sensations too insane to name. But then Michal came to Israel, called him, and asked to meet. She then apologized, telling him she wanted to get back together.

Amit had contemplated staying with her or getting back with Michal, who had so suddenly reappeared in his life. Eventually, he decided that despite the whirlwind romance, despite the perfect storm he'd experienced with her, he would get back together with Michal. All that was left had been to tell her he would be leaving her. A harsh, cruel thing, but he had to do it. When he came to her, ready to tell her of his decision, she hadn't even registered his emotions, and instead stood there glowing, excited and expectant. Her whole body sang.

He knew before she said a word. He was about to become a father.

So, there he was, Amit Koren, at the age of twenty-seven, without a job or degree, and with most all of his friends still single, about to settle down. Amit asked his older brother Yair, the only family he had left, for advice, but in the end, made the opposite decision. It had also been the opposite of his own initial decision.

Amit chose her and told Michal "no."

Though they moved in together, they never married. There had been no pressure to do so from her family, and Amit had no family of his own to speak of. Though they behaved like a married couple, an official document was never signed.

Amit found a job working in a security company, dealing mostly with advising and building security teams. Every once in a while, he'd accompany a Russian oligarch who came to Israel with a young woman who wore a diamond necklace or wristwatch that was worth the equivalence of a three-bedroom apartment.

It was most likely already there, hidden beneath the surface, waiting for the opportunity to emerge. But it waited patiently until after the birth. Amit asked himself what he was doing with her. He asked himself often if he still loved her. Had he ever? He would answer that he probably had. *Probably*. Though he wasn't sure if it was enough to keep him around. One look at her growing belly, however, gave him a clear-cut answer, and that warmed his soul.

The birth itself he remembers as an experience that started with massive excitement and high spirits and ended with a deep devastation and a shattering that could never be mended.

He vaguely remembers how he was taken out of the birthing

room, —the way a doctor ran into the room from down the hallway. Mostly he remembers the silence —the doctors' and nurses' faces. Her face.

He'd asked to see his daughter, even if only once, but the medical personnel wouldn't allow it.

He apparently had no real reason to stay with her. The little he spoke before the birth dwindled even more after it. She, he knew, clung to him as her last anchor to reality. And that, he admitted to himself in a moment of rare, honest self-reflection, was the main reason he would never leave her.

"Why are you doing this to me?" she added as her eyes filled with tears. "If you want to go—then leave. I won't keep you here by force. Don't stay only for the sake of our daughter, embarrassing me like this."

"Embarrassing you?" *What the hell does she want?*

"You were in Nice and met Michal." It wasn't a question.

"What are you on about? I wasn't in Nice. What makes you say that?" he asked.

It happened to be the truth. He really hadn't been to Nice. But he *had* met with Michal. As a security expert, he traveled the world quite a bit. His favorite place to visit was Barcelona, which he used to go to every now and then when he still lived in Nice. Last week, he also made a pitstop there. After all, he wouldn't give up the opportunity to watch a football match. Before arriving, he called Michal and invited her along.

"There are many things I could say about you, but I never thought I'd find you so cruel." Her voice rose. "Something must have changed. Did you decide you wanted to get back together with her, so instead of telling me like a man, you figured you'd simply humiliate me? If you want to go—*leave!*"

He looked at her, unable to hide his surprise. He could see a determination in her eyes that had never been there before. He had no idea what was going on.

"What on earth are you talking about?"

"Oh, please," she said and showed him her cellphone. Her Facebook page was open. On his wall. *His.* His last post clearly showed him and Michal sitting in a coffee shop, the intimacy hanging around them undeniable. The picture may have been in Barcelona, but the status stated *Having the time of our lives in Nice.*

He had no doubt that the picture would forever change their relationship. That seemed to be inevitable. But it also wasn't what bothered him so much. No, that was something completely different. Not only had he been photographed abroad without his knowledge, but that same someone also posted it on his wall. He was a security expert. His privacy settings on Facebook wouldn't allow anyone to write on his wall—not even his friends.

2.

Daniel Rozen looked at the phone resting on his desk. A stubborn red light kept blinking at him. *Does it have to be now— with everything else going on? All I want is not to be surprised tomorrow...*

It was a form of control Daniel had never found appealing. Perhaps it was time to call it in, he contemplated, but finally decided it was too early. Right. When the Director of the Mossad summoned you, you came.

He got up, practically forcing himself from his chair, and left the office. A long hallway, covered in a thick, faded carpet, separated his department from that of the Director of the Mossad's headquarters. A minute later, he walked into the chambers and smiled at Ortal, the Director's secretary. She smiled back.

Who was it who really ran the Mossad? Daniel mused jokingly. Was it Ortal or the actual Director himself? If he asked the man, he would, no doubt, answer that it was Ortal.

"Okay, he's waiting for you. You're not actually waiting for me to call you in, are you?" Ortal said simply and shot him a winning smile that both gave credit to what she said and kept everything casual. She always had a smile on her face—even when she clubbed you over the head with a hammer.

Daniel opened the Director's door and walked in.

"The head of Michmoret,[1] in the flesh," the Director greeted.

"How's it going?" Daniel asked with a quirk of his lips.

"It's all good. All good," the Director replied. "What's going on, then? You tell me. Where do we stand? You know me, don't you? I don't want to hear your report for the first time when we're with everyone during the meeting tomorrow. Give me the highlights."

Daniel was itching to get back to his office. It wasn't that he felt uncomfortable with the Director, but that loose thread waiting for him took precedence. Well, there was no way he could return before completing this ritual. It was better to simply get it over with.

"We'll be starting up close," he began. "The communications we intercepted in Sinai show that, different from our initial assessment, the Bedouin tribes are resisting ISIS taking control. They're fighting back. It's not only a matter of money, it's a long-term strategy, and that means the Bedouins see ISIS as nothing more than a transitory presence in the area.

"And in Lebanon…"

The Director pulled out a box of cigars and offered one to Daniel, a Cheshire cat smile on his face. This, too, was part of

---

1   A village along the Mediterranean coast of Israel; *also*, a fishing boat's net.

the ritual. Daniel had never smoked, and the Director knew that well.

"I have to be polite," the Director said, as if sharing a juicy secret.

"That's you in a nutshell," Daniel goaded.

The Director laughed and lit the cigar.

Danial watched him. The man was sitting behind a relatively small desk, in a far-from-large room. One would expect someone who held such a job to have more space. A lot more. In the corner, there was an oval table twice the size of the desk. It's where the shorter meetings took place. The Director always had one-on-one meetings from behind his desk.

The wall directly behind him was marred by a window with a dark curtain that remained closed at all times. The other walls, however, were almost completely bare. No pictures, flags, or patriotic symbols to be found. There was a world map on one side, and a smudged whiteboard on the other. In front of the oval table was a projector screen, though Daniel knew the Director abhorred presentations and preferred using the whiteboard almost exclusively. A bright light gave the whole room an undeniable warmth. Something that stood in true opposition to everything discussed here.

"Say," the Director asked once Daniel finished his briefing. "What do you think: is the Indian incident the same as what happened in Japan three years ago?"

Daniel remained silent for a moment, his gaze fixed on the table and then on the upper corner of the ceiling as he contemplated his answer. "Honestly, I thought it was exactly the same, at first, but the more I think about it... no. I don't think so. India isn't Japan. The Chinese can't get away with doing whatever they want there."

"The Chinese still don't know we were the ones who screwed it up for them," the Director said, a smile playing across his mouth.

"Neither do the Japanese," Daniel added with no small amount of satisfaction.

"No, they don't, do they?" The Director laughed again. "We saved the Japanese's asses and didn't even get a thank you for our troubles."

"Well, that's always true, isn't it? We save everyone's asses and get no thanks for it. Even the *Shabak*[2] gets more appreciation."

"You're not going to whine about it now, I hope."

"God, no." It was Daniel's turn to laugh. "Anything else? I still have to finish the official report for tomorrow."

"No, thank you. Go on, back to work."

Daniel rose and headed to the door.

"Oh, Daniel," the Director said. Daniel stopped, turning back in his direction. "There is one more thing." The Director kept watching him without a word for a long moment. "Tell me," he continued slowly. "What's his name... Jamil?"

Daniel didn't respond.

"Or is it Eliad?"

---

2   The **Israeli Security Agency** (ISA) is the leading homeland security of the country, akin to the FBI and the MI5.

Daniel's blood froze in his veins at hearing the name.

It couldn't be.

"How do I know, huh?" The Director of the Mossad scrutinized Daniel with a dark stare. Daniel didn't blink, but he couldn't hide his shock. Not completely. And not from a man like the Director.

"What did you think, that you could hide this from me? Come on, now… I'm the Director of Mossad. It's my job to find these things out, isn't it?"

Daniel could have sworn he saw a glimmer of a smile from the man. A little gloating shining through. Satisfaction at having caught him unaware. It was gone in an instant.

"I wanted to…" Daniel tried to find the right words.

"Protect me?" the Director offered. "Are you a child? A politician? What's this bullshit? The prime minister's orders were clear. We're dropping it."

Daniel Rozen, head of the Michmoret unit of the Mossad, stood in front of the Director, feeling as though he were little more than a chastised schoolboy at the principal's office. He had no words. This was a decision that could either grant a commendation for heroic bravery or demote him to little more than nothing. A commendation, now, seemed completely out of the question. Whatever would come next, Daniel could take a guess.

"The next thing you're going to do when you leave this office is send Eliad an abort mission directive. That will also be the last thing you'll do. You can pack up what you like, but then you're out of here."

He didn't say I wouldn't return, Daniel said to himself as he walked out, but he knew that was what would happen. If he was lucky.

Ortal looked at him. She wasn't smiling. She tried to hide it, but couldn't quite manage it—she was surprised, even had a little moisture in the corner of her eye.

If he was lucky, he thought to himself. *If he was lucky.*

The look from Ortal didn't bode well.

3.

He felt his way over the warm body. The darkness of the room swallowed up his smile once he found his mark. He reached downwards, his fingers playing across the surface, trying to find the cavity. When he finally found it, he kept the fingers of his left hand on the opening while palming it with his right. He carefully slid the tip of the charge into the small space.

The charge exploded into action in the host's body, making its fast pace toward its destination. He felt the vibration in his hand—the sign he needed to know the target was achieved. It had taken an age—almost two hundred milliseconds—for the takeover to be completed. His hand hadn't even left the USB device, and the computer was already under his control.

And this was only the first stage. There were three more left.

All that remained for the first stage to be complete was to restart the computer, something that was already underway.

Eliad waited patiently for the computer to finish its reboot. Muffled footsteps could be heard from outside, though it was nothing that sounded dangerous. Even if they entered the room, they wouldn't find him. The true challenge had never been about getting to where he currently was: it was keeping his actions with the computer completely under wraps.

Perhaps that sounded less worthwhile, but it was of the utmost importance. Half of the operation's resources were directed only to that: they had to find the computer that was both farthest away and yet still connected to the relevant network. If the computer really was connected, he would find out in a matter of moments. The important question was how fast the Iranians would figure out what was going on and close in on him.

His program was designed to be as hard to detect as possible, but stealing thirty-four Terabytes couldn't go completely unobserved. The question was, then, "when" and not "if" it would happen. Eliad hoped he would no longer be in Tehran when it happened.

The computer finished its restart, completing the second stage.

Now came the main part. The actual computer with the hostile program meant nothing. It was a computer connected to an outer network, and the protections the network had were relatively weak. It was why taking over this computer was hardly any work at all. The challenge lay, instead, with the impenetrable layers of defense separating it from the inner network that held the coveted information. To penetrate it, it had to jump over it. As Eliad kept thinking things through, the program already put it all into motion.

The action was simple, all things considered. The program

sent out an e-mail to a false account from the outer network. The trick was, the sender's address was one of the inner network computers. Since the address is false, the e-mail is returned, but not to the outer network computer, rather, to the inner one.

He felt another vibration, the signal for the completion of the third stage. The program had taken over the inner network computer.

And now for the fourth stage. The data collection. This stage held the simplest code, but it took the longest time to complete. The inner computer was now his, so everything was accessible. There was nothing left but simple defenses and passwords. Nothing complex. Nothing Michmoret couldn't handle, and easily, besides.

Eliad may have been a part of the Michmoret team, but he had no real clue when it came to computers. He once made the mistake of asking, only to have one of the resident geniuses of Michmoret give him a serious answer. It had been one sentence: "The whole world holds the assumption that P is different than the NP-Complete, but we not only proved that both are equal, we also developed an algorithm that actualizes a polynomial reduction from P to NP-Complete in the order of N^2logN."

Eliad hadn't understood a word of that sentence, and all he had managed to reply was, "Really?"

It seemed like geniuses didn't fully grasp the art of sarcasm, because even that got him a response: "Well, it's not exactly a polynomial reduction, it's still quantum computing, you know. But it's close enough."

"Sure," Eliad had muttered to himself under his breath and quickly learned not to ask again. He merely watched as the algorithm—or whatever it was—cracked each and every existing defense. Terrifying business.

Still, gathering thirty-four terabytes, which was the equivalent of thirty-four-million megabytes, took a while. Now, like dominoes, the defense mechanisms will start alerting the shifting of information from one network to the other. It would take them time to realize what was happening and, most importantly, as far as he was concerned, *where* it was happening, so they could respond.

Eliad found the whole ordeal incredibly ironic. Once upon a time, spies had to sneak into offices in the cover of darkness and take pictures of documents with microfilm. Digital photography, and the digital world and Internet as a whole, made that cliché completely redundant. What his colleagues back in Michmoret had managed to achieve was simply breaking into a computer from a distance and pulling the information through the Internet.

It sure did make things easier.

But then came the double networks, which forced an agent to reach the physical computer and insert a USB device. And, with all due respect to the Internet and progress, gathering thirty-four terabytes took time. A long, long time. It didn't matter how well you encrypted data between different channels, a transfer so big lit up red flags all over the world. In a matter of a fraction of a second, you'd not only be blocked, but found with plenty of Trojan horses to call your own as a diplomatic incident brewed under your nose.

The long and the short of it was that the only way to get that information was to pull out the physical USB device and bring it back the old fashioned way the same as with microfilm: by using the agent.

Eliad found a twofold sense of irony in that, as well as the bringing back of agents to the center of operations coming full circle, just as it had been during the Cold War. Also, ironically, the word irony sounded like *Iran*.

As he continued philosophizing to himself, the door opened. The program wasn't close to completion. They couldn't possibly have found out yet. He lay down under the table. The USB was a small protrusion. To see it, you had to get up close to the computer. It couldn't be removed until the transfer was through.

The light turned on.

There was the sound of footsteps from the other side of the room; a chair moving; a curse. It was nothing but a routine check. He hadn't been caught.

He pulled out his gun, but the silencer had gotten twisted in the shirt, which had gotten caught up underneath him. To release the shirt, he had to get up—something that would result in moving the chair and making noise. There was nothing for him to do but hope he would remain unnoticed.

Nothing I can do? he asked himself, and as if in answer,

remembered Tzukerman, the legendary instructor of the Caesarean cadets. Yeah—he'd grown up in Caesarea[3] before moving to Michmoret a year ago, as per Daniel's request.

"*Nothing you can do?*" he heard the roar of Tzukerman's voice in his mind.

Tzukerman would have never accepted an answer like that.

Once, when Tzukerman had asked him why he was "dead," Eliad had answered that there had been nothing he could do.

Seconds earlier, Tzukerman had closed Eliad in a small room, then thrown in a hand grenade. Eliad had stared at it, wondering what he could possibly do. Right when the grenade had exploded, he had decided he'd had no viable option.

It wasn't a live grenade; nothing but a training one that made noise when it exploded, but caused no damage. Otherwise, Eliad truly would have been dead.

When Tzukerman had asked why he had done nothing, he replied that there was nothing he *could have* done. Tzukerman had leveled his gray eyes at Eliad, who had remained practically paralyzed—though if it had been because of the grenade or that stare, he couldn't have said—then lectured, "There's always something you can do. Always!"

"What?" he'd asked.

"Screw off the detonator," Tzukerman had shot back, and left.

He heard the chair move again—closer this time. Eliad held his breath.

---

3   A division in the Mossad in charge of special missions.

Only then did he realize that while he'd been thinking about Tzukerman, he had managed to disconnect the silencer from the gun. He slowly pointed the gun toward the approaching guard with one hand, while the other worked on disentangling the silencer from the shirt then screwing it back on. Merely a second later, he was ready.

The guard turned back toward the door, turned off the light, then left.

Eliad breathed freely again.

During the next half hour, nothing special happened. Then, the device vibrated for the final time. The information had been gathered.

Eliad looked at the device before pulling it out. Pressing a hidden button made a light appear. *Green.*

Eliad pulled it out then extracted, very carefully, a tiny two-millimeter-by-two-millimeter chip. *Microfilm,* he scoffed to himself. The shining invention from the country that invented the flash—a plastic chip smaller than a fingernail that held thirty-four terabytes of information.

He'd get rid of the actual device later. He safely hid the chip in a plastic encasing that was only slightly bigger than the chip itself, then made his way to the door. He listened for a tense moment but heard nothing. He opened the door and walked out.

He looked to the left and saw nothing.

He looked to the right and found the muzzle of a gun ten centimeters from his face.

4.

Two sticks of margarine. That's all Roni had echoing through her mind. *Two sticks of margarine!*

She wanted to die.

Where were they? she kept asking herself as she beat herself mercilessly.

Not in her belly—luckily, but not her ass, either—to her dismay. She might have gotten away with it if it had gone there. She knew where those rogue margarine packets were. In her waistline. Fighting to destroy her perfect hourglass figure.

The thoughts rushed through her head, tormenting her as she stood on the scales, staring without truly believing at the result shown.

She'd gained 400 grams.

It may not all be fat—but 400 grams! Good God. And less than an hour before she was due on the runway. How could this have happened? What had she been thinking?

I have to change my focus, she ordered herself. *Like in a game.* She had to eliminate all thoughts of her weight and think about how sexy she was. *I'll be on the runway in a matter of minutes.*

It wasn't like she'd actually eaten those two sticks of margarine, and it was only 400 grams. It had to be water weight. Muscle, maybe. The remnants of her last meal, she continued to try and convince herself. She was sure she was cheating, but she didn't have a choice. She had to think positively. Had to delete the stupid decision of getting on the scales before a runway show. She had to look her best there.

No, she stated to herself. It wasn't that she had to look good—she *already* looked good.

Natural blonde, flowing hair, light blue eyes, a pointed, button-like nose, and a small mouth with a killer smile. Though she was beautiful, her face wasn't the most impressive part of her body. It wasn't even her perfect hourglass-shaped figure, or her impressive 5'9 frame. No, it was her profile that put every average, red-blooded male to his knees and got her campaign after campaign. Her natural, perky, small breasts, her buttocks that pushed outwards, giving her that coveted S-shaped profile. That profile shot had become her ticket for worldwide recognition as she looked meekly down, peeking over her shoulder.

Happy with herself for forcing back positivity, she heard Inbar call her over.

"Are we up yet?" Roni asked her.

"Not yet, no. You've got a phone call, though," Inbar replied, handing Roni her cellphone.

"Thanks," she said, taking it. Inbar was the best. She was one of the few Roni allowed to take care of her phone. It may have been locked, but still.

Officially, Inbar was her makeup artist, but she was so much more than that, too. A good friend. A confidant. Someone she could trust in this jungle they called the world of fashion.

The call was from Eran. By the time she picked up, he'd already hung up on his end.

What was he calling for? He knew she was before a show. He usually only sent a few Whatsapp messages wishing her good luck. He never called. *Had something happened?*

"Why did he call and not text, like always?" Roni asked Inbar.

"I don't know." Inbar shrugged. "Maybe he simply misses you." She smiled.

Two sticks of margarine.

Roni pushed away the thought. Everything was *fine.*

Her boyfriend had called and she was stressing over it? What was wrong with her?

She had to stop with all this negativity.

She called Eran. All she needed was to hear his voice and it would all pass.

"Hi, babe, what's up?"

"How's my sexy girl?"

The margarine finally melted away.

"She misses you," she said.

"Good. Remember that with all those models hanging around there."

"Oh, quit it." She smiled to herself. "You know you have

nothing to worry about." She purposefully said it in a tone to make him worry. She liked how jealous he was sometimes.

"I don't, huh?" he asked.

Something sounded off. Something in his tone sounded wrong. Everything was the same, yet still... it wasn't.

"What's up, babe? What did you want? Me?"

"Obviously. When are you up?"

"In about half an hour. I think. I don't know. Inbar knows the exact time."

"Awesome, honey. Good luck, then. We'll talk after."

Awesome? It didn't sound awesome. Roni felt her worry grow.

"Eran, what's going on? Why did you call me?"

"To hear your voice and wish you good luck. What's wrong?"

"Eran!"

Silence.

She was getting annoyed. She could picture him, weighing his words, trying to find a way to say what he wanted in a way that was both dramatic and nonchalant. She could practically hear him talking to himself.

"Remind me, where are you now?" he asked.

"In Bucharest." *What did that have to do with anything?* "Why, Eran?"

The fashion show was supposed to start in only a few minutes at the opera house in Bucharest. Not in the actual hall, but in the lobby—on the first floor. Roni had no idea why someone would choose to have a runway show in an opera house of all places… but the pillars in the lobby were impressive, so she supposed it fit, in a way.

"And then?" he continued.

"Barcelona. Come on, Eran, what's up with the twenty questions? What's going on? Why did you call?"

Another silence. A short one, this time.

"When was the last time you looked at Instagram?"

"Can't remember. Yesterday? Maybe this morning. Why? What's that got to do with anything?"

"Do you not look at the photos you post?"

Actually, she didn't. She used to but quickly grew tired of it. Besides, she wasn't even the one to post most of the pictures, her agent, Sean, took care of that. She'd checked those first few times he'd posted but stopped soon after. She trusted him.

So, what had happened on Instagram to make him want to call her? And be far from nice about it all, too? Sean wouldn't dream of uploading unflattering pictures, and he definitely didn't have any nudes—so what could have made Eran so mad?

"You know I don't," she replied. "Most of them are posted by Sean, anyway. What happened? Did he post something not modest enough?"

"No. No, that's not it. Just take a look. Talk to me after. Remind me—where will you be going after Bucharest?"

He hung up.

Wow. That was really unlike him. And why the sudden interest in where she was going?

Roni opened her Instagram.

Sean had posted a photo from her last campaign: a Spanish lingerie company that had fallen in love with her. Or with her looks, at least. There was another model in the picture with her, a Barcelona football defender. Though no one would say that the photo was "modest"—it was a lingerie shoot, after all—it still wasn't risqué. Quite the opposite. She'd even call it sweet.

Roni felt an undeniable warmth when looking at the defender. Working with him had been fun. It was difficult to curve the smile at the rising memories.

Still, she was no closer to understanding what had ticked Eran off so badly. The photo truly was sweet. Innocent. Not rude or vulgar in the least.

Then, she looked at the comments and instantly felt ill.

Roni had learned the lesson about reading the comment section a long time ago. Though they were usually kind and flattering, oftentimes someone who'd suffered a breakup, or who was jealous, or who simply wanted to spew the darkest parts of their soul at her, wrote there, too. And it always seemed that her attention zeroed in on that particular comment. So, really, why bother? Not reading any comments was a better and safer decision.

The few times she did look, was when someone pointed her attention to something specific. Like now, with Eran. And it wasn't merely one mean comment. They all were.

If she could sum up the total comment section in a word, it would be "whore."

There was always one comment to start it all off, Roni knew.

She swiped up, ignoring the mounds of scum on the feed, looking.

The comment wasn't exceptionally vulgar, and perhaps that's what made it so cruel.

No, it couldn't be. She was barely breathing.

She sat down heavily on the chair next to her.

Remind me, where will you be going...? Eran's voice echoed in her head.

5.

"Hi, what's up?"

Yair was in the middle of a meeting. He'd seen that the call was from Amit, so he'd answered. He'd intended to quickly say that he couldn't talk, but merely hearing Amit's tone of voice in those few words made it clear hanging up wasn't about to happen soon.

"Hang on, I'm in the middle of something. Let me finish this and I'll call you back."

"Sure."

Yair hung up. He looked back at the directors. They were all looking at him questioningly. They'd heard what he said and probably didn't understand. Yosi was the one to voice what was most likely on everyone's minds. "What are you planning on finishing up? The conversation or the meeting?"

Yair remained silent for a moment. "I'm sorry," he said as everyone gathered their laptops and papers and left the room. "I really have to take this call."

"What are you apologizing for?" Yoni tried to cheer him

up on his way out. "The fewer meetings, the more time they have to work." Yoni laughed, but he was serious and probably right. This meeting truly had been something they could have avoided all around.

I'm only excusing my bad behavior, a little voice in his head said, but Amit came first. Which meant that... well, that would surely come up in the conversation.

Yair watched the last of the managers leave the boardroom. *His* boardroom. His company.

He wasn't quite the owner anymore, but he was still the founder. The company, headed by him. had been one of the first to recognize the potential of the Internet cloud services. It quickly grew, building itself from the ground up, and became highly profitable. There was no great exit, nor was there a foreseeable IPO, only some investments that had severely limited his hold on the company. During the final investment round, which had been... seven years ago—God, how time flies—the company finally made a profit. Since, it had even become *highly* profitable. Not enough to be sold off, but enough to hire almost 150 employees and have them make good salaries.

Amit first. He made the call.

"Hi, what's up?"

"You sound like a broken record. What's up with you?"

"Nothing. Everything is great," Amit replied.

"Sure." Yair grunted. "Sounds like it, too."

"I really don't know if it's a good or bad thing."

"Why don't you tell me and let me decide, then?" Yair offered.

"I don't even know where to begin."

"Like you always do—from the end, then slowly make your way backward."

"Okay," he agreed. "So, I think this is it. We broke up. This time for real."

Yair was silent.

"So… nothing to say?" Amit asked him, sounding more than a little annoyed.

"You know what I think," he said. "I know you feel like shit now, and I'm sorry for that. But I can't say it isn't for the best."

Yair sighed. His heart went out to his little brother, but Yair's head was already working three steps ahead. Their relationship had been strong even before their parents both died in a car accident, and it only grew stronger from then on. Yair saw Amit as both a brother and a son. He'd practically raised him, after all.

Amit, though he had a vastly different personality than Yair, followed him all the same. Yair's life went by the books: graduating high school; going through *Sayeret Matcal*—the Elite Forces—in the army and finishing as an officer; completing a BA and MA in business; building a successful company; having the perfect family with a loving wife and three children. He even had a short amount of time serving in the Mossad somewhere in his resume.

Amit, though, handled himself differently. He indeed served in the same unit in the army as Yair had, and even made his way through to team leader, but on a more personal level, he never seemed to truly find his feet. He even left the army under unflattering circumstances. No one had told him he'd had to leave—he'd made the decision himself. Officially, he was still on reserve, but he hadn't been called up even once.

Amit still says he did the right thing, but that wasn't the conclusion written in the final report of the investigation. Yair was sure Amit had acted as he should have during that incident, but he'd been torn between that knowledge and his obligation to the system.

Fortunately, the commander didn't put him in a situation where he needed to make the decision of where his loyalties lay. Amit left the country for Nice, where he met Michal, who started this whole mess he was in today.

Even so, Yair's opinion regarding Amit and Michal's relationship was positive. He'd attributed their last fight to that of the "big blowout" before a proposal. The relationship Amit was in now… well, he'd been against that one from the start. And he'd stayed consistent with his opinion. He believed that Amit should be with Michal, not with the woman who'd almost become the mother of his daughter. He figured if their relationship would end, it would be best for all parties involved. So, with all the pain he felt regarding Amit, it was hard to say he was sorry for the way things had gone down.

Yair figured that their conversation would start with his little act. He assumed that Amit would be onto him rather quickly, and if he wouldn't, then Yair would tell him. Either way, Amit was going to lash out at him. Still, Yair was sure it was for the best.

"There are a few things to hash out here," Amit said. "First, the fact that we broke up, then how we broke up, and finally a security breach I can't figure out."

"Yes?"

"'Yes,' what?"

"Go on, I'm listening."

"That's it. I don't know how to carry on. I started from the end, like you asked. What do you want from me now?"

"Okay, so you've broken up, and probably not in the most amicable way. I got that part. Add a few more details. And what's the security problem?"

"Two weeks ago I had a work trip to Germany."

"Right."

"I came back through Barcelona."

"What was it? The *Superclassico*?"

"Yup."

"Okay, so I feel like I'm losing you a little," Yair said.

"I invited Michal to come, too."

"To Barcelona?"

"Yeah."

"Well, Hallelujah for that. Maybe you're not a complete moron."

"She wasn't really interested in the game, but we sat at a café and spoke quite a bit."

"And...?"

"And nothing. That's it. We spoke—*only* spoke. I swear. I'm not that much of a jerk."

"No, that's not what I meant. You spoke in the café, and what? There should be some kind of security problem here or something. Some people actually have to work for a living, you know. Get to the point."

"Oh, shut up," Amit grumbled halfheartedly. "And we were photographed."

"Oh, the travesty." He huffed.

"That's not funny."

"Sorry, it is, though. That's not a security breach. It's not professional, it's personal. A private investigator that specializes in adultery. She got the photo of you and made a scene—rightfully, I should say—and dumped you. With all the sympathy I have for you, and, you know, even the sympathy I have for *her*, it's for the best. Start living already!"

"It's worse than that."

"What do you mean worse?"

"The picture—it was posted to my Facebook wall."

"So?"

"*So?* No one can write on my Facebook wall, not even friends."

"Are you planning on taking on Facebook then?"

"No. But there's something rotten here. Only I can post on my wall. And, seriously, spare me your jokes. It wasn't me who posted *Having the time of our lives in Nice*."

"So, someone used your username and password."

"No way. No one could have got it."

"You don't say… come on, Amit. Of course, they could.

What did Sherlock Holmes say? 'Once you eliminate the impossible, whatever remains, no matter how improbable, must be the truth.'"

"Stop fucking around. You're no Sherlock—what does he even have to do with this? You can't get my password. No one has it except you and me…"

Silence.

"You son of a bitch."

"A son of a bitch, indeed."

"And here you are, acting all high and mighty—the understanding, helpful older brother. 'Security breach,' 'people work here'—and you knew the whole time. *Knew*—you were the problem in the first place!" Amit fumed.

"I stopped an important meeting to take your call."

"Thanks so much for that, then. The truck carrying your medals is on its way."

Yair figured it would be best to hold his tongue.

"What were you thinking, for fuck's sake? I never asked for this screwed-up patronage. Who the hell gave you the right to ruin my life?"

"Hey, hang on a second," Yair cut in. "Let's keep this in proportion. The one screwing up his own life here is *you*. Not me. I was only trying to fix it for you."

Amit was quiet. gathering ammunition for his next attack.

"Okay," Yair carried on, "what I did might not have been the most moral or politically correct fix, but it was done with the intention of helping you, not to ruin your life. You're not going to like what I have to say to you, but I'm going to throw it out there anyway: you're a coward. You're scared of her—scared of yourself, too. Scared to live your life. You sneak around, meeting Michal behind her back, and why? You love her! Make the move already, you pussy!"

"Why like this, though?" Amit asked, most of his anger fading. "Why in a way that humiliates and hurts her? It's not her fault. That's just cruelty."

"Because nothing else *worked*. Truly, I have no better answer to give you. I've been trying to get you to wake the fuck up for ages, and it's like talking to a brick wall. So, yes. I poured some cold water over your head. Not my finest hour, and I'm sorry. I would have preferred to have made it more subtle, but this got the job done. And know: my conscience is clear. With how awful she must be feeling now, too, in the long run, it's what's best for her, as well. I honestly believe that."

Amit remained silent.

"I know you want to throttle me now," Yair said, "But in your heart, deep down, you know I'm right."

"How did you get the picture?"

"Come now, you can't think that was so complicated. Some-one from the Mossad did me a favor. I hate to say it—and I know you'll want to kill me over this as well—but they had two junior agents do it as a practice mission."

"You're an unbelievable bastard."

"You've got that right."

"So, what am I supposed to do now? I was meaning to—"

"Come stay with us?" Yair laughed.

"Right, like I have any other choice. Fine, bottom line—despite being an absolute shit, let Hadas know that I'll be coming over to stay at yours for a while."

"No, you're not."

"What? What's that supposed to mean?"

"You're not coming to us. Seriously—is that how you know your brother? Half-assing a job?"

"Half-assing…what? What are you… No. *Really*? You bought me a ticket to Nice."

It wasn't a question.

Yair only laughed in response.

"You're an asshole. A stubborn, obsessive shit who's even worse than me, and I've got no idea how I put up with you."

"I love you, too."

"Fine. Tell Hadas I'll be over to take a shower and change my clothes."

"Tell her yourself. You're not the boss of me. Besides, the three monsters are home today, so you've got a rough evening ahead of you." He smiled. "Your flight is tonight, so I'll be leaving here early to say goodbye."

"I can't believe I'm going to say this…"

"Say what?" Yair asked.

"Thank you."

Amit hung up.

6.

Holding the gun so close to my temple is a fatal mistake, Eliad thought to himself. But the thought rushed through his mind long after he moved. His body fell into action the moment he registered the muzzle of the gun. *The man is right-handed,* he quickly deduced, and that was why he shifted to the left—keeping away from the man's wrist. His center of mass followed the angle of his head, shifting left so he was on the guard's right side. At the same time, opposite his body's movements, his right hand rose in a half-circle to the right. It hit the guard's hand and pushed it to the right—away from Eliad. His fingers gripped the guard's wrist as his forefinger rested tightly between the gun's hammer and striker. His arm completed a full circle, angling the man's hand down and bending it backward.

The vague pain in his finger indicated that the gun had fired. His finger had taken the kickback from the hammer, so that it didn't complete the shot, though. The pain, however, did not stop him from breaking the man's shoulder joint. His right hand loosened its grip on the gun slightly, and it fell to the floor with the hammer closed.

His left hand quickly came up to cover the guard's mouth to muffle his shout of pain. Without breaking contact, he pulled the man's head to the right so it rested on his left side. Eliad shifted back to the right, as his left hand pushed the guard's jaw to the right. Eliad's right hand, now free of handling the gun, came up from the right to grip the back of the man's neck.

The power of your strike comes from your center of mass— your hips, Eliad heard Tzukerman's voice echo in his head. *In all Eastern fighting styles—karate, kung-fu, and even ballet—if you want to make a sharp, strong movement, you have to start it in your hips.*

Eliad shifted his hips, the movement traveling up until it reached his arms. His right hand pulled as the left gave a mighty push. The guard's head could do nothing but surrender to his ministrations, making a fast 180-degree turn.

There was a dull crack.

The guard's neck was broken.

In Caesarea, they called it the Frontal Sentry Removal.

From the moment Eliad had found the gun aimed at him to him snapping the guard's neck, no more than a second and a half had passed.

He let the guard's body, which was currently hanging from his arms, gently fall to the floor. The struggle had been almost completely silent. Eliad had even managed to stop the falling gun by angling his foot just right.

He looked down the hallway. Both sides. Then he opened

the door again and pulled the guard's body inside, hiding it behind a table at the far corner of the room. He slowly made his way out once again, this time more carefully.

There was no urgent shuffling, no quick footsteps or sounds out of the ordinary. He didn't think he had been made. Not yet. The unlucky guard most likely had nothing to do with him. He had merely been unfortunate enough to fall into Eliad's path.

Eliad, at that moment, felt nothing. The amount of adrenaline coursing through his veins made sure of that. But it would hit him—he knew. He may have been forged into the best soldier he could be in the halls of Caesarea, but actions such as the ones he just took did not come without a price.

Eliad stood for a moment at the entrance to the building, looking out to the street. Everything was calm. He exited and started walking.

The street was relatively busy, and Eliad quickly blended in with the masses. He reached his car and got in.

The ride to the airport, too, he knew, would be a non-issue. The challenge would be at the actual airport.

The drive took close to an hour due to the excessive traffic, and Eliad was starting to feelpanic. Despite the drive going smoothly, with each passing moment, the breach was closer to being discovered. The risk to his life grew.

He parked in the airport's parking lot. They would eventually find the car, but wouldn't be able to tie him to it in any effective way. It definitely wouldn't be connected to Israel. He made his slow way to the entrance.

Eliad had arrived in Tehran through a German airline, Lufthansa, and he intended to leave the same way. As he waited to check-in, he saw security guards huddled up close by. His first thought was that he'd been discovered, but he quickly dismissed it. After all, it made no sense. If he had been made, the whole airport would have been shut down, and dozens upon dozens of officers would have been dispatched.

No, this was something else.

Still, it was better to implement plan B than walk into the lion's den unaware.

Plan B included buying plane tickets to a European country. Any entry into a hostile country required an exit visa. Each purchase of a one-way ticket to such a country instantly brought up red flags. The ticket in Eliad's possession now was bought by one of the other agents of Michmoret, one who looked very much like him. He'd come into the country and then left in a different manner—non-aerially—and had left his passport and ticket for any European country of his choosing as the plan B exit strategy.

The ticket he had was for the Romanian airline Toram, thus leaving him the option of a flight ticket to Bucharest. Liftoff was in approximately an hour and a half.

Eliad approached the attendant at the reception desk and greeted her in German. Luckily, she knew German, too. He preferred not to talk in English.

The attendant looked at his ticket for a long moment. "Why aren't you flying Lufthansa?" she asked.

"Because Lufthansa isn't flying to Bucharest," he replied.

"And what business does a German have in Bucharest?" she pressed.

"Most Austrians work in Austria, but not all of them. Some of them work in Romania."

The attendant apologized and twenty minutes later, after going through passport control and the security, he already sat in the departure lounge. There was still an hour for him to kill. And it passed slowly.

Very slowly.

But that, too, reached an end, and he finally boarded the plane.

As Eliad sat in his assigned seat, and moments before the plane was set for liftoff, he felt a vibration on his thigh. His cellphone was a regular device, even considered old by certain standards, but it had been altered by the Michmoret team. The change was undetectable unless the device was sent to a special lab since the alteration was so minor: the addition of a longwave transmitter.

The longwave transmitter had three key elements: first, it could receive and transmit practically anywhere on Earth—even places without satellites. The long waves bounced from the atmosphere to the ground, then back again and again, thus making the wavelengths' ability to travel across vast distances possible. Second, they were weak, so detecting them was very difficult. And third was the price you paid for the first two points: the amount of information you could transmit through the waves was limited.

In fact, Michmoret transferred nothing but a number—a code of some sort—through the *Green Device*, as it was referred to. A simple program on the phone translated the number—the code—into a coherent message.

Eliad looked at the green phone and started to laugh. He'd received an abort mission order.

He had no way of replying, so the only thing he could rightly do was sit there and laugh at the irony. He looked around, thoroughly proud of himself, and soon after felt the plane rise up into the air.

As Eliad received his abort mission order, dozens of kilometers from him, another man received a very different directive. A junior analyst in the traffic monitoring division of the cyber command center of the Islamic Revolutionary Guard Corps was nervously standing in front of his commanding officer, struggling to find the words he needed to explain.

"Stop and breathe," the commanding officer said. "Give it to me in a sentence. What happened?"

"I can say with a seventy-eight percent certainty that we were hacked and that they successfully managed to steal information."

"And what are you basing this on?" the commanding officer demanded. "You found no clear break in or hacking signs."

"True, there were no signs, but we noted a massive amount of data collection—of *classified* information. That can only mean one thing."

"I don't think so," the commanding officer said. "Find me

proof that the system was hacked."

"But, sir—"

"Shut up. I can't get everyone up in arms over a *hunch*. Give me proof."

"Yes, sir."

The commanding officer of the traffic monitoring division of the cyber branch of the Revolutionary Guard Corps stood by his decision. On the one hand, he really couldn't get everyone fired up over information shifts. A break-in had to be proven before that was done. On the other hand, if he missed alerting a hacking attempt—or worse, a successful hack—it would spell his end.

The commanding officer decided to call the commander of Internet control, a close friend of his.

"Hi, how are you?"

"Hello, hello! What an honor."

"Look, I'm sorry for dropping this on you now, but we discovered a massive shift of information—without any break in signs. It looks suspicious, but we don't know if we should alert the upper levels of command. What do you think?"

"When you say massive, how big are we talking?"

The commanding officer lowered the receiver and asked the data analyst, "How much info was moved?"

"I can't tell you exactly, but more than twenty terabytes. Maybe even thirty."

"Between twenty and thirty tera," the commanding officer repeated.

"Holy— That's definitely a security breach," the Internet control overseer said. "Get everyone on it—now! I'm shutting off the Internet. Tell me what's going on."

The commanding officer of the traffic monitoring division hung up; the blood drained from his face.

"You're staying here—right here with me—and you're not going anywhere," he yelled at the data analyst.

"Yes, sir." Then, a little more quietly, added, "But... sir, there's another thing."

The commander was no longer paying attention. He took a deep breath and called the cyber command division of the Revolutionary Guard on the red phone.

"I need to speak to the commander," he said, his voice shaking.

"Yes," a deep voice finally answered.

"Sir, we have a serious indication of a security breach."

"I see. And your evidence regarding this... indication?"

"We found a large transfer of information. Between twenty and thirty tera. We immediately shut off the Internet, and now we are reporting to you."

"Closing it was the right call. Absolutely fantastic." The cyber commander gestured to his aides while continuing the conversation. "Tell me, why did you shut it off, though?"

"To prevent information leaking outside of the country."

"Ah, very good. Clever." *I am dealing with idiots,* he thought to himself. His aid handed him another red phone—the one that would connect him to the commander of the Revolutionary

Guards. He pulled away the receiver connecting him with the head of thetraffic monitoring division and gave his attention to the commander.

"Greetings, sir. I'm sorry to be the bearer of such news, but it seems we've suffered a breach. I suggest you close the borders then perhaps consider implementing 'Fox and Grapes.'"

"I see," the voice from the other end said gravely. "Keep me updated with each development."

"Of course, sir. I'm beginning the process now."

The call cut off and the cyber unit director turned to his aid. "Contact Internet control and have them re-connect the Internet immediately. When Baharam calls, have it directed straight to me."

"Baharam? Who is that?"

"You'll find out."

"Are you still there?" he spoke into the other red phone, directing his harsh words at the commanding officer of the traffic monitoring division.

"Yes, sir."

"Who discovered the breach?"

"A junior analyzer, sir. No one important."

"I see. Let me speak to him."

"Yes, sir."

The commanding officer of the traffic monitoring division turned to the system analyzer, explained to whom he was about to speak, and warned against embarrassing him. He also made it clear just who would suffer the consequences if he did.

"Sir?" the junior analyzer asked in a shaking voice.

"You were the one to recognize the data transfer?"

"Yes, sir."

"Go on, then. Give me the facts: how much information, to where was it transferred, and from where, how long? Everything you know and in as much detail as possible."

"Yes, sir. The data transfer was approximately thirty terabytes, possibly more. I'll be able to give you a more accurate number in half an hour. The information includes many subjects, but mainly concerns nuclear plans—including highly classified information. The gathering of the information was done through the inner network and it took approximately twenty minutes. My guess is that there is a point where it skipped over to the outer network, but that hasn't been discovered yet. We're working on it. The only thing I can say with any level of certainty is that the point of origin was here in Tehran. There has been no leak outside of the country, sir."

"Good. Yes, I don't believe there has been movement outside of the country. Tell me, if you'd been the one to steal the information, what would you do with it?"

"Upload it onto a hard disk and take it physically out of the country."

"How?"

"The fastest way possible. By plane. I'd hope that the breach would only be found after the plane took off."

"Yes, that's what I would do, too. Listen to me: you keep identifying every bit of information you can out of this breach.

As of this second, you report only to me. All the tools of the Cyber Command are at your disposal. I'm passing you over to my aid, he'll give you the additional information you need."

"Yes, sir."

"Remember—everything you find out, you report directly to me."

"Of course, sir."

The Cyber Command division's aid nodded at the director to indicate he'd understood his orders, and held out his hand to take the phone. As he did, he held out another device and simply said: "Baharam."

"What are you doing to me, man? Tell me this is a false alarm." Baharam's voice came through the other end.

"Sorry to disappoint, this is real. We're implementing 'Fox and Grapes.'"

A few minutes later saw Baharam up to speed. He took a deep breath and picked up the phone. After the cyber attack with the Stuxnet worm, he built a grand plan called "Fox and Grapes" which was made precisely for this scenario. He'd desperately hoped he would never have to use it, but was still well prepared if the situation indeed called for it. And this certainly did.

The most elite unit of the Revolutionary Guards was at his disposal—the crème de la crème. People both from inside Iran and overseas, exceptionally talented in a wide range of subjects: people from the logistics world who were practically capable of drawing water from stone, world-renown cyber experts, and agents who would be a significant boon to any country. Each of them had a small device that started to work once the codeword "Fox and Grapes" was sent through. Baharam dialed a number and the code was distributed.

Half an hour later, he already had all the information: what, how, and where it all happened, what was stolen, the dead security guard, and the flight the hacker took to leave the country.

Now, Baharam had the time to build the tactical headquarters. It was too late to stop the plane, but one of the agents would wait for him in the Bucharest airport, and the other agents would arrive soon after. But still, not before operation "Breadcrumbs" began.

7.

The music of UB40 enveloped her as she walked into her house. Her favorite music. Layla closed her eyes and gave herself over to it. A muffled sound came through from the kitchen. Steve was making dinner.

There was a single lit candle on the heavy wooden dining room table giving the cozy room a gentle aroma of lavender. Their place was a small, intimate flat in the heart of Antwerp, Belgium. The furniture was a little dated, but it still suited them perfectly.

Layla loved arriving home when Steve was already there. Arriving before him meant walking into an empty flat, arriving after him meant coming home.

Layla had lost her parents when she was young, and the feelings Steve gave her were of a home she'd never had before.

She wasn't born in Belgium, but had spent most of her adult years there, nonetheless. She'd met Steve a little over a year ago at a job function. All she'd told him at the time was that her job was boring and didn't elaborate much else. It must not have bothered Steve much since he never pried. To be honest, she was probably conning him just a little—and herself, too. Still, she assumed he was doing the same.

She had a heart-shaped face, hair as black as coal, and piercing green eyes. She was only 5'2, but her body was lithe, with cat-like flexibility. Steve, however, was 6'2, had Slavic features, and a slightly long, upturned nose, blond hair, and light brown eyes.

Meeting Steve had been a twofold surprise. First, she hadn't believed she'd been capable of falling in love—that she'd ever *allow* herself to fall in love after everything she'd been through. It had been shocking when it happened. Second, she was constantly surprised at how much and how fiercely she loved him. It was as if the falling-in-love stage had never ended. If asked, she'd say she was so fiercely in love with him that it was painful, and that it was more passionate than words could say.

It seemed that Steve felt similarly, which made their lives together full of burning heat. There were times when she asked herself whether her feelings for Steve would interfere with her work, and she fervently hoped she would never have to put that to the test—still, if asked, her answer would always be as blunt and fervent as could be.

Layla made her way to the kitchen and Steve smiled without turning to her. She couldn't see his face but knew he was smiling all the same. She crept silently behind him and plastered herself to his strong back, inhaling his distinct, comforting scent, hugging him with all her might. Her Steve.

He gasped in mock surprise, and she knew his smile grew even wider. She loosened her hold on him a little and he turned to her.

"Wow, I didn't hear you come in," he said, grinning down at her.

She raised her head and stretched so she could reach his face. He, in turn, bent and kissed her. She put her arms around his neck, letting him take her weight until her feet no longer touched the floor. She kissed him back, their tongues meeting, dancing together wildly. His hands grabbed her ass cheeks, grinding their hips so the flame between them burned hotter by the moment.

Long seconds later, she pulled away a little, her eyes closed and a smile of true happiness spread across her face.

Steve watched her, feeling like nothing less than the luckiest man alive.

She stayed as she was for a while, enjoying the closeness, before smoothly separating.

"What are you making us, love?" she asked.

"Nothing special," he replied, his eyes shining with mirth. The dreamy look he gave her was not far from that of a lovesick sixteen-year-old.

"I'm going to shower," she said and turned her back to him. His gaze remained glued to her behind as she walked away.

An almost imperceptible vibration from a small device in her belt stole her attention. She pulled off her belt as part of her disrobing ritual, stole a quick glance at the inner part of the belt, receiving the message. No muscle in her face revealed her tension, yet still, she was glad her back was to Steve.

For a moment she didn't know what to do, but her mind was made up practically before it even became conscious. She'd do anything for Steve, the love of her life.

She paused, spun back to face Steve, and said in a tone that spoke for itself: "Actually, I'm not going to shower."

In a quick, practiced move, she pulled off her pants, then stood in front of him, showing off the blackest-of-black triangle of hair between her legs.

Steve stared at her pubic area, entranced, before she ran at him and jumped.

She hung on to his neck again, kissing him as her legs wrapped around his waist. She gyrated against him, feeling desire pool in her lower belly until she was panting with need. Steve leaned against the kitchen counter, moaning with her movements. One of his hands raked through her hair, exposing the long column of her neck to his lips and teeth, while the other squeezed her ass so hard her breath caught in her chest. He worked his way down to her breasts and she purred with pleasure.

She didn't let him reach his mark, however. She slid down his body until she was kneeling in front of him. She pulled his pants and boxers down until they reached his ankles, then focused on his hard length.

She let the head of his cock brush against her lips as she tickled his low-hanging balls, and only when she heard his cut-off moan did she allow him to sink deep into her mouth. She sucked him noisily, allowing him to thrust to the back of her throat with increasing vigor. When he was squirming under her ministrations, she replaced her mouth with her hand. She pumped him fast to the counterpoint of her lips slowly trailing down his length until she'd expertly swallowed one of his balls, sucking it and tickling it with her tongue.

He was ready for her, she knew.

She rose and helped him tear off his shirt. She clung to his hairy chest, kissing him until she couldn't stand it anymore, and climbed back on him—her arms back around his neck and her knees momentarily on the counter for balance as he helped her out of her shirt.

She was so hot for him, the evidence of her arousal wet all the way down her thighs. She reached down and helped him find his mark, and then she finally—finally—slid down onto him.

They both sighed in pleasure as the familiar feeling of becoming one washed through them. She slipped out of her bra and started to move, small circles with her hips, at first, before need became too overwhelming for them to be gentle or slow. He pinched one of her nipples and directed it to his mouth, sucking hard then pressing his tongue in rough circles. When she moaned with an undeniable burst of ecstasy, she could feel his lips form a smug smile against her breast.

She directed his hand back to her ass, and he knew what she needed. Both of his palms now where she wanted them, he squeezed and gently pulled her cheeks apart, his fingertips brushing over her other hole, but not trying to work themselves in.

It felt like electricity running through her whole body—pleasure more potent than words. *God, I'm so close,* she thought, tightening her muscles and pulling a litany of curses and moans from Steve.

He was close, too.

The love of her life, the most important person to her in the whole world, was about to come inside her. She wanted to give him this, this last gift before she took everything else from him.

The loss of his rhythm and feeling him get impossibly harder inside of her let her know he was moments away from orgasm. She pushed her breast back into his mouth, then with her other hand took the knife he'd used to cut the vegetables for their dinner.

She slashed on an angle from his left jawline to the back of his head, the movement accompanied by a strangled cry from her own lips. She was coming, too.

The tip of the knife reached his brainstem, as planned, killing him instantly. The result was immediate. His body went slack and fell to the floor. Layla went with him, but remained standing, legs spread, over him. He lay on his back on the kitchen floor, his cock still hard, semen still leaking from the tip. Layla's body was still shaking with the pleasure of her orgasm, the pleasure still pulsing through where he'd been inside her mere moments ago.

It had all gone as planned except for them coming together. Layla hadn't planned on coming at all. The contractions from her pleasure had caused the knife to shift a little so that before it reached his brainstem, it also nicked his artery. Massive gushes of blood were spraying everywhere, reaching Layla's body and pooling on the kitchen floor.

A single, transparent drop fell from her eye, slid down her nose, then reached her lips. For a moment it clung to her as if suspended in time, but then it fell to the space between her breasts, slipping slowly down her body, down to her pubic hair, down between the lips of her vulva. It mixed with Steve's semen, turning pink with the residue of blood. The drop kept its course, falling down her thighs, and down…

So she stood over her beloved, sobbing helplessly. The knife remained in her hand, the tears kept falling, his cooling blood left on her chest. His semen didn't stop dripping down her thighs.

8.

The Tarom Airlines plane landed in Bucharest, however, Eliad knew that the danger was far from gone. He may not have been in Iran, but nor was he in Israel. Chances were that the Iranians had found the breach and had discovered him, too. The main question was whether or not they had the ability to send agents here, and just how good the agents were. Once again, time played in their favor rather than his.

The longer he stayed in Romania, the greater the chances of meeting Iranian operatives grew. The simple *kind* of information he'd stolen was enough to mean that they'd send anyone they could after him.

Eliad preferred to stay far away from them all.

He mentally laid out his options: The first, getting on a plane to Israel. The second, reaching the Israeli embassy. Any other option meant getting caught up in a surefire interaction with Iranian operatives.

Unfortunately, the option of catching a plane to Israel was impossible since there were simply no flights leaving from the airport. If he'd flown, as per the initial plan, to Germany, there'd have been a connection flight to Israel right as he'd landed and he would have had two agents from Michmoret waiting for him there, able to replicate the chip.

He'd not wanted to contact them and get them to Bucharest instead since the risk had seemed too high at the time. Still, they'd see he wasn't on the prearranged flight and arrive at Bucharest all the same. They would probably beat the Iranians here, too.

He momentarily contemplated reaching Israel by flying first to Paris, but ultimately decided the risk still too high. His flight would be marked instantly, and once he landed, there would be throngs of Iranian agents waiting for him. A flight out to Israel was out of the question.

So, plan B, yet again. He had to get to the embassy.

The chance of an Iranian agent waiting for him before passport control was low, but not entirely impossible. Eliad stayed alert, but no trouble awaited him there. The luggage claim added a whole other element of danger, however, especially since so few people had been on his flight.

The chance of an Iranian agent waiting at the baggage claim was much higher, and, most importantly, Eliad hadn't even flown out with any luggage. If he left the airport with no luggage, he'd be marked in seconds flat. If the agent sent through had any kind of experience, he would look for key behavioral elements rather than external queues. If the agent was shit at his job, on the other hand, he wouldn't even be a problem...

Eliad assumed he was good at his job. *It's better to anticipate your opponent being better than they are in actual fact,* he heard Tzukerman's voice in his mind.

Tzukerman, Tzukerman, he kept up the imaginary conversation with him. *What would you do in my shoes?* As it happens when you talk to yourself, he knew Tzukerman's answer before the imagined voice replied: *I'd meet the risks head on.*

Eliad could take someone else's luggage and leave the airport. It could work, though it very well could *not.* The biggest danger in this scenario was the fact that Eliad was a passive player, waiting only for the Iranian operative to make the first move while being incapable of striking first. If, assuming the agent had even a modicum of talent, the attack on his person could come from anywhere. The risk remained too high.

The other option, as per Tzukerman, was to initiate attacks. To "invite" the enemy to make a move when, in actual fact, Eliad would be ready. It was called initiating risks. By so doing, Eliad would make the attack come sooner, but it would be under his control.

The simplest way to kickstart an initial risk was to go to the restroom. The agent, if he'd already been marked, would follow him there.

Eliad passed the baggage carousel and feigned interest in when it would start. Then he fluidly made his way toward the restroom. He didn't notice anyone following him.

He leaned over the first sink in the row and turned the tap, pretending to wash his face while actually keeping his gaze firmly on the door.

He heard a muffled knock while someone bumped into him. But the door was closed, and no one had come in. It didn't make sense. *There no such thing as something not making sense!* Tzukerman's voice screamed at him in his mind.

Eliad changed his perspective of the door and noticed a small hole in the center.

The Iranian agent had shot him! *Through the door!* And he'd hit his back.

There went his hope for an untalented operative.

It wasn't more than a second since the shot, and Eliad knew he had no more than two or three seconds until the agent came in. He had to act, and quick. Eliad tore off his shirt and hung it on the sink counter, then leaped in the direction of the wall next to the door. *Change your standpoint!* Tzukerman shouted. He didn't have the time or ability to climb, so he lay down.

The change of standpoint meant switching the place the enemy would expect you to be—height-wise if not the location. Being at such a distinct disadvantage made your position one of the few things you could use as an asset. A talented agent could guess the places you'd be, but daily life was most often conducted at eye level. If you wanted that half-second advantage, never meet your enemy at eye level. Eliad had little hope of the agent being non-impressive anymore. He might even be very talented indeed. So, all he was asking for, was that half-second, and with all due respect to the Iranian agent, Eliad had been forged by fire in the halls of Caesarea—he knew how to fight, and how to fight well.

The door opened and closed after less than a beat. Two slight whistling sounds accompanied the movement, and broken ceramics shattering to the floor came right after. The agent was in and out—and managed to add two shots through Eliad's discarded shirt. He wasn't merely talented, he was excellent.

Without giving Eliad another moment to think things though, the agent came back in, spun in Eliad's direction, and fired another five shots. The shots were directed for his center mass, so narrowly missed his head.

The Iranian instantly corrected his shooting, but it was too late. Eliad had his half-second advantage.

He gave the agent's leg a vicious kick, causing him to lose his balance, spin, and land on Eliad with his back to him. The Iranian moved his head so he could keep Eliad in his focus and tried to align his gun to get another shot at him, but Eliad was faster. He avoided the flailing of the Iranian, getting both arms around the man's head. He swiveled his hips, the movement traveling up to his shoulders, and snapped the man's head in a 180 degree violent move.

The operative fell back on Eliad, dead before his body touched the floor.

A groan burst from Eliad at the dead weight hitting his diaphragm. He noticed a few splatters of blood on the man's head, which was odd. It took him a second to realize the reason for it. It was his blood—not the agent's—spewing from his mouth. His lung was punctured.

He rolled the agent off him and tried to get up. He could barely breathe. He looked down at his stomach and couldn't see an exit wouldn't. *Great. Hemothorax due to trauma.* First things first, though. He had to take care of the body, only then could he focus on himself. He dragged the Iranian into the farthest cubical, got in too, and locked the door.

He really couldn't breathe. There was no avoiding this— it had to be done *now.* Luckily, the agent had a knife. Eliad snatched it and quickly stuck it between his ribs, biting his lips to keep from screaming out in pain. A sound not unlike a balloon losing its air echoed around him. Air and bubbling blood came out of the incision, letting him breathe again.

One more test. With the placement of the wound, he had to worry about his lung being the least of his problems. He stood up and made himself pee. *Positive.* His urine was pinky-red. The bullet had hit his kidney. He had to receive medical attention. Now. This would kill him otherwise.

He fumbled over the bathroom stall, put on his shirt, hid the stolen gun, and looked at himself in the mirror. He looked a lot better than he felt.

He left the restroom and looked around the baggage claim area. No one had noticed a thing. There was no immediate threat to his person, but he was wounded badly. Getting on another flight would mean a death sentence. Going to a hospital would eventually mean the same. The agent who had attacked him had been a pro. The ones who had let him off his leash would only send more—many more—like him. The embassy was out of the question, too.

There was only one thing he could do now. A move far from anything logical, and nothing like what he'd been taught. It was the only way to stay ahead of the people hunting him. Naturally, he had no idea what to do.

He looked at one of the airport billboards and smiled. He walked out and did the one thing he thought he would never do—the one thing he was most definitely not allowed to do. He had no idea how much time he had left, so he didn't have much of a choice. He opened his Green Device application on his phone and pressed the button.

9.

"What happened?" Inbar asked, looking almost as pale as Roni did.

Roni sat down heavily, barely breathing. Endless scenarios rushed through her mind. In some, Eran dumped her; in others all her campaign deals revoked their contracts with her—and those were the better ones.

Inbar was clearly distressed at seeing Roni like this. Roni gave her her phone.

Inbar looked at it, noticing the Instagram picture. She scrolled through the comments. Someone had written: *by looking at that pose of theirs and the way they're looking at each other, they'd clearly just finished fucking.*

"Wow," Inbar covered her mouth with her hand, muffling her gasp. "You should probably delete it, right?"

"What's the point?" Roni said despairingly. "After all those comments? It would only double the media coverage. Besides, I couldn't care less about what they write there. What I care about is what Eran thinks, and if he told me to read the comments, it's all pointless."

"Do you think he knows?" Inbar asked.

"Knows what?"

"You know... that—"

"Don't make me strangle you. He doesn't know anything, because nothing happened. And if you say something that could make him or anyone else think otherwise, I don't know what I'll do."

"I didn't say anything. Not to anyone. Ever. I was only asking whether—"

"Enough. Stop it. It happened once, and even then only because I was drunk. It didn't mean anything and it won't happen again. If you kept your mouth shut about it next to Eran, then he doesn't know anything."

"Of course I haven't said anything!"

"He suspects, I'm sure, that's true. But he's a jealous guy and is suspicious about everything, so you can't really tell."

"But you'll be going to Barcelona from here," Inbar pressed.

"So?"

"So—so he must be freaking out."

"Come on. Big deal. They're not there, anyway."

"What? Who's not there?"

"The Barcelona team."

"What do you mean?"

"The players. They aren't in Barcelona. They're playing an away game."

"Oh."

Inbar kept silent for a moment but didn't look away from Roni. Roni's cheeks flushed. She'd only realized the significance of what she said once the words had left her mouth.

All right. Yes. It was true. There had been mad chemistry between her and the football player during that photoshoot. Now, she told herself it only happened because she'd been drunk, but she honestly hadn't drunk that much. She never did, after all. So, no. It hadn't been meaningless, and the worst part was that she didn't even feel too sorry about it.

She still didn't follow the Barcelona games, nor had she become a football fan overnight, God forbid. What she did was merely make sure that during the times she arrived at Barcelona, the players weren't there at the same time. It wasn't always within her control, but if possible, she preferred to keep herself out and away from temptation.

In her mind, that showed loyalty. At least, that's what she kept telling herself.

Besides, specifically with this—it even added up.

"Have you forgotten where the show will be there?"

"Oh, right." It seemed like Inbar calmed at that. "For a moment, I actually thought you started following sports news." She laughed uncomfortably.

"What's going on with the show?" With the Internet drama, she preferred to simply get on the runway.

"Just a couple more minutes. Here, let me check your makeup." She scrutinized her for a moment before giving Roni another smile. "No smudges. You look beautiful."

"Thanks." Roni smiled back. She needed the reassurance now.

As if by magic, as Inbar pulled away, one of the fashion designer's helpers called her in to get dressed. Inbar walked her in.

Fashion shows were usually boring. Roni was at that point in her career where she could dictate what she would and wouldn't wear. Sean also did a great job when it came to things like that. She could ask to showcase only one set, and designers still fought over having her. It wasn't that she didn't want to have more than one set, it was more that she *hated* the stressful behind-the-scenes changes. She preferred getting dressed for one set only, thus avoiding the millions of people getting underfoot and the general hysteria.

Being as she only did one set, designers usually used her for the finale, ending their show on a high note, if you will. She mostly avoided talking with the other models, conversing instead only with Inbar. Sean never went into the dressing area. He was very good at what he did, but there were red lines. All Roni had needed was one look when he had come in to ask her a question one time, for him never to make that particular mistake again.

The current fashion tour was not being held in the typical halls, which created a buzz with the viewers and made the overall experience quite impressive. The main runway in this show was in the lobby of the Romanian opera house. It was surrounded by impressive columns and fantastic stairwells that were an architectural marvel. The models came up and down the stairs wearing the extravagant outfits, but watching them did nothing for Roni's nerves this time. She wouldn't even talk to Inbar as they waited. Luckily, Inbar was the kind of person who took the hint after merely one ignored comment. Roni kept thinking of Eran.

What was she really doing with him, anyway? Did she love him? She was quite sure she did. Being with him was fun, for the most part. He was an easy-going guy to be around. A little short-sighted, perhaps, but still funny. And the sex was good. That said, he was rather predictable, and their relationship lacked any kind of excitement. There were times when he tried too hard, as if he felt unworthy. It was those times when Roni abused it—not too much, but enough. She wasn't proud of it, but she couldn't stop.

It seemed that the most accurate answer was that she was simply comfortable. She saw no reason to make waves or any significant changes as long as it remained. Eran was, she figured, a man to have fun with. Not marry.

The designer called her in and Roni forced all thoughts apart from the show as far from her mind as possible. She had a show to put on.

And that was exactly what she did, and she did it well. She was radiant as she stood out there, milking the crowd for applause and compliments. At the end of the runway, she turned to flash her profile, lowered her gaze, and allowed the camera flashes and cries surround her.

She returned backstage before walking back out, hand in hand with the designer and all the other models.

It was finally over.

Sean met her as she walked out the dressing room, wearing her own clothes once again.

"Wow, you were incredible. Simply beautiful—gorgeous. And what a show! You made heads spin, sweetheart. You're the... what's wrong?"

The show was over, and so was the act. She was back to thinking about Instagram. And the margarine.

"Nothing, Sean. It's fine."

Inbar gestured to Sean from behind Roni's back to drop it.

Women's drama, Sean thought to himself. He'd been representing them long enough to know when to stay well away from their shit.

"Right, I see. I'm at your disposal, if you need me, though. Take a breather and we'll see what happens. You were wonderful tonight. You made me proud," he said.

"Thanks, Sean." Roni smiled at him. This whole mess was far from his fault. He did a good job, overall.

Roni felt claustrophobic, the walls were closing in on her—suffocating.

"I'm going out for some air," she said, not talking directly to either of them.

"You haven't started smoking again, have you?" Sean asked.

"No, Mother." She smiled at him. "I just want a bit of peace and quiet. Chill out, would you?"

"Sure. Inbar, go with her, please."

"No," Roni snapped. "Sorry, Inbar." She turned back to Sean. "Calm down. I'm in Bucharest, no more than a few steps away from the opera house and our hotel. Just take it easy, Christ... you're not actually my mother, you know. What's wrong with you?"

"I just worry, that's all. I'm sorry. Go on. Go have some air. Inbar and I will be here."

She did.

It was cool outside. The early hours of a spring night.

There was a small garden by the opera house, before the large parking lot behind it. On the right, she could see the Hilton hotel. She knew, down the corner of the street, was another hotel: the Radisson Blu. Most of the Israelis who came to Bucharest stayed in the Radisson because there was a casino there. The same reason Roni preferred the Hilton.

She took a deep breath and felt herself calm down a little. She would have liked to have been able to have left the show for a bit of air before, but, of course, she wouldn't have been able to. Still, better late than never.

Five minutes later, she figured she was as calm as she was going to get. She turned and started to walk back to the opera house. It was only two steps after that she felt someone's hand roughly cover her mouth. She tried to scream but to no avail. An arm snaked around her body in a vice. She couldn't move. She could barely *breathe*.

Then she felt them drag her into the bushes.

10.

In the Kirya Tower,[4] six floors below the ground, in a small room that was filled to the brim with electronics, one of the control boards' red lights blinked on. The screen next to it simply showed a name: Jamil. A muffled alarm accompanied it.

A sleepy soldier raised his gaze from the book he was reading—"Macro Economics"—and mumbled to himself, "That can't be right." The soldier had been serving for more than a year, most of it stuck in this particular, stagnant room. It was mind-numbing, but allowed him to study not only for the Psychometric aptitude test, but for his BA. He really couldn't complain much. Most of his unit preferred to work in the office outside, approximately 100 meters from the tower. He was happy in the small room.

Everything here dragged lazily by, with no more than one or two incidences popping up per hour. The most complicated occurrences required approximately 20 seconds of work. That

---

4   A skyscraper in Tel Aviv housing many military functions under one
     roof.

is, until this moment. During his whole service, he'd never seen a Red Alert. More so, neither had the solder who'd served here before him. However, the significance was clear, as was the required action.

He picked up the phone and quickly dialed the number. When the other side picked up, he said, "We received a Red Alert regarding Jamil." He listened for another moment, said something else, then hung up.

In an office not far from there, the director of the Mossad hung up the phone and whispered, "Fuck, oh fuck, oh fuck." He stared at the phone for another second before resting his head on his desk. He allowed himself a moment to bang his forehead against the wood a couple of times. He put his hands on the back of his neck, contemplating pulling his own hairs out.

He raised his head and pressed the intercom button.

Ortal's voice replied, "Yes?"

"Who do we have here from Saar's unit?"

There was nothing but silence as an answer.

"Ortal!"

"Umm, yes, sorry, what did you ask? I didn't quite catch that."

"Who do we have here from Saar's unit?"

"I… I think Avi is here."

"Call him. Now. Have him come in here at once."

The head of the Mossad heard heavy breathing on the other side.

"Ortal?"

"Yes, of course. I'm calling him now."

The Director closed the connection.

Three and a half minutes later, Avi came into his office.

"Listen," the Director started and quickly filled him in on what happened and what had to be done.

Thirty steps away, Daniel was busy packing his things. Twenty-three years of serving his country down the drain, about to be dishonorably discharged. And hopefully, it would only end in being fired. It was justified, of that, there was no question. But his decision had been the right one, too. If he had asked permission, he never would have received it.

Was being dishonorably discharged worth putting through this operation? Yes. No question about it. The only issue lay with where and at what stage Eliad had received the abort mission order. If everything had gone according to plan, the revoke had come in too late to be of any use. He didn't bother letting the Director know that particular detail. There was no point in that. He'd simply sent the code, no arguing. Everything else was in Eliad's hands.

More than he cared about his own fate, he worried for the operation. The crown action of his service. Eliad couldn't handle the Iranians all on his own. He needed help. And it seemed like he wouldn't be able to get any.

It was fair to say that Michmoret was Daniel's. It wasn't that there hadn't been a cyber division in the Mossad before, even if it hadn't been named as such back then, but it had only been at Daniel's insistence of combining the computer geeks and the operatives of Caesarea that truly built Michmoret. With all due respect to the hackers and intel personnel, to reach Stuxnet levels of success, someone had to physically reach the centrifuges. Daniel had supplied the perfect answer to that particular need and others like it, thus resulting in Michmoret. So, yes, Stuxnet was his baby. True, many of the algorithms of the code had been developed by Americans, but the pasting, the skipping between networks, the camouflaging... that was all Michmoret. Beyond the algorithms, the Americans only supplied the digital signature, which allowed for the initial deception.

As he was packing, Daniel heard the door slam open. He turned and saw Avi.

Saar's guys! The Mossad was sending Saar's guys after him.

"You don't waste time, do you?" he said in utter despair. *What was the Director thinking? That I'm such a security risk?* Was this truly how he would be repaid for over twenty years of service?

Avi didn't respond.

"Do you want to do it here or are we going somewhere secluded?"

"The Director wants you in his office now," Avi said rather than answering his question.

He's nuts, Daniel thought as he left his things on the table. Packing was meaningless now, anyway. He followed Avi down the long hallway.

When he reached the Director's office, Avi on his heels,

Ortal quickly averted her gaze. But she wasn't fast enough. Daniel still noticed her eyes were red.

He strode forward and entered the office.

The Director looked at him and shook his head. "What am I going to do with you, Daniel?"

"What's the problem? What do you want from me? Pity?"

"Oh, shut up." The Director looked at him and said, "We received a Red Alert from Eliad."

"*What*?" Daniel couldn't help but feel shocked at that. Eliad would never send in a Red Alert from Tehran, so that means that at least he got out. "Where from? Frankfort?"

"Bucharest."

"Plan B," Daniel mumbled to himself.

"What's the meaning of all this?" the Director pressed.

"The meaning is that everything I've worked for in the last three years is shot down the drain. That's what it means. That's why Avi is here, isn't it? To clean up for you?"

"Have you lost your mind, you idiot? Who do you think we are, the Stasi? You think I'd deploy one of Saar's men to take care of one of our own? That is so backwards I don't even have the words."

"Why is he here then?"

"Because all his other people are in Africa, and I figured someone had to be sent over to help Eliad. If I'm sending anyone, it's probably best to have someone who knows how to hit back, wouldn't you say?"

"And to torture me on the way."

The Director smiled. "I have no idea what you're talking about."

Daniel didn't play along.

"So, from what I understand," the Director changed the subject, "he failed to extract the information from Iran."

"The opposite, in fact. He managed to get it."

"So, him pressing the button—what does it mean?"

"If you really want to help him," Daniel ignored the question, "one of Saar's people isn't enough. You need to send the whole of Caesarea to Bucharest."

"But what does him pressing the button mean?" the Mossad's director asked again.

"It means he's dead," Daniel replied.

11.

"Just so you know, I was against this," Hadas said as he walked in and moved to hug him tightly. "But you know your brother. He's more stubborn than a mule and thinks he lives in a spy movie."

"He also knows me far too well," Amit added.

"Well, that's true, but the question isn't about the 'what,' it's also the 'how'. He's still got a lot to learn."

"He means well," Amit suddenly found himself defending his brother.

"That he does. But you know where that path leads." Hadas shot him a smile.

"*Amit!*" the happy shout from three little people sounded from down the hallway, followed quickly by them running toward him.

"At least he got three things right," Amit said, just as said "three things" jumped on him.

He made his slow trek to the living room with Shir, the eldest clinging to his waist, Dor, the middle child, hanging from his shoulder like a sack of potatoes, while the youngest, Gal, wrapped himself around his leg like a snake.

The next half hour, Amit didn't think of a thing other than hide-and-seek, catch, and a Greco-Roman style wrestling match. And he enjoyed every second of it. The house, however, looked like… like a house that had four children rough-playing in it for hours. Hadas, in the meantime, had managed to make dinner, tidy up some of the mess, and even draw up another sketch for one of her clients.

Amit loved being at Hadas and Yair's. He was always wanted there, no strings attached. It didn't even matter if he was in the middle of a fight with his brother. Hadas made sure to allow the brothers their freedom without giving up on the things that mattered to her, and Amit was well included. All that, and no judgment, besides. In a way, Hadas filled in that space his mother had left in his heart, so, really, there was no other truth than him knowing that their house was home.

After the stillbirth, when his partner had been as broken as he, when the two of them had been unable to find any form of solace with each other, Hadas had been the one to give him the strength he needed to get back on his feet.

Another man might have stewed in jealousy over Hadas and Yair managing to build a home with three children, but jealousy had never been one of Amit's vices. He loved his nephews fiercely, loved playing and staying with them.

"You're such a girl," Yair teased him about it, making him chuckle. Amit saw playing with them as nothing less than a win-win situation: fun all around, and no need to be the disciplinarian. Nothing but delighted joy.

After that half-hour came shower time. When they were done, dinner was ready and Yair was home. Amit became restless and impatient as they ate. Hadas and Yair obviously noticed, so they simply let him be. An hour later, he was finally on his way to the airport.

He called Michal a few times, but there had been no answer. He sent her a Whatsapp message, but it remained unseen. For a moment, he worried that she might be with someone else, but if their last conversation in Barcelona remained true, that was far from the truth. Perhaps she had simply gone to sleep, he calmed himself.

The plane landed in Nice a little past midnight, per France's time, and by the time he left the airport and arrived at her house, it was well on the way to 2:00 a.m.

He walked slowly down the narrow street. A few years back, Michal's parents moved to Paris and left their daughter their home in Nice. She'd insisted she wanted to stay in the city and paint. That's what it was like to have rich parents, though. There was no real reason to work.

The neighborhood wasn't particularly high-class, and the houses were relatively small, but the place was quiet and picturesque, close to the center of town, so overall, an attractive location.

The sound of the Mediterranean Sea could be heard, despite it being rather far away, the salt in the air ever present. The bustle of the city didn't reach this place, so at such an hour, the neighborhood was completely silent.

The front of the house was painted different shades of gray. The yellow streetlights gave it a faded, mustard color.

Michal still wasn't answering. He called her house phone but only got an angrysounding busy tone. It seemed that the receiver hadn't been put back to the cradle properly. He opened the gate to its slight screech and walked into the front yard.

The house door was locked. He knocked lightly so as not to disturb the neighbors, but there was no answer. The bell was broken, he knew, but he tried it anyway. Unsurprisingly, it did not work.

Right, he said to himself. *This won't be the first time I do this.* He took a few steps back, rounded the protruding window of the dining area, then climbed the narrow space between the supporting beam and gutter. A minute later, he was outside Michal's window. He pressed against the side of the glass to open the latch. The tricky part was not falling off. It was only three meters, but still—a fall from that height would be unpleasant.

Two tries later, the window gave in to his mechanisms and opened. He leaned back a little, opened the window, and climbed in.

It was empty.

Of course, Michal didn't actually sleep in this bedroom anymore. She'd moved into the master bedroom.

Amit slowly made his way down the second-floor hallway

and opened the door where he knew she would be. His heart swelled with love as he lay eyes on her.

She was curled up in bed, facing the wall, her dark, wavy hair covered almost half of her body. The moonlight came in diagonal beams and reflected on the wall opposite her.

"Sleeping…" he whispered to himself.

He lay down carefully next to her and gently stroked her body. Alarm bells shrilled inside his head. Something was wrong. Something was very, very wrong. For a moment he couldn't put his finger on what, but then it hit him.

She's cold.

He shot back and reached out to turn on the light.

He grabbed her and spun her to him. She stiffly rolled to her back. Her face was white as chalk and her eyes were glassed over, unseeing. The left side of her neck had a three-centimeter hole that still bled sluggishly. On the sheet, on the place where her head had rested, was a large, red stain.

12.

A few hours earlier, Guy David was excited. It may not have been clear by looking at him, but he was. The week before had seen him lead a group of Caesarean cadets to a highly impressive achievement. They'd broken through the final test of the *Midrasha*, the grueling training of the Mossad.

Who'd have thought possible... Him, of all people—with everything he'd been through, the place he'd come from, all his hardships—and he was such a success.

He could have easily been a part of the crime world. Easily.

Nir, his close friend from back then, had decided to join the crime organization that rules their neighborhood to this day. Nir was doing quite well for himself. Every once in a while, they would get together to catch up. At least regarding the things they could share. "Both sides," as Nir put it, laughing. Proud of himself.

"You could have done great with us, you know," Nir had told him last week.

Nir was a big guy, one who enjoyed eating. In fact, he liked consuming everything—food, women—and even those who didn't pay on time. Despite his stature, he was capable of moving surprisingly fast, as those who preferred to give up on his "protection services" quickly found out. The same way those who underestimated his round, friendly face did.

"I think I'm doing pretty well where I am," he'd replied. "Which do you think is better?"

"That's hardly fair," Nir had grumbled. "You—you could do really well with us. Me… I would never have managed with your people."

"How kind," he teased, but he knew Nir was right.

"Unlike me," Nir had continued, "Who is shit on the inside and looks like shit on the outside, you look like a good boy. Left-wing-do-gooder liberal. You can't tell by looking at you that your insides are just as shit as mine."

"You didn't answer though," he'd pressed. "What's better for *me*. Not you."

"Mossad—obviously, you idiot. You're our pride and joy. And I'm not even bullshitting you." He became serious. "Are you trying to milk compliments out of me, man?"

"Not at all, I… sometimes I just don't feel as sure that I—"

"You can't really be that stupid," Nir had grumbled at him. "Every single person in this neighborhood would kill to be in your shoes. What's going on, Guy? Do you think they're going to kick you out? Why are you pussying out on me now?"

"Kicking me out… that's off the table now," he'd said, smothering a smile.

"*What?* You son of a bitch! You graduated and you didn't even tell me? Such a shit. Come on, the next round is on me. And no pansy-ass beer, let me get you the good stuff."

Guy had looked at him with a pinched face.

"What? What's the problem, now? Talk to me, brother, what's bothering you?"

"You…"

"I, what?" Nir looked at him questioningly. Disbelieving and pitying at the same time.

"You fuck all the time."

"I what? Fuck? Of course I do. Why wouldn't I? What's that got to do with anything?" he'd paused for a moment, staring at Guy. Stupid, the man was not. "Shut the fuck up! Guy David, prom king and virgin eliminator isn't allowed out."

Guy had given him a bitter smile.

"I get you," Nir had said, grinning. "You've got a ten-inch, diamond-encrusted and gold-plated dick, and you're keeping it well hidden in your pants because you can't go waving it around the 'hood."

"Right."

Nir hadn't stopped laughing for five straight minutes.

Someone sat next to him and in a split second, he was pushed back into the here and now. He still had half an hour until the briefing, then an hour later he would be off for his first mission.

Fuck, it wasn't a simple someone who'd sat next to him. It was Shaked Yossef.

"What's up, Guy?"

"Good, good."

"You excited? Nervous?"

"No, why? Should I be?"

"Very nice. You always were an excellent liar."

Guy couldn't tell if Shaked was smiling or not.

Shaked Yossef, in the flesh, sitting next to him. He was slimly built—skeletal, some would say. He had a big head with ginger hair, or at least it had been ginger, once upon a time; now, it was more white. At least what was left of it. The top part of his head was bald, with only a sparse amount of hair surrounding it. Most men his age would have started shaving their heads, but Shaked had opted not to. It made him look much older than his years. Guy couldn't tell how old that would be. It could be anything between thirty-five and fifty. He had no way to tell. Perhaps he was even sixty.

Shaked looked like a man from the fringes of society. Someone who most likely walked around with a stolen supermarket cart and slept on park benches. Nothing about his appearance showed the man he truly was: a sophisticated killing machine. The best Israel had to offer. Maybe even the best in the world.

Rumors about his hit count shifted from somewhere in the thirties to over one-hundred. That was most probably far off, but it made him a legend all the same.

And there he was—next to him.

"You know why you managed to crack the final test?"

"I don't, actually," he replied, telling the truth. He had asked himself more than once how exactly he'd managed to do what he did, and had always come up with absolutely nothing.

"Because you think differently. You think like a criminal."

"Is that a compliment?"

"That depends." Shaked's brown eyes bore into him. "If we're talking about things like creativity, or freedom, or things as restraining as morality, it's an advantage. And it's also what made you get to where you did last week."

"But—"

"But the crime world acts according to a certain code of conduct. We don't. You still think by those codes, and that makes you vulnerable. When we realized that, it was already too late, and you made it. But if we'd have figured it out an hour sooner, you would have failed. In the real world, it's tough to accurately estimate the enemy. We're not talking about your trainers. We're talking real life. You can be dropped on someone who can read you, and that would be the end. You'd be done. Take me for example—I'd take you down no problem."

"Could you really? No way." Guy found himself laughing out loud.

Even Shaked laughed.

"Honestly. This is the real deal. You don't want to fail because your head grew too big to go through the door."

"It's not—" Guy started to say, but Shaked cut him off.

"Quit trying to pull the fake-ass humility. I know you know

my history. I grew up in Tevel,[5] not in Caesarea. I can read you like an open book. Besides, my head would have grown two sizes, too. You're smart. Make that switch in your mind. Force it to happen. We usually send off rookies to minor missions at first so they can build up some real experience. We don't have that luxury right now. I don't sit down to pass on my wisdom to just anyone, you know. So, pull yourself together, cut the shit."

"Is this what they say to everyone before they are deployed for their first mission? To keep them on their toes?

Shaked looked at him. For a moment he seemed to be contemplating something, then said, "Sometimes. Other times, no, not really. And it's never given by me."

Shit. "What's going on in Bucharest?"

"I have my speculations, but we haven't been told anything. If they think you need to know, you'll be told."

Guy looked at Shaked and couldn't decide whether he was telling the truth or not. One thing was for sure, and that was that Shaked was involved in this. Shaked kept looking right back at him and said, "Yes, I'm going out there, too. But two hours later. I need you there. Do me a favor, and hang tight until then. Don't fuck it up."

It's not only because he needs me, he said to himself. *He cares.* He thought for a moment before saying, "You were against me going on this mission and they didn't listen." It wasn't a question.

---

5   A division in the Mossad that handles diplomatic and intelligence-based matters.

"Listen to me, you little shit," Shaked's answer was different than he expected. "The only reason you came to the conclusion I care about you at all is because I let you read me. You're not listening. You're predictable. Cut that shit out or it will get you killed."

Half an hour later, he was already on a flight to Sofia, and a couple of hours later he was in Bucharest. His orders were fairly simple: a triple report. The first report was due as soon as he landed. He did so. The next one required that he confirm with the Mossad station commander in Bucharest.

Guy took a taxi to the old city. He got off about 100 meters from the Old Church and walked from there. He was holding a map and looked like nothing more than one of the tourists who were milling about.

It was early evening at the end of the winter, and the locals were already home. It was only the tourist centers that were packed full of people. The dichotomy between the empty streets and the pubs and restaurants in the old city center gave off a magical atmosphere that Guy completely ignored. He had a mission to do.

Guy recognized the station commander from afar and closed the distance between them nonchalantly. They made the needed confirmation and Guy sent in the second report.

He'd been told they'd yet to receive orders from above, but knew there was some kind of trouble. They had to wait for later, for when everyone arrived. "More people need to get here, did they tell you?"

Yes, he'd been "told." There hadn't been anything about it in the briefing, though. Only Shaked's words.

"We'll wait for them at the pub out back there," the station commander said while pointing to the alley behind the Old Church. "It's out of the way for it not to get too much attention, and central enough to not be suspicious."

Guy joined him in walking towards the alley, but on his tenth step, he fell.

He felt nothing.

The thin blade that dug into his brain from under his right jawline hit his brainstem, killing him before he reached the ground.

The "station commander" lifted him and put Guy into the trunk of an old Toyota Corolla that was parked nearby. Half-an-hour later, there was no evidence of what had happened.

Guy never sent in the third report, only a quarter-of-an-hour after confirmation.

In a small office in the Kirya Tower, a young man raised his head from looking at the computer screen and addressed the man beside him. "Jaybird didn't call in the third report."

"How long since his last?" the commander asked.

"Twenty minutes."

"Let's give him another ten."

Ten minutes later, the commander lifted the red phone, pressed a button, and said quietly, "Bucharest has fallen."

13.

The Director of the Mossad grumbled under his non-existent mustache.

He really didn't need this. Avi was long gone, but Daniel still remained. He'd sent Daniel back to his room. It would have seemed too suspicious if he'd been asked to stay.

Daniel sent him a questioning look and the Director practically yelled, "Are you stupid? Get the hell out of here, and come back when he's gone. I need you here."

"Will Ortal call me or are you planning to simply set Kidon[6] on me?" Daniel asked, allowing himself, for once, to give as good as he got.

"Are you still here? He'll be there in a minute."

Ortal smiled as Daniel left. "I'm very close to throttling you," she muttered.

Daniel couldn't quite hide his smile as he returned to his office. This would work.

---

6   Kidon is the unit within Israel's Mossad that is allegedly responsible for the assassination of enemies, and is the Hebrew word for "bayonet."

One minute to the dot later, Ortal told the CIA representative standing in front of her, "You can go in now. He's waiting for you."

"Hi. How's it going?" the Director showed true excitement at seeing the CIA representative. He was excited. He'd convinced himself ahead of time that he would be excited. They'd been working together for a while and knew each other well. If the head of the Mossad wasn't excited, the head of the European CIA branch would notice.

"Everything is good, you know how it is." The CIA representative smiled.

"Are you here for a vacation? Planning on visiting the Dead Sea, perhaps?"

"A vacation? Here?" he huffed. "You don't get one day of peace around this place. Vacationing for us is in New Zealand." He paused.

"Or maybe Antarctica," the head of the Mossad added.

"Right, huh… well, at least I'm not being asked to spy on the building going on in your settlements. Hard to believe what your politicians decide to deal with on a daily basis."

The Director laughed. That was true. The Americans had the heaviest kinds of artillery, and they decided to focus on things that couldn't be more redundant. "I've got a photo for you to see," he said. "Someone in Ariel built a balcony against regulations."

The representative laughed. "Right, well, this time the reason I'm visiting is of my own volition. And it's serious, no political bullshit. And since we were talking about photos… here's one for you." The representative took a picture out of his pocket and handed it over to the Director. "You know her?"

The Director looked at the photo. It was of a woman—a beautiful woman, with black, flowing hair. What was truly arresting about her were her eyes: piercing green. Enchanting. But, no. He didn't know her, and the representative figured it out from his expression.

"You're looking at one of the most sophisticated war machines—one of the deadliest ones, too—that humankind has ever managed to create."

"Who is she?" the Director asked.

"Her name is Layla."

"And…?"

"And she was born in Lebanon to an Iranian father and Lebanese mother. When she was three, she moved to Iran, and at around the same time, also lost both her parents. We're not sure about the exact details. What we do know is that when she was sixteen she returned to Lebanon and that in the last few years has been living in Belgium. Her training regimen isn't completely clear, either. She clearly began as a child in Iran, but it most likely continued in Lebanon, too. She's uncommonly intelligent and highly proficient in many different kinds of martial arts. All that, however, isn't the significant part. She's got exceptional systematic vision and management capabilities. She can make others act as a mere extension of herself."

"How have you reached all these… conclusions?" the

Director asked slowly.

"She ran 'Luminary Eclipse' for the Iranians," he stated.

"Bullshit. That was Baharam's work."

"No, it was Layla. Baharam was the agent in charge, but he worked out of Tehran. Layla was the one who did all the field-work. She works for him."

The Director pondered the new information the CIA representative gave him. There was no reason for him to give him misinformation, and if the CIA representative was the one to hand over this information, the matter had to be well researched. That made the woman in the picture the very war machine he'd said her to be, and definitely not someone you would want to meet. He couldn't figure out the angle here, though. "So, is she the head operative of the Iranians in Europe?"

"Not exactly."

"Meaning?"

"She's the head of the Iranian European task force."

"What kind of task force?"

"The one in charge of the threats against their nuclear development."

"Okay. You've got my attention. How is it you're back to keeping us in the loop regarding Iran's nuclear doings?" the Director asked.

"Nothing has changed on our side, but I'd be happy to hear what you have."

"Regarding?" He was *not* planning on sharing the current

ongoings with the CIA.

"Honestly, I've no idea. I was hoping you would tell me."

The Director shrugged, saying without words, 'I've no clue what you're talking about.'

There was a tense silence before the representative continued. "What do you know of 'Breadcrumbs?'"

The Director shook his head. He was less and less happy with the direction this conversation was going. The CIA representative was throwing him too many bits of information he was unfamiliar with.

"'Breadcrumbs' is a cleanup order."

Cleanup? This was getting from bad to worse. Cleanup orders were given to sleeper agents to "clean the field" moments before they were deployed for their dormant missions. It was done not only so they could operate without disturbances, but also as a way to "burn bridges," so to speak. So that they wouldn't have anything to come back to. If this truly was an Iranian cleanup mission, then there were two things they could expect: the first was a huge amount of dead bodies: some of their own, and some from other agencies. The second was that Bucharest was about to be flooded. Daniel, that son of a bitch, was right. He had to get the whole of Caesarea there. Even that would probably not be enough.

The Director looked at the CIA agent speculatively, not even trying to hide his emotions.

"We had Layla covered, of course. She had an agent—one of our better ones—on her case. Then something rather...

surprising happened. They fell in love, and I mean really in love."

"No, they didn't."

"It seemed problematic at first, but the more we thought about it, it actually seemed like a good thing."

"But..." the Director hedged. "You said cleanup action, no?"

"I did."

"Poor guy. But if she really loved him, at least she did it straight up. She probably didn't let him suffer," he continued.

"Well, I wouldn't call the scene clean... but at least she let him come."

"Sharon Stone?"

"Exactly."

"I don't think I'd like to meet this woman." The Director chuckled humorlessly.

"But your boys are about to," the representative got them back on track with jarring seriousness.

The Director remained silent.

"Look," the head of the European division of the CIA continued. "Many, many Iranian operatives are on their way to Bucharest as we speak—if they're not there already. But you know all this. What you may not know, is that they're of the highest caliber, and they're *good*. I know that some of your Cesarian agents are on their way there now, and I highly doubt that will be enough. I have no idea what you've done, but it must have been something right because the Iranians are pulling everything they have short of starting an actual war with Romania."

The Director carried on glowering at the representative.

"Let me help you."

"With what?" the Director kept playing unaware.

"Come off it. Seriously, don't tell me what you're doing, but let me help. My guys are already on their way to Bucharest, and I've asked the Germans and British to help, too. I'm not leaving you hanging, if you want it or not."

The Director didn't shift his gaze.

"Look," the representative continued. "Our default action is to assist you. We're on your side. I'll also talk to the Romanians once this gets out of hand—and it will get out of hand. If you don't want me interfering, if you want me to pull my men back, give it to me straight. Tell me now, do I drop this completely?"

The Director remained silent.

"Good." The representative rose, the Director followed his action. "May luck be on your—and our—side. And though your sharing the information you have isn't a condition to our continued help... I'd still appreciate knowing what the hell is going on at some point."

The Director reached out and shook the man's hand.

"Thank you," the Director said softly, only just loud enough for the man to hear. He paused, gave the Director a quirked-lip smile, and left the office.

The Director remained standing. He took a deep breath.

There were multi-level actions that had to be done. He had to reinstate Daniel and get him back here, he had to get the entirety of Caesarea to Bucharest, get Saar's guys out of Africa and to Bucharest too, and many more things.

He sat, picked up the phone, and said to Ortal, "Get me the Prime Minister, please."

14.

Rajan was sure he was about to save humanity—nothing less. Perhaps not quite literally, but at least that was how he felt.

In only a few moments, he would be presenting in front of the committee. It was merely a symbolic act since, practically, his doctorate had already been approved. They'd read it all already, had asked their numerous questions, and by their interest, he knew they liked his concept. Really liked it.

Still, you couldn't have your doctorate approved without presenting it to the committee and going through their grueling questions. Which was fine. He was prepared for this. There was no part he was unfamiliar with. Some things he even knew better than some of the distinguished professors. This—this he would pass easily.

Rajan thought about his parents and five brothers and sisters who were back in India. He knew they were incredibly proud of him, waiting to hear back from him once this was approved. He— the boy from New Delhi who'd grown up in the slums with no real future in front of him—would be getting his doctorate today.

It had started small—nothing more than a triviality for Westerners—but for him… for him, it had been monumental. Rajan had managed to apply his outstanding mind to find a place at the train station to sell his mother's samosa. And so, for years, from the age of six until he was seventeen, he'd upped his family's income, improved his location, and increased his sales more and more. One day, a distinguished man gave him a new, two-thousand rupee bill, and asked him how much he could buy for such a sum. Rajan had completed the division in his head, telling the man the answer in an instant. He also added how much change he'd have left. The man had been shocked. He'd needed a minute to confirm Rajan's mathematics. The real answer—that Rajan couldn't possibly have enough samosas to sell two-thousand rupees worth of them—he didn't share out loud. In the end, the man only bought three pieces. It took Rajan fifteen minutes to find someone who could give him enough change.

What Rajan hadn't known was that the man was a part of the MIT faculty, and so, half a year later, Rajan found himself with a scholarship to MIT in Boston, USA. He improved his English as time went by.

He found his interests lay in geology, of all places, rather than mathematics, and so he learned the subject's ins and outs. What he found most fascinating was geography, and in particular, the issue of worldwide overpopulation. Geology became nothing but a means to an end. Rajan may have left New Delhi, but it would forever be a part of him.

His doctorate dealt with the creation of artificial islands that have a volcanic base. The theory he'd developed based itself on his ability to evaluate the stability of ancient, hidden volcanoes in such islands. Once the volcano was deemed to be dormant, and would not erupt in the coming decades, the island would be able to be artificially expanded and manned.

The majority of his measurements, deductions, and conclusions he'd extracted from working on an island in the Pacific Ocean: I-752. The results had been incredible.

Rajan entered the committee hall.

He was familiar with all the professors present. They were all sitting behind a heavy, antique wooden table, but the hall itself was practically empty. His footsteps echoed in the large hall. He saw his doctoral adviser sitting on the far right of the table, smiling awkwardly. As tradition dictated, his adviser was present, but not active in the discussion.

The head of the committee invited him to sit in front of them, then started firing away questions no more than a moment later. They were polite, but the questions came fast and unremittingly. Still, he always had enough time to give his full answers.

As expected, he dealt with it all with relative ease.

Toward the end, the questions started repeating themselves, all centered around one issue: how could he be sure the dormant volcano wouldn't erupt? He'd expected this, and Rajan merely repeated his answers.

At some point, he realized that though the professors appreciated his work and were willing to "believe him," he was falling short of truly convincing them.

The head of the committee stopped the discussion to summarize. "Rajan, I have—we have, that is, two things we'd like to say. The first is that it's uncommon to tell a doctoral graduate whether or not their dissertation was accepted right away. Rather, we allow the doctoral advisor to later give them the news. In your case, however, we will share the news immediately. The second thing is, and I'm sure I speak for everyone here, is that it's been a long time since we've encountered such a thorough piece of work, and such unique and fascinating ways of thinking. In fact, the whole committee is already very much ensnared, so we will be foregoing an additional discussion without you present."

The head of the committee fell silent and let Rajan process his words. Rajan wanted to smile at his praise, but the serious expression on the man's face made him believe the word "but" was imminent. It did not bode well.

"But," the head of the committee indeed said, "despite all that, we cannot approve your doctorate."

Rajan was shocked. So shocked he couldn't even ask why.

"I'm sure you must be confused regarding our reasons," he added, "and the answer is here." He held out an aerial photo.

Rajan took it with shaking hands and studied the picture. "No, it can't be," he muttered.

The picture showed island I-752, there was no doubt about that. But there was another indisputable fact, and that was that the island's volcano had erupted.

15.

Shaked Yossef asked himself how he felt. He didn't give it much thought or deliberation, it simply happened naturally.

If anyone was looking at him from the side, they would never have noticed a thing.

So, how *did* he feel? He was sorry. He was. And not only because now he now had one less agent in the field in an escalating, dangerous fight. He honestly felt sorry for Guy.

However, he didn't feel any guilt over it. He had done everything he could—everything in the realm of possibility—to keep him alive. If he'd lost his focus on the mission itself, perhaps the result would have been different, but there was no room for such feelings now. Not only regarding the situation at hand but also directly related to Shaked's job in this crisis.

He figured that if he could have arrived merely twenty or thirty seconds sooner, he'd have managed to change the ultimate result. But he hadn't, and that was life. Another man, perhaps, would feel increasing frustration at that, but not Shaked. There was no crying over spilled milk, nor could there be any regrets. There were only lessons learned and the storing of information in his mental archive. Now, all he was focused on was what would come next. How could he use what had happened to his advantage?

All this passed through his mind as he watched the man posing as the station chief eliminate Guy. Shaked had been too far away to act, and he had no way of saving Guy, but the one who had killed him would live to regret it. No, Shaked wouldn't kill him. His life had no room for vengeance, only the never-ending fight to best his adversaries.

Shaked had suspected that the first move of the Iranians would be to impersonate the station chief. It was what he would have done. The operation itself must have been planned well beforehand and executed exceptionally fast once the order was given. Guy must have taken it for granted that the head of the Romanian station was one of the Mossad's. Shaked would have found him to be the first person worth suspecting.

The Mossad agent who'd come from Iran would have been unable to get to the embassy, after all. It would be the first place the Iranians would have closed in on. The next logical step would have been to go to the local man in charge. And that, he knew, would be where the Iranians would have waited. However bright Guy had been, there was no price for experience. He hoped—no, he *believed*—that the agent who'd started this all was well experienced. On the one hand, the simple fact that he had destroyed his phone—the phone that had started this whole mess—meant he was on a high enough level not to fall prey to elementary traps. On the other, it also made finding him that much harder.

From the first moment he'd landed in Bucharest, Shaked had made sure to secure an apartment that would act as their headquarters. That would also be where the "head of the station" would be staying. Shaked waited only a little longer to make sure no other Iranian agents were around.

The alleyway where the "chief's" car was parked was shrouded in darkness, but things were still visible. The road was newly done in ugly, generic asphalt, rather than the expected old cobblestones. It opened up into a main street, about 100 meters from where the car was. Absurdly, the alley was actually wider than the main street, and the bustle and mere amount of people there made it look packed. Tourists, for the most part, sat at outside-pub-tables, drinking and clogging the way, making everything move slowly.

Shaked hadn't noticed any enemy-side backup, so he went under the assumption that there was none. This being such short notice, the Iranians were limited with their resources.

He re-holstered his gun and pulled out his "blowgun." If his assumption was wrong, he would miss this golden opportunity for handling the Iranian agent, but at least he would have time to pull back. Shaked was far from an altruist. He had no intention of putting himself in harm's way merely for the operation. Especially if it was uncalled for.

The "blowgun" got its name from the weapons used by indigenous people of South America who'd used thin tubes to shoot poisoned arrows at their prey. The poisoned darts and a vague resemblance to a tube were all that remained in common with the original weapon and the "blowgun" Shaked had pulled out.

It was made from a thin, short tube that had an air-pressure blower on one end. In that regard, it looked more like an air gun. The tube had a laser-assisted aim, and the darts held a powerful anesthetic that dissolved into the bloodstream once they hit the target body, leaving no other trace. The dart was shot using air pressure, while the laser aim measured the distance to the target. It also automatically adjusted the barrel. When shooting in a wind-free area, it was hard to miss a target when it was less than 80 meters away.

The interesting part was in the way the dart hit its target and created an effect similar to a hypodermic needle. The target felt little more than a sting, and since the substance used targeted the nervous system, it took no longer than half a minute for them to fall into a deep sleep.

Shaked watched analytically as the agent first rubbed at his neck, then soon after folded slowly down to the ground. He gave it another ten minutes to be sure there was no backup coming, then strode toward him.

Just like in Beirut, he told himself.

The alley remained quiet and empty during the time he loaded him up, and the "head of the station" shared the trunk space with Guy. Shaked removed all hearing devices and other electronics from the man, and though he desperately wanted to be able to bring them along to Israel for further analysis, the risk was simply too high. He found it hard to believe they didn't have trackers in them, anyway. He left them, entered the car, and simply drove away. There had been no disturbance or questionable incident besides.

Shaked parked in a dark, narrow alley, about 300 meters from the safehouse. He assumed the Iranians would manage to track the car, sooner or later. Three-hundred meters gave him enough disconnect for the given situation. By the time the Iranians would close in on the apartment, the whole operation would be well and done. Shaked pulled out the man and tied him up so that his whole weight rested on Shaked, but if someone was looking at them, they would merely assume that Shaked was assisting a friend who'd had too much to drink. Shaked had plenty of experience with getting things like this done. He'd walked half of Beirut that way.

Guy, to Shaked's regret, would have to stay in the trunk. Not only did Shaked not have the time to move him to the apartment, but if the car was eventually found by the Iranians, they would not believe the agent had been caught by Israelis.

Ten minutes later, he was at the apartment, and in the last 50 meters, he was joined by Dor. The security cameras were already installed.

Dor, who was younger than Shaked by approximately ten years and practically twice his weight, easily lifted the "head of the station" and got him into the flat. Two minutes later, the Iranian was tied up in one of the small rooms.

Shaked rested his palm on the secure communication device, and ten seconds later, it opened. He gave a half-minute update, then simply listened.

He had grown used to not asking questions when the higher-ups didn't share what was truly going on. He did so now, too. However, what was actually going on here seemed a lot more significant than the tidbits he'd been told: that an agent stationed in Iran had gotten away and was now being followed by practically the whole Iranian force. He couldn't quite say what was going on. Things refused to add up. The man in charge was Daniel, the head of Michmoret—an educated guess since he hadn't been told. The assumption wasn't hard to come by, since the agent in question wasn't one he was familiar with. With the effort and show of strength the Iranians were putting in, he also concluded that what was going on was still well underway. He couldn't understand why the agent couldn't call from a regular phone and simply pass on the information, or, alternatively, if he had stolen physical data—they *were* talking about Michmoret, after all—why he didn't simply connect to the Mossad network through a coffee shop Wi-Fi then pass on the information. And the thing that made the least amount of sense, was how the head of Michmoret believed him to be dead… so why on earth were they still calling the cavalry to save him?

The Iranians clearly hadn't reached him yet, or they would have been long gone. So, the mission was to find the agent before the Iranians, to figure out what help he needed, and to give it. It was going to get dirty. And the Europeans were about to get involved, too. Dirty *and* messy.

But, there was a time and place for everything, and first, the Iranian in the other room needed to be interrogated.

As if the man was listening to Shaked's internal monologue, he opened his eyes.

16.

"We can't tell yet," Layla said.

She glanced back, studying the movements in the little apartment they'd chosen for the headquarters. The people behind her were the spearhead of the Revolutionary Guards. She'd worked with a few of them during "Luminary Eclipse." The rest she was merely familiar with due to her position. She'd activated them, as she knew well to do, then found the time to speak to Baharam.

"It doesn't make sense," Baharam replied.

"Yes, I thought so at first, as well. But it's what's going on. It seems as if there's been a complete compartmentalization on their side, and... I believe he surprised them, too. We can see a growing force, but it's slow. There are fewer than us."

"What have you done so far?"

"The embassy was closed up before I even got here," she said. "We haven't seen any activity. I'm guessing they were expecting us to be there, so it's been kept outside the loop. I left only a small group to watch for any change, and though they'll maintain their position, I highly doubt that will be the grounds of any altercation.

"We also activated the "Station Head" procedure. According to his last update, he only caught one junior agent—which is surprising. I don't know why they sent someone so green. It doesn't fit, and I need to understand what the hell is going on there. Anyway, he's in position, but I don't think the thief will try and approach him."

"I see. What's your plan?"

Layla asked herself the same. She'd been working automatically to this point. She'd done so according to procedure, and blocked all ways the thief could contact help, which included train stations, airports, and the like. She erected a blockade that would eliminate Israelis once they arrived… and they were arriving a lot slower than she had expected. It took her a while to figure out, but like she had told Baharam, the thief had caught the Israelis by surprise, too.

She thought back to earlier this afternoon. It seemed like it had happened a month ago. She'd received the order through her belt buckle. She'd killed Steve. *Her Steve.* The only person she'd ever loved. She'd known it would have had to happen one day, yet still, deep down, she'd hoped it never would. She'd given herself ten minutes to grieve but then had forced herself to act. The loss of Steve mingled with the dull ache of Nadine. She smothered her sadness, though she knew it would hit her later tenfold, and pushed all her energy into exhaustive actions.

Then, she worked like a well-oiled machine. She'd activated

her field agents before she'd even arrived in Bucharest. Some had arrived before her and had already started closing up the city per her orders: Hassan had "changed places" with the head of the Mossad station; the embassy was closed, as were the train and bus stations. Bazad, her top agent, was sent to wait for the thief at the airport. He'd yet to contact her, and he'd better have a damn good reason.

So... what were her plans now? Layla had indeed asked herself that well before Baharam did. Practically her whole force was on the ground, spread throughout the city. They were all ready for the Mossad, who was, for some unknown reason, late for the party. They would get a warm welcome when they did, of course.

Now, it was time to plan, and the way to do that was simple: she had to think like the thief. There was no doubt he was a talented, experienced agent. Every action he'd taken up to now was evidence of that. Putting herself in his shoes, in that case, was no hardship. What would *she* do in his shoes?

"Give me ten minutes," she said to Baharam, "I'll lay out the plan for you th—"

"You've got to hear this," one of her agents cut in.

He raised the volume on the communication device. Excitable Romanian came through the speakers. Unfortunately, she knew little Romanian. "Translate," she ordered.

"...he was in a closed bathroom stall... no, no signs, but the sink was broken... there's a bullet hole in the door..."

"What is this?" she asked the agent, and before he replied

said to Baharam, "Hang on, I'll update you in a second."

"It's a police report from the airport. They found a body in a bathroom stall."

Layla did the math and immediately arrived at three different conclusions. That kind of fast thinking was one of her hallmark attributes. It was part of what made her such an excellent agent, capable of analyzing situations, predicting dangers, and finding solutions even for particularly tricky conditions.

The first conclusion lay with Bazad. A body in the airport restroom… if it wasn't him, Bazad would have updated her already and she wouldn't have been hearing about it by listening to Romanian police communications. Since she hadn't, there was no other explanation. The hope he hadn't called in since he was too close to the target snuffed out.

The second conclusion was that whoever had killed him was the thief himself. It had to be. Reading the ground as she was, there was simply no other explanation. The Israelis were well behind them, so there was no chance they would have arrived at the airport before them. So too, as per Baharam's intel, by checking security cameras in the Tehran airport, the thief had entered the country via Germany and had left to Romania. That meant that something had gone wrong on his side, which made the reasoning of him having no agents waiting for him there logical. The way the Israelis were handling this whole mess seemed rather… amateurish. They were doing everything solo and under the radar—which was unlike their usual course of action. She wondered what they were hiding.

The final, most important conclusion was that if the thief had managed to overtake Bazad, he was exceptionally talented. Well, clearly—since he'd managed to gain entry and steal state secrets—but that was all child's play next to going up against Bazad. Still, there was no way he had gone up against him without getting hurt. The broken sink added to that assumption. But then, he'd managed to lock Bazad in a stall and get away, so the injury couldn't be too bad.

The fraction of a second it took for her to come to these conclusions meant she could update Baharam the moment the agent who'd filled her in stopped talking.

"What's your plan, and does this change things?"

"Ten minutes," she repeated, and hung up.

What would you do? she wordlessly asked the intruder. *You're alone, no one is here to help you. You've already been attacked at the airport—and if you were found there, you already assume the city is closed off to you. The embassy, the Mossad station... everything. Getting on another plane would be just as dangerous... so what do you do? Trains? No, not your style. No. You would do something different. The questions are, then: What and whether or not you're badly wounded. You know you're alone and we're on to you, you're running out of time—you know this. You've taken on Bazad, and though you came out on top, you now also know what's coming for you. You can't handle it alone. You need help.*

That was it—that's what he would do. *You'd get help in any way possible, still assuming we would block you at every corner.*

Would you go to the American embassy?

For a moment she panicked. That wasn't guarded. But no. No Mossad agent would go to the American embassy. It simply wouldn't happen. *No… you'd look for Israelis. That's what you'd do. There are many Israeli businesses in Bucharest. You'd go to them for help.*

"We need a list of all local Israeli businessmen. They have to be eliminated." She'd shot off the order before she'd even spun around to look at the agent.

His face!

Beside him stood Ahmad from the deep infiltration unit. Layla counted at least four bullet holes in his body, but he was still standing. *Good for him.*

There wasn't much he needed to say, she understood. The deep infiltration division had been eliminated, and he had crawled out by the skin of his teeth. How could that have happened? A whole unit? The Mossad had barely arrived!

"What happened?" she demanded.

"Ambush," he answered. "Down by the Old City. There were two agents with Ruger snipers. In the crowd. They took us out like flies."

Rugers? An ominous feeling spread throughout her entire body. Rugers, 0.22 calibers, were known to be highly accurate, but rarely ever deadly. That only happened if you caught your enemy by surprise. That was the only reason Ahmad stood before her now. He'd understood what was happening while his comrades were taken out. Moving quickly wouldn't stop you from getting hit, but it might reduce the chance of it being deadly.

That, however, wasn't what bothered her. Not at all. How could she have been so stupid? She had to make a quick shift in her planning. It was becoming clearer now—obvious, in fact: why the thief had surprised the Israelis, why the Mossad wasn't present. Who said the thief had been *Israeli*?

Their assumption, from the moment the breach had been discovered, was that it had been done by either the Israelis or the Americans. No one else could have pulled off an operation like this. Apart from them, only the Russians had the needed technology, but that wasn't their MO. They did things completely differently. The Russians also had most of the stolen information, and anyway, if it was the Russians, the thief would have flown straight there and this whole ordeal would have been done with a long time ago. No. The Russians weren't at fault. She was sure of that, at least.

So, the only two other suspects remaining were the Americans or the Israelis. They'd assumed the Americans wouldn't dare, despite their criticism regarding the Deal. The Israelis most certainly would. The guard found at the break in point had been taken out by an Israeli—they knew since the Americans liked to work with technology. They didn't get their hands dirty.

Thus, the given assumption: Israelis were responsible for the breach.

But perhaps the Americans were the ones behind this, after

all? Perhaps they'd killed the guard by snapping his neck—mis-leadingly pointing them in the direction of the Israelis? That seemed to fit better with what she saw on the ground here in Bucharest.

Once again, she came to these conclusions in a blink of an eye. It had been the fact they'd been killed by Rugers. That wasn't a weapon the Israelis used. Maybe only in a meticulous-ly planned operation—not when things were so up in the air. When the Israelis wanted to show strength, they did just that. Rugers they deemed nothing more than crowd control guns. It was, however, highly effective in taking out agents in places where there were many people—the Old City, for example. The whole weapon was silenced, and, if hit right, the target simply fell. It made it look like a heart attack.

No. Whoever had taken out the deep infiltration unit was not connected to the Mossad. That—that had been the work of the CIA. Which meant that the breach hadn't come from the side of the Israelis, but the Americans. What a serious mistake she'd made.

Layla looked at Ahmad, contemplating for a moment her next course of action. At least one good thing had come from all this: because of her mistake, if the thief was in good condi-tion, he would have long since reached the Americans. Since the Americans had bothered to take out the unit, that had most likely not happened yet. The thief, in that case, was badly in-jured. Possibly even dead. Now all that was needed was to find his body. *Thank you, Bazad.*

17.

Roni knew she was about to be raped.

The terror clutching at her faded.

After the initial paralyzing fright, and a fruitless, short struggle, she came to terms with that unfortunate fact. Surprisingly, she was even relieved. The shock, the hysteria, the anxiety... they fell away once she realized there was nothing she could do, and it would happen regardless. The clarity that had come with the knowledge gave her back a little control. As low as she currently was, at least she knew what kind of low it was. Her rapist wasn't going to kill her. At least not right away. How did she know that? Because she was still breathing.

She held onto that ray of hope.

So, she was going to be raped. It was horrendous, but it was going to happen. There didn't seem to be anything she could do about it. Once accepting that, she felt as if her spirit disconnected from her body. She looked at her bound hands, held by her would-be rapist as if she were someone else.

She thought about what she *could* do.

He was incredibly strong, her rapist, so struggling was useless. But she refused to lie back and wait for it to be over. She *would* fight. How did you fight without fighting?

The answer came to her right away. She would throw up. The thought of being raped went from being terrifying to utterly disgusting—abhorrent. She didn't think throwing up would be particularly hard.

Her rapist wouldn't take his hand off her mouth during the whole time he'd be raping her so she wouldn't scream. Once he'd… finish, he'd probably hit her hard enough for her to lose consciousness as he ran. She would have to throw up through his fingers. If she did it right, he wouldn't be able to stop it. Then they'd see if he could even get it up.

Roni hadn't got to where she was merely because she was beautiful. And she *was* beautiful—even very beautiful. And she had a body to die for. But there were prettier girls than her around. No, she got to where she was because she was incredibly ambitious, she had an extraordinary amount of resilience and an uncanny ability to make things work as she wished. True, things became easier when you had a lovely face, but it took more than that. The *drive* was necessary, too.

Once acceptance came, the pressure fell away, and it gave way to determination and resourcefulness. She recalled the few acting tricks she'd learned in acting school and planned to use them. Unfortunately, the smashing of her knee into the TA's groin would probably not be recreated, but the throwing up reflex… that she could do.

Roni began with visualizing it and already felt her stomach churn. As she went limp and continued to try and focus as hard as she could, the rapist brought his mouth close to her ear. She froze again at the feel of his breath against her cheek. It smelled of death.

Then he whispered in a quiet, steady voice, "Mossad."

What? He spoke Hebrew? What did he say?

Her plans shattered.

"I'm Mossad," the man whispered in her ear again.

Mossad?

Her stomach heaved and the thoughts rushed through her mind. A Mossad agent? The man who had her was a *Mossad* agent? So, there would be no rape.

She felt furious.

Furious at the way he'd jumped her, at how he'd ruined her plans.

She'd been prepared for being raped, and by the time she'd come to terms with it, the rapist—a Mossad agent, of all people!—went and changed everything. But, most of all, she was furious with herself. Instead of thanking God for her not being about to be raped, she was angry for having her plans foiled. It was insane. How stupid could she be?

"I'm sorry for jumping you like that," he carried on whispering. "I need your help."

She tried to muddle through the mess in her mind. He was Israeli, there was no doubt about that. Not only was he speaking Hebrew, but he didn't have an accent. On the other hand—was he really Mossad? His grip on her didn't falter.

"I'm going to let go of your mouth, please don't scream."

Roni waited.

An age went by, though maybe it wasn't so long. She didn't think she could trust her sense of time. It had felt like forever since he said he'd remove his hand, yet it was still there.

Finally, slowly, slowly, his hand loosened from around her and fell back. She barely dared breathe, let alone talk. She didn't dream of screaming.

A long moment passed during which her mouth was free, then the agent loosened his grip on her body. She was completely free.

She wondered if she was allowed to look at him—the remnants of thinking he was about to rape her were still very much present in her mind. If he truly wasn't a criminal and instead was, as he'd said, a Mossad agent, then she was probably allowed. Still, she couldn't find the courage to turn around.

"What do you want?" she whispered, terrified, not looking anywhere close to his direction.

"I need your help," he repeated.

"Why?" was the first thing that popped into her mind, and she belatedly realized that she'd also asked the question aloud.

"Because I need help, and I don't have anyone else."

For a moment she considered she might be getting pranked. Could it be that Eran had got something together? No. No, that wasn't like him at all. And anyway, this whole scenario was too terrifying for it to be part of a mere prank.

Roni was used to being asked things. Selfies, in particular. But she'd never thought she'd get a Mossad agent asking her for help.

The terror of being raped had faded, but she still held on to the mindset of resourcefulness and drive. Thoughts, plans, and questions flew through her mind. To her disappointment, they all boiled down to one, childish question, and she found herself asking it regardless.

"Why me?"

"I told you," he said. "I need help, and I don't have anyone else I can ask."

"That still doesn't explain why it has to be me. Is this because of the way I look?" For a moment another worry crept up her spine, but she didn't let it linger.

"I've got two options," he replied. "Either I can go to someone I know and trust, or I can go to someone I'm sure is Israeli, and who I know cares about Israel and wouldn't sell it out at the first opportunity."

Roni slowly turned to the agent as he carried on talking.

"There is no one here I know, so the only thing I can do is go to someone famous. At least I'm sure you're Israeli. Like I said, I need help, so I don't have many choices. This is about your being famous. It has nothing to do with the way you look."

"Right, I'm Israeli, but what makes you think I wouldn't sell it out?"

"It would hurt your image, so I can only assume you won't. But that's not the truthful answer."

"And what is?" she asked.

"That I don't have a choice," he ground out. "The only option I have is to hope you'll help me."

If he's playing me, he's doing it exceptionally well, she thought. He sounded incredibly believable. She looked at him. He had a slim face, and with what she could make out in the darkness, had dark eyes and hair. He looked tired. Exhausted, actually. He'd probably been through quite a bit. *Whether he's playing me or not, he seems like someone who needs help.* The fear that had turned into readiness, which had in turn transformed into interest, shifted to pity.

"What do you need me to do?" she asked.

"Do you see this?" he asked, raising his hand. Between his fingers, he held something small that looked like a SIM card. Smaller, even. A micro-SIM card.

She looked at it in interest. *What does he want from me?*

"This holds a huge amount of highly classified, incredibly important information that is vital for the country."

"And what am I supposed to do with it?"

"Keep it safe! With everything you've got!"

"It's tiny, it could get lost," she muttered.

"So keep it somewhere where that won't happen."

"Where?"

"Have you never seen a spy movie?"

Roni looked at the agent, and any bit of pity she'd felt for him evaporated. *What a shit.*

It's what you asked for though, isn't it? a voice in her mind said. *You were ready for this—you were even angry about him not* raping *you. Here's your chance, then.*

All men were bastards, she concluded to herself.

It was possible that the agent could read her like a book, but he didn't show it. He carried on. "Good. You keep this safe and bring it to Israel. They'll contact you and take it."

"But I'm not going to Israel from here," she said. "I'm off to Barcelona."

"And after Barcelona?"

"After Barcelona, I'm going back to Israel."

Eliad imagined the possibility of the Iranians getting on her trail if she suddenly changed her plans.

"You know what, it's better if you don't change your schedule. Don't change anything."

"And in the meantime?"

"Like I said, you ke…" he paused for a moment and closed his eyes, wondering how to continue.

After a long pause, when it didn't seem like the agent was going to continue, Roni cleared her throat and touched his shoulder.

In response, the agent fell to the ground, landing on his side.

Her breath caught in her chest. She checked his pulse, but couldn't feel a thing.

18.

Dor glanced at Shaked, saying without words that he will take care of the man. Shaked nodded almost imperceptibly, and Dor dove into action.

It started off simply. Dor asked questions in English, and the Iranian answered in Farsi. It continued a minute longer—going nowhere. Shaked waited patiently for the minute-mark to pass, then said in English to the Iranian. "You killed the head of our station here, and you killed our agent who came to you about an hour ago. You shoved his body into the trunk of your car. The agent you killed couldn't speak Farsi, so there would have been no other way for you to communicate with him other than in English."

Shaked paused and looked at the Iranian, who still kept a questioning, puzzled expression plastered on his face.

"As you wish," he allowed. He turned to Dor and said, still in English, "Cut off his balls. Put a tourniquet on, though, so he doesn't bleed out."

"Yes, sir," Dor replied, and Shaked left the room.

He waited just outside the door and listened in. After a short series of screams, the Iranian began speaking—in English this time.

Well, Dor did know what he was doing.

Shaked looked around the small apartment. He wished to be outside, in the "field," so to speak. But he had to make sense of this mess beforehand.

The flat was small, as Shaked preferred. There were three bedrooms. In one, they were interrogating the Iranian, and in the living room, they'd established the control center of operations with a desk, a computer that showed views from numerous cameras positioned in the vicinity of the apartment, a few pieces of paper, a secured communications device, and a map of Bucharest. Nothing else. No more was necessary. Shachar and Yoav were bent over the map, sectioning it off. There were almost ten other people outside in different places around the city asking, looking, trying to find a lead. None of them, though, knew what they were actually looking for, let alone how to start.

Shaked was not a fan of these kinds of operations. He felt similarly about the mustard-yellow color the apartment was painted… but the others back home were determined, and that was the important thing. It wasn't so much what they were saying, but how they were saying it.

The flat had another room that Shaked had insisted stay empty. It had two beds in it and not much else. Having a place to rest was important, and no one truly knew how long this operation would take. He'd also insisted—practically forced—Shachar to go grocery shopping. It was amazing what a little food could do to improve cognitive thinking, and that's not even touching on the effect it had on one's mood and general well-being.

"What's going on?" he asked.

"Not much," Shachar replied. "The guys are all scattered around, but it's like finding a needle in a… well. You know, if we actually had any idea what to look for…"

"They still being passive?"

"Yes."

Shaked watched Shachar, thinking it through.

"Should we activate them?" Shachar asked.

Shaked remained silent. Shachar looked at him. He'd never seen Shaked so indecisive. It was surprising.

"Soon," he finally replied. "Not yet. I need a moment to think, then I'll go out there. We'll activate them once I've left."

Shaked went into the third room and sat down on the bed. It was rather dark in there, and it made the mustard-colored walls even uglier in the dim lighting. Shaked remained oblivious to it. He was too deep in thought.

Where are you? he asked the agent who'd come in from Iran. *You're alone and need help. You* need *help. You might even be dead, like Daniel seems to think. If you are, where's your body, and what do we need to do with it?*

You arrived in Bucharest. You realized the Iranians were on your tail and we were far behind, so you give up on pursuing any of the more obvious ways of alerting us and do something else, but what? How do you expect us to figure it out?

What would I do? he asked himself. *I'd go for help from someone I was sure would help me—someone as far from the Iranian radar as possible.*

That left two options: another country's agency—of a friendly nation, maybe even an agent I know personally. Then again, I've got something incredibly valuable, so I wouldn't trust someone else—a foreigner from a friendly nation—not to act against me. No. That's not a good idea.

So, I'm left with the second option: an Israeli I can trust who is not on the Iranian radar. A businessman, perhaps. An Israeli who came to Bucharest for business, someone I could find enough about on Google to know that he's a patriot—a sped up, shallow security clearance.

That would be my move, he said to himself. *Merely because I lack an alternative.*

He thought for another minute before coming to the conclusion that that was exactly what the Iranians would do, too. There was no time to lose.

It also strengthened his resolve to activate all the agents in the field.

When looking for someone who was being hunted by a common enemy, there were two ways to go about it: passively or actively.

If you looked for them passively, you would attract less attention. The search was less effective, but you would more than likely avoid confrontation with the enemy forces. The issue was that passivity fit into situations when you were in contact with your agent, or at least close to finding them and not wasting time. The search was useless, otherwise.

Searching actively was based on the following principle: if you didn't know how or what to search for, make sure to disrupt the enemy's search as much as you possibly could. Doing so would, hopefully, give your agent additional time and a greater chance at survival. It was also important to make as much noise and fanfare as possible so that the agent eventually reached you on their own. The downside to this, of course, was that you ended up practically inviting the enemy into a serious confrontation with you. Based on the quality of the Iranian agents around here, that meant this would end with casualties, and many of them.

Damn, he sighed. *Where were Saar and his guys when you needed them?*

Shaked went back into the living room and asked Shachar and Yoav, "Where are most of the Israeli businessmen in Bucharest?"

"At the Raddison Hotel," Shachar replied.

"Then that's where I'm heading."

"What? You think he'll try and contact Israeli businessmen?" Yoav asked, then added without waiting for a reply, "I'm coming with you."

"Son of a bitch," Shachar growled. Yoav had beaten him to it by a second. "Shaked, what about the call order?"

"Activate them," he said. "And you're not to leave here. Keep listening in to what's going on in the other room. Make sure Dor has it all handled."

As if Dor had heard Shaked's words, a loud scream sounded from the other room. Shachar, Yoav, and Shaked all looked at the closed door and listened to the roaring silence that came from within. A second passed, then Shaked walked up to the door and pulled it open. Dor was standing over the imposter who was laid out in an unnatural position on the chair.

Dor looked up, seeming apologetic.

"I don't give a shit," Shaked said, "Just give me the information."

"Well," Dor said back, "Then I don't even think I screwed up." He seemed relieved.

"What was that scream we heard?"

"The finale. The moment before I got what I needed, and before I sent him to meet Allah."

"Then come out here and brief us."

Dor followed him into the living room and shared the focal points of the interrogation. The agent had been part of a special, elite unit, which had been created for the sole reason of protecting leaked information regarding the Iranian nuclear plans. He'd given up a little information about the unit itself and their commander, Layla. The most important part, however, was their actual mission: catching the man who'd left Iran with highly confidential information.

"So, why did you kill him?" Yoav asked.

"Because that mother fucker laughed at me?"

"What?" Shachar didn't seem to follow.

"You see, I was interrogating him, and he realized that we knew nothing. And that's the truth—we know nothing because no one tells us shit," Dor rebuked, directing his words at Shaked.

"Are you a child?" Shaked shook his head. "In the same way we caught him, they might have got any one of us."

"And…?" Yoav cut in, motioning for Dor to continue.

"And then he started laughing, saying how we'd been fighting them for hours, not even knowing what we were after."

"So you killed him. Because he pissed you off," Shachar summarized. "How very mature."

"But the most important thing—the actual thing we're looking for—you still don't know," Shaked added.

Dor shot him a smile. "I told you, that was the last bit of information I managed to extract from him."

"So," Yoav drawled.

"It's a hard disk," Dor replied. "But a hard disk with a huge amount of information. I'm not sure I got the complete picture, but it most likely includes the whole nuclear plan. It's such a large amount of data, that it can't be uploaded to the Internet."

"Good God…" Yoav breathed out.

"All right. That explains this, then. It also explains why this guy of ours is so important, even if he's dead," Shaked said, his eyes down.

He quickly processed the information. It meant that if the

agent who had arrived here from Iran was seriously wounded, he still only had two options for action. One was hiding the hard disk and somehow getting in touch with them to let them know its location… but Shaked highly doubted that would be his plan of action. It definitely wouldn't have been Shaked's move, the reason being, the Iranian agents were extremely well trained, so they'd have to assume any contact with Israel was being monitored. No. That only left him one other option, which was finding another Israeli and handing it to them. That was, most likely, Daniel's assumption, too, but so too the Iranians'. It meant that the mission now was to find the businessman the agent had found.

"Right, this is what we're going to do. Shachar, have you got everyone activated?" Shaked asked.

"Not yet. Doing it now."

"Good. Dor, update the offices back home regarding the investigation. Keep it about who exactly we're dealing with. After that, go get Guy's body from the car and make your way back here. You're both staying here. Keep vigilant, this is going to get messy. I'm going to the Radisson Hotel. Yoav, you're with me."

19.

Yair was silent.

His stomach churned and the wheels in his head spun dizzyingly fast. He didn't bother with checking the time, all he knew was that it was the middle of the night. He may have been torn from sleep, but he was completely alert.

He had to reply, to say something, but he didn't know what. He hadn't fully processed what had happened, hadn't yet understood the complete meaning of it, let alone the consequences—and, most importantly, all his plans had fallen through. And in the worst way possible. His actions, the damage he'd caused... the injustice of it all!

Hadas reached for him, looking at him with questioning, terrified eyes. She hadn't heard a word, only saw his expression in the moonlight as he clutched at the phone.

"Amit?" she finally uttered her biggest fear, her voice so hushed he could barely hear it.

Michal. His lips moved but no sound came from his throat.

Hadas covered her mouth with a shaking palm, her eyes

filling with tears.

Yair was still on the phone, listening, though Amit was no longer talking.

"I don't know what to say," he said weakly. "It's just... it's awful."

It was much more than merely awful, and that was because there were two things that were seemingly completely unrelated here.

Amit had just finished telling him what he had found.

It was *awful*. Illogical. But Yair did not believe in coincidences. Not in the least. So, the question remained, should he share his knowledge with Amit?

"What do I do now?" Amit asked, his voice still echoing his uncontrollable tears.

Hadas took the phone from Yair. "Amit?" she asked with a broken voice.

"Hadas..." Amit couldn't force himself to talk and burst into tears. Hadas cried with him. "She was cold when I touched her... cold!" Years of repressed emotions burst forth, memories both beautiful and painful mingling in his mind, choking him.

Hadas began sobbing and Yair rose and started pacing the room.

He took back the phone, took a deep breath, and said, "You have to get on a plane back home to us. You can't be alone right now. Get back and we'll see what we can do."

Amit took a few moments to calm himself before saying, "I don't think so."

"What?"

"It's not you—don't take it personally." Amit took a deep breath and forced the words out. "I can't come back to Israel. I just can't. I wish I could be with you both right now, but there's no way... it's not possible."

"Then what are you going to do?"

"I'm going to Barcelona. I need a break. I'll watch some football, breathe a bit. Then I'll see what's next. Don't worry. I'll keep you posted."

Yair was silent again.

"Say something."

"I don't know what to say. I only ever wanted you to be happy, I can't seem to manage to make it happen for you."

"It's not all your fault."

"Of course not, but the bottom line is that I simply don't know what the right thing to do is."

"Not everything is a high-tech project, you know," Amit said somberly.

"Yes... so, I mean... if what you think is right for you right now is Barcelona, then that's what you should do. I'm still offering you the both of us, but if that's not right for now... you have to find what is."

"Right."

"And, of course, we're always here for you. If you need anything, you call. Even if you want me to come over to Nice or Barcelona. Anything."

"Thank you. There is something, though..."

"What? There's *more*?" he asked, failing not to panic for a moment.

"Not that... look. If I were an officer, I'd be my first suspect, you know? I foun—"

"Don't you worry about that."

"What do you mean, *don't worry about that*? This whole place is full of my prints. And I didn't exactly come in throu—"

"You climbed in through her *bedroom window*?"

"Of course I did! The house was locked, and she wasn't exactly up to answering the phone." His voice choked up again.

"Okay, look... this—"

"It's not even her room anymore. She'd moved to her parents' bedroom and..."

"Amit!" Yair almost raised his voice. He would have to tell him.

"What?"

"Don't worry about that. I'll handle it. I will. You've got enough on your mind. Let that go. I know how I can fix this."

"What? Mister Fix-It? Baby brother cries and you make everything better?" Amit started crying again.

"No, it's not like that. Unfortunately—or fortunately, I don't even know anymore... this, I can fix. But that's not what I need to tell you."

"What? What did you want to say?" Amit repeated himself.

"There's something I haven't told you, simply because it hasn't been relevant until now, but the circumstances...."

"What do you mean? Is this another one of your tests?" Amit

practically hollered down the line.

"No, no! What are you talking about, of course not! Listen for a second…"

"What? Anything else would just make this whole mess worse."

"Amit, it doesn't have anything to do with that, and I'm sure Michal would have told you. She should have been the one to say it, not me, but it looks like it might be relevant now, so you have to know."

"Was she pregnant?"

"*Pregnant?* What? What are you talking about? Umm, I mean, maybe, I don't know—no—why would she be pregnant? How did you even get to that from what I said?"

"You told me she had something she needed to tell me!"

"How could I possibly know if she's pregnant? You think she would have told me rather than you?"

"What then?"

"Look, I don't know if this means anything, or if it has anything to do with what's going on there, but you need to know. And you need to be careful."

"What? Careful of what? Of the police?"

"No, not at all. Let me just ask you this: Who killed her?"

Amit was quiet. He hadn't even thought in that direction until that question. It hadn't been important enough to stop and wonder about. Michal was dead, and that was all he cared about. He couldn't even think of anything else.

"Exactly," Yair continued. "It wasn't a robbery. You won't find signs of a break-in or anything missing."

Amit looked around, but it wasn't really necessary. Yair was right. Whoever had killed Michal was a pro.

"What are you saying?" he asked.

"Like I told you—I don't know if this means anything, but…"

"But?"

"Amit, Michal was an agent for the Mossad."

20.

Roni slowly walked back into the lobby. The agent's rough handling hadn't left a mark on her. She also wasn't as pale as she'd been when she'd read that nasty comment on Instagram. Yet still, her eyes couldn't hide what she'd just been through.

Inbar looked at Roni and asked if she was okay. Inbar was quite sure she looked worse now than she had before she'd left. Why had the time outside, alone, not calmed her? She'd been there close to half an hour. That's what happened when you occupied yourself with nothing but trivialities, Inbar figured. And now she had to tell Roni that... she decided to steer clear from that.

Sean walked in and Roni preferred to address him instead. "When are we flying to Barcelona?"

"Tomorrow morning at eight, I believe. Why?"

"Can you check if we can have an earlier flight?"

"Earlier? For when? Why?"

"As early as possible. If there's a flight out now, then now."

Sean looked at Roni. *What on earth is wrong with her,* he

wondered to himself. Inbar had indicated for him to keep his distance before, but now with the flight... should he be worried? Roni had given the same standard of show that she always did, so... Sean looked at Inbar who merely shrugged in answer. *Whatever.* "I'll see what I can do," he said and left to handle it.

Inbar turned to Roni again and said, "Eran called again when you were out."

"Great," Roni muttered, thoroughly impatient with everything. Including Eran.

Inbar glanced around them. They may have been standing in the corner of the entryway, but there were still quite a few people milling around them. None of them spoke Hebrew, she believed, but it lacked any kind of privacy. Inbar turned to one of the pillars and motioned for Roni. "Come here for a moment."

Roni looked at her. She had no idea what she wanted.

"Come here for a second, come on."

Roni took slow steps toward her. *What were these games about now, then?*

Inbar closed the distance between them and whispered, "I'm not supposed to tell you this, Eran told me not to."

"Not to tell me what?"

"He said he was buying a plane ticket over here. He'll be landing at six a.m., before our flight to Barcelona."

That's all I need, Roni thought. She was still far from recovering from having the Mossad agent die in her arms, she'd still not decided when and how she would handle this bloody SIM card, and now she also had to deal with Eran's jealous fit. She couldn't be bothered with it.

For a moment, she contemplated passing the SIM card to Eran, for him to be the one to take it back to Israel... but it was *Eran*. He was, quite possibly, the least qualified man for such a job. Not that he wasn't a patriot, he was simply incredibly irresponsible.

Well, she had to find some kind of good excuse to get out of meeting him.

As if he'd heard her wish, Sean came back with a smile on his face.

"What?" she asked, unable to hide her own smile while looking at him. His smiles were contagious.

"I love it when you smile," he said. "You know I'd do anything to see you happy. "

"What? You got a plane to turn around?" Inbar asked, shocked.

"Well, not literally," Sean replied.

"Inbar... seriously," Roni muttered.

"We can fly out at four in the morning. I got us seats. You need to get back to the hotel right away and pack. Then it's straight to the airport."

"You mean only us?"

"Yeah, there were only two seats left and... I know you love me and all, and parting from me is torture... but I can see there's something going on with you, so it's probably better you go with Inbar. I'll get there later on."

Roni hugged him. "Thank you."

Now all she had to do was talk to Eran.

She dialed his number and he picked up right away.

"Hey, how's my beautiful girl?"

"Eran, what are you doing?"

"What? You're the one who called."

"Yeah. Right. Cut the crap."

"What? What's wrong, babe?"

"Quit your games, okay? What's this nonsense about coming here and meeting me? What's gotten into you?"

"Inbar couldn't keep her mouth shut, then, huh?"

"Stop blaming everyone else and take responsibility for yourself. Grow the fuck up."

"I wanted to surprise you, is that not allowed? If she hadn't said anything to you, I'd have managed, too. What's wrong with that?"

"*What's wrong with that,*" Roni mimicked him. "Plenty! You idiot! I'm leaving in a couple of hours. Would you prefer it if Inbar hadn't told me you were planning on showing up the next morning? Unlike you, people here think about others, not just themselves."

Eran was silent for a moment before saying uncomfortably, "Weren't you supposed to be flying out at eight a.m. tomorrow? That's what Inbar told me. I bought a ticket according to that."

"That was the plan, yes, but then it changed. It's not like you told me you were coming here. You planned it all in secret with Inbar—so I knew nothing about it!"

"But you just said Inbar told you I was coming."

"After the ticket was already bought, so that you wouldn't come here for no reason," she yelled.

"Then why didn't she say anything before?"

"Because you told her not to tell me! What's *wrong* with you?" Her patience was officially running out.

"I see," Eran said, then paused for a second. "Why did you get an earlier flight?"

"Because I'm sick of this place and I want to get the hell out of here." And that was the truth. After "meeting" the agent, Roni couldn't stand being in Bucharest. The even more honest answer was what the agent had shared with her.

"You can tell you're fucking with me right now, right?" he said angrily.

"What?" Roni shook off her distractions. What was he going on about now?

"You giving me this bullshit about wanting to get the hell out of there and shit—it has nothing to do with Bucharest. You just can't wait to get to Barcelona. That's the truth."

"Okay, you've lost it."

"Maybe. I may have lost it—but I'm still fucking right!"

"Is this because of one stupid comment on Instagram?"

"It's not only the comment, it's about what *really happened.*"

"Which was *nothing*! You nutcase. *Nothing!*"

"That's not what the person who wrote it said."

"*What?*" she practically shrieked into the phone. But then she fell silent, trying to figure out what on earth he meant with that. *The one who wrote it told him something had happened? Who could have... Inbar.* Eran wouldn't have put any weight into what anyone else had said.

It couldn't be, though. Not her. Not Inbar. But she had been talking with him secretly. *Behind my back.* Inbar had said he'd called when she was outside—*but he hadn't called me!* She realized. She'd seen no missed call from him. That meant he'd called Inbar. Had she told him what had happened? Had she been the one to write that comment? *How could it be?*

"Right. I can hear you thinking. Not bad for an idiot, huh?"

"You... what? How did you even get..." She was confused. She felt betrayed. She looked up from staring at the floor, her gaze stopping on Inbar, whose expression hardened by the second.

"How did I come to that conclusion? Easy. I've got a special key that opens up any girl of my choosing. She told me about it so she didn't have to feel guilty about my spreading her legs and fucking her. Yeah, that's right. You think you're the only one?"

Roni couldn't talk. Her stomach roiled. A look of utter shock and horror spread over her face.

"You what? Who?"

She pulled the phone away from her ear and stared at Inbar disbelievingly. Inbar hadn't heard a word of what Eran had said, but she could read enough from Roni's expression. She stood there, pale and frozen in place.

Roni looked at her and started crying. "How could..." then

she threw her phone straight toward Inbar. She ducked, letting the phone sail above her head, only to smash loudly against the pillar behind her.

The extravagant pillar built in 1888.

21.

Layla ordered unit 3 to either catch or eliminate the group from the CIA. She gathered up unit 4, then left. She was heading to the Old City while still keeping in touch with HQ back at the apartment.

Achsan, the commander of unit 3, hadn't needed Layla's order, but was glad he had it, nonetheless. The last fifteen minutes saw him tailing two people, one relatively tall with blond hair, and the other of average height and with mousy-colored hair. They were both wearing jeans and graphic T-shirts, and they looked just like the dozens of other tourists who were still walking around the Old City. It was only now, due to the late hour, that the pubs were finally starting to empty.

In fact, the two "tourists" wouldn't have even seemed suspicious if it hadn't been for him noticing them put their two Rugers in their bags and melting into the crowd. Right after, Achsan met Ahmad and urged him to go to HQ. He'd been tailing them ever since. Both of his fellow agents from unit 3 were on his right and left, keeping a twenty-to-thirty meter distance. They still kept eye contact with him, though. They were prepared to halt any attempt at escape.

Despite the late hour, there were still too many tourists around, so Achsan planned on eliminating the two agents, not capturing them. Layla's order, as put, came on time, and Achsan started closing the distance between him and the CIA agents. When no one was looking, he picked up a beer glass from one of the tables, pouring a good amount of it all over himself. He walked faster toward the taller of the two, wobbling drunkenly, still holding the beer mug in his left hand.

Achsan came right up to him. The tall man turned, and it seemed like he was unaware of what was about to happen. Achsan held up the silenced gun, aiming it straight at the taller man's head.

The taller agent followed the movement of the gun, as if hypnotized, but seemed to be too paralyzed to act. He still didn't move when he saw Achsan's head explode in front of his eyes, nor when Achsan's body was flung against his.

He watched Achsan's body fall to the ground, and only then registered that he'd heard a gunshot. But it hadn't been from the gun in Achsan's hand. Instead, it was from the gun that had shot him dead. A gun without a silencer.

There was screaming from every direction. There was a charge of fleeing men and women. The tall man turned to his partner and saw him on the ground. It was the last thing he saw. Achsan's second quickly closed the distance between them. After he killed the man of average height, he aimed and shot the taller man, too. Achsan's third closed in on the agent who'd shot Achsan, and killed him. Seconds later, with people running in every direction, another agent killed Achsan's third.

Achsan's second could see what was going on, but couldn't get any closer because of the sheer amount of people rushing down the street. He reported to Layla that the CIA agents had been eliminated, but that they'd been attacked by another group and that the entirety of unit 3—including Achsan—were gone. Right after that, another agent came up behind him and took him out.

Unit 2 heard the report and made a fast pace toward where all the people were screaming and running. They could hear the shots fired, and they saw the agents who'd taken out unit 3.

Unit 2 spread out and quickly went into action. They remained unseen, thanks to the rushing crowd. For some reason, the agents stood their ground and didn't run. Unit 2 managed to take them by surprise, and a shootout ensued. The agents were good, but they were no match for unit 2, and ten minutes later, the fight was over.

Layla heard the gunshots and rushed to the scene, arriving only ten minutes later.

What she saw was not encouraging. The passersby had abandoned the scene. There were bodies everywhere: the two CIA agents, the three members of unit 3, four additional agents, and one agent from unit 2 who'd been hit in his stomach. He was still alive, but wouldn't be for much longer. None of them was the thief—that she knew—which meant that they were wasting time.

She glanced at the foreign agents and again was struck with a sinking feeling. She'd at once been right and wrong. The two agents she'd suspected were American were indeed that, but the four others were Mossad. She was sure of it. And if she went by what the head of unit 2 told her, they hadn't tried to run like the Americans had. No, they'd tried to draw fire to themselves. That could only mean one thing: the thief was Mossad, just like they'd thought at first. The Americans were merely helping them.

They had to go back to the original plan. Layla ordered unit 1 to prepare to raid the Radisson Hotel. Her orders were clear: they were to situate themselves 200 meters from the hotel and wait for her.

She started organizing the scene. It would take time for the Romanians to get there. The Mossad would be here first. Layla wanted to make sure that those who arrived would not be leaving with their lives. She instructed the commanders of units 2 and 4 to stake out the place, then took a step back and surveyed the site. *What a mess.*

"Okay," she said. "I'm going to join unit 1 at the Radisson. Keep me updated."

She started to walk up the street, then paused.

She put her fingers against her ear and asked, "Are you sure?"

She listened once again, then pressed, "According to what evidence?" silence.

"I see. Wait there. I'll be right over."

The leader of unit 4 looked at her. "What happened?"

"Unit 1 was situating in the bushes next to the opera house," she replied. "They found the thief. He's dead."

"Should I come with you?"

"No. Stay here, stick to the plan. I'll meet unit 1 and keep you updated."

She reported back to HQ then left in the direction of unit 1.

22.

Shaked stopped to listen to the communication device. He was 100 meters out from reaching the Radisson Hotel. Yoav, listening too, watched him.

"So… we giving up on going to the Radisson?"

"Looks like it," Shaked answered. "All the Iranians seem be in the Old City."

They turned back and ran through the university campus in the direction of the Old City.

Everyone had been activated. According to the report he'd received, they'd attacked an Iranian squadron somewhere along Str Șelari in the Old City. The attack had been successful, at least so far as Shaked understood, but now the agents were stuck there like sitting ducks. Shaked was almost tempted to order them out of there, but that meant that their chances of finding the agent grew smaller. He gritted his teeth and told them all to stay put. He told them to be careful, as if that meant anything.

"Shachar?" Shaked called on the secure line as they continued their quick pace toward the Old City.

"Yes?"

"Connect me to the headquarters."

"Right away, hold on a second... here. Right. You're being put through."

"Office?"

"Yes."

Shaked recognized the voice. It was Daniel. The Director of Michmoret.

"Have you received our report on the investigation?"

"We have."

"So, what's our next step?"

"Find him."

"And..."

"It's not a hard disk. It's much smaller—and that, the Iranians don't know. When you find him, make contact with us. I'll tell you what to look for."

"And what about him?"

"He's dead."

"How do you know that?"

"I'm not going to say it on a phone call."

"I see. What can you tell me, then?"

"Two things. The first: the Iranians have no idea he's dead, but they know he's badly wounded."

"And how did you reach that conclusion? Can you tell me that much?"

"Because they're still trying to keep you from finding him

instead of searching for his body."

"Okay. And the second point?"

"Is that he didn't leave the device on his person."

"Why is that?"

"Because he assumed that the Iranians would reach him before we did."

"I see," Shaked said again and took a moment to think. "What do you think he did with the device?"

"The way I see it, there are two options for this, too: the first is that he hid it somewhere—but I would say the chances of that are slim since he didn't get in touch with us to let us know its location."

"And the second?" he pressed.

"That he found someone to give it to, and did."

"To whom?"

"That, you're going to have to find out. Find them and contact me. Then—"

At that moment, they heard a barrage of shots from down the road, not far from them.

"—there's another thing you need to kn—"

Shaked didn't wait to hear what Daniel had to say further. He hung up and ran ahead, Yoav at his side.

It took them almost fifteen minutes to arrive. They could see the stragglers of the crowd running in each direction. When they closed in on the scene, they slowed and looked around. They were about 100 meters from the place. There were overturned tables, discarded chairs and glasses, plates and mugs were strewn about—and bodies. Shaked couldn't count how many.

For a moment they stood staring at the carnage. Then it happened. It had been years since last it had happened to him, but sure enough, there was Tzukerman, yelling in his mind. That, Shaked knew, could only mean one thing: Tzukerman's words were pointless. He already knew on his own. He acted instinctively, grabbing Yoav and pulling him down.

The rest, Yoav, who quickly caught up, did on his own. They both rolled to the side and plastered themselves to the brick wall at the corner of the street. Shaked heard Tzukerman yell, "*Trap!*" right as the first bullets whizzed by.

The place they'd chosen was relatively secure. The bullets hit above them and to their sides, but none of the shooters could hit them. The problem was that they were penned in. There was nowhere for them to move—not down the street, or up, back where they'd come. Going out to the main street would be certain death: the bullets were coming from down the street and above. *You yelled too late,* Shaked said to Tzukerman in his head. *We're already deep in the trap.*

He would be surrounded by the Iranians in a matter of seconds. There was no doubt about it—that would have been *his* next move. Yoav had come to the same conclusion and shared a heavy glance with Shaked. They'd both accepted their fate. They wouldn't be leaving this place alive, but they would not go out without a fight. If they were going, they'd take out as many Iranians as possible.

The whistling and angle of the bullets changed. The Iranians were starting to move. To close in on them. Then they heard a mighty barrage. All the bullets, so far, had been fired from a silenced gun, but they were filled to capacity with gunpowder, meaning that they were shot with maximum force, far beyond the speed of sound. The silencer may have muffled the shots, but the sonic booms of the bullets still sounded like thunderclaps in their ears. No, the sound was different. It was a mighty attack. But then everything stopped, and silence fell.

Yoav looked at Shaked questioningly. *Are we even alive?* he seemed to ask.

Shaked gave him the same look back. They peered over at the street, but couldn't see anything. Could this have been part of the trap? Were the Iranians merely luring them out? Shaked didn't think so.

The Iranians could have taken them out—no games, no muss.

Was this another force? Was it friendly? As far as Shaked knew, there could be additional CIA and MI6 agents on the ground, but in relatively small units. That had not been anything like what they'd heard. *So, what the hell was it?*

The street was still empty, and the silence deafening. They finally saw a man walk in their direction. He was smiling. A sweet, mightily annoying smile. Shaked couldn't quite believe he lived to see that smile again. There was no way he could be in Bucharest now, because he knew for a fact that he was in Africa. Saar and his smile.

Saar! How was it even possible that he was *here?*

Shaked wasn't supposed to know—but there were many things that he wasn't supposed to know and did. The fact was that Saar and his men *were* in Africa, so, what was he doing here?

Slowly, shadows disconnected from parts of the building and joined Saar. And it *was* him. *Those poor Iranians. They didn't stand a chance.*

"Saar?"

"Shaked Yossef! As I live and breathe."

"I can't believe I'm saying this… but am I glad to see you."

Saar merely laughed.

"How did you get here?"

"Know the app GetTaxi?" Saar asked.

"Yeah, so?"

"Well, you use it, then press a button and you get an F-18 on your head."

"Shut up!"

"We're here, aren't we?"

Shaked's mind spun through too many thoughts to count. Saar's guys arrived from Nigeria to Bucharest, with the Americans flying them over on F-18's. It was insane. That was unprecedented assistance from their end. That couldn't have happened through the use of Mossad connections alone. It had to have come straight from the Prime Minister. Nothing less than that. So, that also meant there was a price. A steep price, most likely. And it would most definitely be collected at some time in the future. He didn't have time for that now, though. There were too many unknowns and too much urgent business right here.

"Okay, listen up," Shaked said, "Thank you, but we don't have much time. Look over the bodies here, check to see if any are a woman."

"None," Karen said, giving him a reproving look.

"That wasn't what I meant, Karen. One of theirs."

"I meant that too," she replied. "There isn't. I've already checked."

"So, she's not here."

"Who?" Saar asked.

"Her name is Layla. She's their commander."

"What now, then?" Saar asked.

"We can't get the bodies because the Romanian police will be here any moment. You're coming with us to the Radisson Hotel. It's the key. I'll fill you in on the way."

23.

The Director of the Mossad looked at Daniel.

Daniel had just finished talking with Shaked. "They already know quite a bit. The Iranians, too. He hung up because there were shots fired."

"Saar's group will be with them in a minute," the Director said. "I hope they get there on time."

Daniel looked at the Director for a long moment.

"What do you think?"

"About?"

"All of it. How is this going to end?"

"The Iranians are a step ahead. They're going to beat us."

"What do you mean beat us?"

"It means that they will figure out who has it before we do, and they will also reach them before us. It'll take them a while, but it'll take us longer," Daniel surmised.

"I can order Saar to shoot everything that moves."

"The Iranians aren't idiots. That's not going to give us an advantage."

"Then what the hell are you saying? Give me *something!*" the Director exploded. "I don't need you to tell me where I fall short when put against the *Iranians,* I need you to tell me what to do so we can beat them to it!"

"Yes… I wish I knew." Daniel looked him right in the eye, contemplating his next more.

"What?"

"Look…. It's not something we know how to do."

"*What?* What don't we know how to do?"

"Finding someone and protecting them. It's not what we practice doing. Iranians find things like that easier. It's classic search and destroy. They simply need to hunt. *We* need to protect. It's not in our DNA. But…"

"But?"

"But other units… other units, that's exactly what they train for."

"The unit for personal security in the *Shabak?*"

"For example."

"Don't give me clues. What are you suggesting? Should we involve them?"

"Maybe. It's not your call to make, though."

Daniel fell silent and let those words fully penetrate.

"You son of a bitch," the Director muttered.

He did listen, Daniel thought.

"Ortal?" the Director spoke into the intercom after taking a deep breath. "Get me the Prime Minister, please."

The Director updated the Prime Minister on the happenings

in Bucharest and added Daniel's insights.

"And what do you think?" asked the Prime Minister.

"That there isn't a difference between ours and the Iranians' missions."

"Explain."

"We—and they—want to reach the person who carries the device and take it from them. We want to get it to Israel, they want to destroy it. That's the only difference."

"Okay. You've done an excellent job so far, but you're not alone. Like Daniel said, just as Israel has other assets we can use, so too does its Prime Minister have more options at his disposal."

"So, what now?"

"Now, carry on as you are. I need to get some advice, then I'll get back to you."

24.

Layla arrived at the large parking lot outside the Hilton Hotel. To her left, around the bend and a little ahead, was the Radisson Hotel. To her right was the Opera House, which was now silent and empty. Between the parking lot and the building, was a small garden. It was lit by faint streetlights and nothing more.

Layla went into the dim garden and reached unit 1. The squadron members were doing peripheral security as the unit's commander leaned over the body.

"Are you sure it's him?"

"He looks just like the man in the security cameras. He hasn't even changed his clothes."

Layla looked at the thief. He had been stripped entirely of his clothes and been meticulously searched. She looked at the gruesome wound in his stomach and thanked Bazad once again.

By the time she'd arrived, unit 1 had searched the whole small garden, hoping to find the hard disk. She didn't believe they'd find it, but not searching was a mistake they wouldn't make.

"We didn't find the hard disk," the squadron leader told her. "It wasn't with him or in the garden."

"Yes, clearly."

"Why? Where else would it be?"

"He gave it to someone. Someone he could trust."

"How do you know he didn't hide it somewhere?"

"Because then he would have had to make the call to tell them where it is. He doesn't have a secure line, so we would have intercepted any call he'd made and found it before them. No. He didn't hide it. I wouldn't have hidden it, either. I'd have passed it on to someone else."

"Who could it be?"

"An Israeli businessman who's here in Bucharest."

"And how are we supposed to know who it is?"

"All the Israeli businessmen are staying at the Radisson. We'll find them. Every last one of them. Leave the thief and get ready to raid the hotel."

"Could the Mossad already have the hard disk?"

"No. They're still here, looking. The Mossad hasn't found the businessman yet, and we will find him before they do."

The unit spread out and made its way to the Radisson Hotel. Two passersby were strolling past the road leading up to the hotel. You could still hear the police sirens heading toward the scene in the Old City.

Layla and the unit leader waited as the couple went on their way, then entered and went straight for the reception desk. One of the unit members stayed by the doorway to guard the entrance. The second member took up position down the hall. The hotel's lobby was silent this time of night, the casino was closed, and no guests were milling around.

Layla turned to one of the two receptionists, asking for a couple's suite for two nights. She leaned over the desk a little, giving the receptionist a perfect view of her accentuated cleavage. The man valiantly tried not to stare while working to find them an available room.

The main purpose of Layla leaning forward the way she was, was so she could look at the computer screen and make sure he got into the system. Accentuating her breasts was nothing more than a bonus. Once confirming he was in, she pulled out a gun with a silencer and shot the receptionist in the head. The unit leader followed her lead, and a split second after, shot the other receptionist, too.

Layla got behind the desk and made quick work of scanning the guest list and room numbers. She sectioned them out according to country of origin, then printed the results. The hotel currently had eight Israelis staying with them. Layla quickly went through the list, adding two more guests who had a German passport—their names seemed Israeli. Ten people overall.

She divvied up the guests, three for the unit leader, three for the man guarding the hallway, and four for her. The unit member who'd guarded the entrance slipped behind the reception desk.

Layla issued out the keys and the three of them went on their way.

Layla went up one floor and turned to the first room. She opened the door with her keycard and found the door to be locked with a chain from the inside, too. She pulled out her silenced gun, shot the lock, and the door opened.

Layla made her way to the bed and saw an old, white-haired man sleeping deeply. *No, he's not the man I'm looking for.* Still, she gave his leg a kick. The man woke and looked at her with glazed eyes. At first, he seemed alarmed, but once he focused on her and realized that a beautiful woman stood in front of him, he smiled, pulled the blanket aside, and exposed his wrinkly, old body. He was naked. He patted the bed invitingly.

Layla was partly amused with the situation, partly frustrated with the result—this man was definitely not the one she was looking for. Layla shot him in the head and continued to the next Israeli guest.

The second Israeli didn't repeat the same surrealistic response as the first, but reacted in a way that could not be misinterpreted. He had no idea why she'd appeared in his room, so he'd clearly not met the thief. The same happened with the other remaining Israelis.

Something seemed off. All squadron members reported the same outcome. It was a complete surprise—and she didn't understand it. Anyone who'd received the hard disk from the thief would not react the way these people had. Something was wrong. She was doing something wrong.

Layla ordered everyone back down to meet at the reception desk. The scene in the lobby was not appealing. Three unlucky guests who'd walked in while they'd been eliminating suspects had been shot by the agent at the front desk. The unit leader reported having met another guest on the seventh-floor hallway, who'd also been shot. He'd dragged the man's body into the room of the final Israeli on his list.

The hour was, indeed, late, and the shots had been silenced, but the carnage they'd left behind would mean that the Romanian police would arrive sooner rather than later. Two unit members dragged the bodies into a side room, but that wouldn't give them more than an hour. They had to leave the hotel. Now.

When the whole unit met back up, she asked, "What's wrong?"

"It doesn't seem like any of them had contact with the thief," the unit leader replied.

"Maybe he spoke to someone in the Hilton, instead?" offered one of the team members.

"No," Layla stated. "No. I think we're missing something."

The members of unit 1 watched her silently.

"He must not have turned to one of the Israeli businessmen."

"So, who then?"

"I don't know," she replied. "Come, let's go back to the beginning."

Layla led the unit back to the thief's body in the garden.

We're wasting time. They spread out and Layla looked around. Since she'd ruled out the Radisson, she didn't notice Shaked, Yoav, and Saar's men sneaking into the hotel.

"What are we looking for?" the unit leader asked her.

"Whoever the thief had looked for here," she said. "Unlike what we initially thought, he wasn't looking for a businessman. But he was still searching for someone. The question is, who."

"But there's nothing here," one of the men said.

"Now," Layla shot back. "But there may have been when the thief arrived. Was there an opera show?"

"No, just a fashion show. No opera."

"A fashion show?" Layla asked aloud, though didn't actually address the question to any of the men in the unit. She walked toward the opera house. It was dark now, but still had a large banner, front and center, proclaiming the fashion show. She looked at the banner, feeling an inescapable sense of déjà vu. She'd seen the same poster—at the airport.

The writing on the poster described the fashion show itself, but that wasn't what had drawn Layla's attention. On the left part of the poster, was a prominent figure that drew her attention. Layla looked at the woman on the poster and figured out the thief's move.

She was well known in Belgium, and even in Iran.

"Roni Carmi," she said.

"What?"

"Roni Carmi, the Israeli model. She was here, at the fashion show. She was the one the thief was looking for. She's the one who has the hard disk."

"Roni Carmi? The model? What's the angle? Why would he choose her?"

"Two reasons," Layla replied, "The first being he was sure she was Israeli. The second is that she would have been the last person we suspected. It's an excellent reason to choose her. Anyway, it's what I would have done in his shoes."

Layla called someone on her phone, talking with him for about a minute. "Go." She ended the call then turned to the unit. "Barcelona."

25.

The Director of the Mossad looked at Daniel and cursed.

"This is all your fault," he complained.

"Yes, it's all my fault. Or it's all thanks to me. But in the end, the Prime Minister approved the mission, despite it being done against his specific orders, and I took the whole risk on my own shoulders."

"I'm not talking about that."

"I know. The decision to turn to him now was also the right one. His response was annoying, I'll give you that, and I'm not sure he's right about it, either. But it was still the right call to contact him. You know that, too."

"Let's hope they know what they're doing."

"Can we help them?"

"You heard the Minister of Defense. They were rather determined."

The second call with the Prime Minister had come mere minutes after the first. The Prime Minister had gotten back to them with the Minister of Defense with him. They didn't bring in the *Shabak*, no. They passed the mission straight on to the Israeli Defense Forces.

The IDF? On European soil? Daniel still found it hard to believe.

But as the Director had said… they had been determined.

26.

Roni rested her head against the headrest and sighed. The plane angled for the runway—a moment of quiet—then the engines roared and it began to gain speed.

She asked herself what exactly she was doing. Going—alone—to Barcelona. No Sean, naturally, no Inbar, and no Eran. Most importantly, she didn't even have her phone. And, with all those other problems plaguing her mind, the mission the dead Mossad agent dropped on her loomed darker than all. The constant reminder—the discomfort in her pubic area—didn't allow her to think of much else.

Inbar had apologized over and over, had sobbed that Eran had seduced her. She'd said that she had tried to resist, but didn't manage. Roni was thoroughly uninterested in hearing a word. She didn't want to see her, not ever again. The sheer magnitude of the insult, the humiliation, and betrayal of them both wouldn't allow her to even think of forgiving them. She wouldn't even listen. Roni simply wanted Inbar out of her life. Simply so. *Poof.* Inbar had offered Roni her phone so she wouldn't walk around Barcelona without a way of contacting someone, but she'd refused that, as well.

She left Inbar and the remnants of her broken phone in the opera house, which had, by then, been almost completely deserted, then went back to her room at the Hilton. She'd thought about who she could call, but everyone back home was asleep. Sean's number she didn't know off the top of her head, nor had she remembered which room he was staying in. She'd tried to get the room number from the front desk, but they'd kept mum. They'd agreed to call him, but there had been no answer when they'd tried.

She hadn't even had the flight information at hand, not the airline, flight number, hour, or ticket. Everything had been sent to her phone. Inbar's too, but that had been moot. She'd refused to ask Inbar anything at all. Anyway, Inbar seemed to have let her be since she'd not tried to contact her in any way since.

Roni had allowed herself to wallow in her misery for a little while before pulling herself together. In the same way she'd dealt with the non-existent rape while she'd been held by the Mossad agent, so too had she handled this crisis. She assumed the worst was behind her and thought only of how she could improve herself going forward.

The Mossad agent… thinking of him made her heart twinge. He'd sacrificed his life for their country, and his body had been left there like a discarded dog. He was lying in the bushes, far from any loved ones—all of whom didn't even know he was gone. She'd felt sorry he wasn't there with her, supporting her… comforting her, perhaps, and, most importantly, telling her what her next move should be. Realizing she'd only been thinking of herself made her feel even more sorry. She'd let the guilt overwhelm her for a moment until she smothered it all back down. If the guilt and self-pity came at her together, she wouldn't stand a chance.

A plan! I need a plan, she'd thought to herself.

The flight had been set for four a.m., so it hadn't left her much time at all. She'd packed and planned: *drive to the airport, search for the airlines that had flights out to Barcelona, reach the check-in with the hope that her name would be on the flight list…*

Before she left, however, there had been one more important thing she'd had to do. She reached into her pocket and pulled out the micro SIM card, thanking God she hadn't lost it with all the emotional turmoil she'd been through.

She'd stared at it, wondering what she could do with it. It wasn't large… but still…

She took out a tampon, and with the help of a pen, made an incision large enough to stuff the SIM into it. She'd then put the tampon into a condom she'd had in her bag—one there for "just in case"—let out the remaining air, and tied it. She'd looked at her "masterpiece" with a sense of utter disgust.

She didn't have a choice though, she'd agreed with herself. It was a dying man's last request.

A minute later she walked around the room, muttering to

herself and the dead agent, "How pleasant and comfortable this all is—they don't share all of *this* in spy movies, do they?"

The uncomfortable feeling in her pubic area wouldn't be going away any time soon, but she'd forced herself to get used to it and move on to the next order of business. The Barcelona football team wasn't even in Barcelona... so it mattered none.

She'd cleaned up, and then ordered a taxi and went downstairs.

The receptionist told her that her taxi was already waiting outside, and she'd left. She'd already been outside when the receptionist came running after her. For a moment she'd panicked, but then realized that she hadn't checked out. Honestly, there were so many things she had gotten out of the habit of doing because of the help from Sean and Inbar. They'd completely spoiled her.

She'd apologized, paid, then got in the taxi.

The taxi turned right. Roni sat in the back, on the right-hand side, but kept looking left to the Radisson Hotel. Perhaps choosing the Hilton had been a mistake, she'd thought. Maybe if she'd been in the Radisson, she could have found a nice Israeli businessman to spend the night with. She'd looked at the security guard standing at the entrance to the hotel, and for a moment had thought he was holding a gun. *A gun! In Bucharest, not Israel.* None of the security there was armed, but the guard had been holding a gun—it hadn't even been holstered! The guard had looked right at her, and she froze. *He can't see me,* she'd thought to herself. The windows were tinted and she was sitting on the far side of the taxi. Yet still, she hadn't been able to escape the uncomfortable feeling trickling down her back. She knew that whoever had injured and eventually brought about the death of the agent could possibly already be looking for her.

She convinced herself the armed guard was merely there because of the casino at the hotel, and that she had no reason to worry. *Goddamn lucky I didn't decide to stay at the Radisson. And even better that I'm leaving this city.*

The drive to the airport had taken almost three hours, and the time seemed to move backwards, it dragged on so slowly. She'd felt close to losing her mind. When they'd stopped, she saw that those three hours had in fact been twenty-two minutes. It was a good thing it hadn't been her watch she'd decided to throw at Inbar.

Roni had walked into the airport, finding that there was only one airline flying out to Barcelona at around four a.m.—at four a.m. exactly, in fact. That left her with twenty minutes to spare, so she'd really had to hurry.

Luckily, there had been no line, and her name had indeed been listed.

"Are you flying alone?"

"Yes."

"There's another name listed to be flying with you an... Imber?"

"Inbar, yes. She decided not to fly to Barcelona in the end."

"We cannot give a refund with tickets that were bought at

the last minute, I hope you unders—"

"It's fine," Roni had cut in. "I understand the ticket is nonre-fundable. She decided not to come. Let's not delay the plane."

"You're right," the attendant said, and less than a minute later Roni had been on her way.

Her heartbeat had skyrocketed when she'd passed security and the metal detector, trying to believe that there was no way for them to find the SIM card. Still, she'd held her breath until she was through, but had immediately been stopped by security. He checked her and saw that she was nervous.

"Everything all right?" he'd asked politely but firmly.

Roni, still relieved about the metal detector not picking up on the SIM, answered, "Yes, of course, I'm simply a little over-tired." Then she'd smiled. An honest smile.

Her smile had melted the stern exterior straight off the guard's face, and he smiled back at her.

She'd carried on to the boarding gate and waited her turn.

She hadn't even been the last one on the plane.

At that same time, in a different area of the airport, hidden from passersby, a man answered his phone.

"Yes, yes, I saw her," he said. "She's kind'a hard to miss."

The man listened for a moment, then replied⊠ "Barcelona. I don't have a ticket, but I can reach her."

"Go," came the voice on the other end of the line.

The man closed the phone, threw his firearm into the trash, got the flight ticket to Cypress he'd got beforehand so he could reach the departure lounge, then made his way to security. He quickly noted the gate number of the flight to Barcelona and then walked fast—as fast as he could without drawing undue attention—after Roni.

Roni reached the front of the line and held out her plane ticket to the flight attendant. The woman slid the ticket into the ticket reader, then wished her a good flight. Roni started to make her way into the passenger's boarding bridge, but then heard a commotion behind her. She'd turned and saw a man walking—almost running—in the direction of her boarding gate. He stopped once he was twenty meters away, but he was staring at her. *Staring. At her.*

Her blood froze in her veins. The look on his face had looked exactly like that of the guard at the Radisson hotel. Only... this man was looking right at her, and he could see her looking back at him.

She'd turned back and rushed through the bridge.

He doesn't have a ticket. He doesn't have a ticket, she'd repeated to herself.

The plane sped across the runway, and Roni muttered a little prayer before slowly calming. She was on the way to Barcelona. She was safe. For a moment, even the discomfort *down there* was forgotten.

27.

Yair couldn't fall back asleep.

The conversation with Amit had left him completely drained. He was consumed with guilt. Hadas had noticed and had told him that he'd meant well and that not everything was under his control. He agreed, yet still couldn't fall asleep.

Amit told him he was planning on flying out to Barcelona that night. He'd be there soon. Yair promised him he'd take care of everything. He reported to the Mossad about Michal's death after the phone call with Amit. They'd listened to him politely, but he didn't feel as if they'd taken it seriously enough. And that seemed odd. He made a note to look deeper into that particular problem the next morning.

Hadas had fallen asleep with her arms around him. He gently extracted himself from her hold and rose from the bed. At least none of the children had woken up. Yair walked to the kitchen, poured himself a cup of cold water, sat in the silence of the sleeping household, and took slow sips. He tried to muddle through his thoughts of the last day, of how he'd tried to fix a life that was not his own, even though no one had asked him to do so.

He was deep in thought when his phone rang.

Yair was sure it was Amit, but the name on the screen depicted Chen Friedman. The Unit leader. The commander of *Sayeret Matcal*. *How could he have heard about Michal so fast?*

"Chen?"

"Hi, Yair. I'm sorry about the hour."

"It's all right. I'm not sleeping. But you probably already knew that."

"Yeah, you answered rather fast. But no… why? What do I already know?"

"About what happened in Nice."

"In Nice? What happened there?"

"Michal?"

"Michal? Which Michal? What happened to her?"

"The Mossad agent who was killed. She happened to be my brother's girlfriend. Amit's."

"God, what a mess. I'm sorry to hear that. I didn't know. Is it connected?"

"Connected to what?"

"Yair, why do you think I called you?"

"I don't know. Not about Michal, I presume?"

"I don't know her and I haven't heard about the incident. She's one of yours. Out of the two of us, I'm the one who wasn't in the Mossad."

"So, why *did* you call?"

"Look, there's a serious mess in Bucharest. It may have something to do with what happened in Nice, though I can't see the connection just yet. Anyway, that's not why I called you."

"Why then?"

"I can't say over the phone. Can you meet me? I'm in the car already, I'm ten minutes from your place."

"Okay, come here. I'll be waiting downstairs."

Yair went back to bed and hugged Hadas.

"Can't sleep?" she asked without opening her eyes.

"No, but there's something else."

That made her open her eyes, looking worried and confused.

"No, it has nothing to do with it. Something else. Chen wants to meet me and talk about something he couldn't talk about over the phone. He's coming here."

"Have him come up."

"Of course not. I'll meet him downstairs."

"Okay, wake me when you get back, then." Chen Friedman conferred with Yair every once in a while, so Hadas didn't think it odd—not even when it was the middle of the night. She definitely didn't think it was something worth staying awake over.

"I will," he said, kissed her, and went downstairs to wait.

Three minutes later, the Hummer belonging to the commander of the *Sayeret Matcal* rolled into his street and parked next to him. Yair got in and shook Chen's hand.

"What am I doing inside my car two meters from your house at this hour, huh? Isn't that what you're asking yourself?" Chen said.

"Something like that."

"I've just come from the Kirya. Met with the Minister of Defense, no less."

"There a war coming?"

"No. Not that. It's your guys from the Mossad who are in trouble. Caesarea is getting kicked all to hell in Bucharest."

"What's going on?"

"I wasn't told the whole story, but from what I understood, the Mossad had a mission go too well. So well that they weren't prepared for it. The Iranians are onto them, and now Bucharest is full of dead bodies. The Americans are involved, and we've quite unhappily had to update the Romanians."

"What's it got to do with us?"

"Apparently one of our agents managed to get something out of Iran—pinging the radar of the whole world while he was at it. The Iranians are after him, we're trying to find him and protect him, and, most importantly, we're trying to get our hands on that *thing* he got out of there. The Americans aren't clear on all the facts yet, but going by the Iranian's reaction, they saw the potential and helped us big time. In the meantime, we're all going in blind. The most recent rumors peg the agent as being dead."

"I still don't see what this has to do with us."

"The Prime Minister decided to get the Mossad out of there, and get us in instead."

"What? *Why?* What's the logic in that kind of a move?"

"It's the Prime Minister. What does logic even mean to that guy?"

"Come on, seriously. What's the plan?"

"The same as with changing up a special investigative unit in the police force, I believe. The Mossad isn't delivering, and they're looking for someone who will. The official excuse is that Caesarea isn't trained in finding and protecting people. The Prime Minister is looking for someone with counter-terrorism experience and personal security detailing. Long story short, it's either the *Shabak* or us. He won't let the *Shabak* out of the country, so we're what's left."

"Military force on European soil…? Does that make any kind of sense to you?"

"No, but the Prime Minister is determined, and the Minister of Defense jumped on the political side of it, so now it's all falling to me."

"And what's that got to do with me?"

"There's something I don't understand, and I need your view on it," Chen said.

"And that is…?"

"Look, it's not only that this was dropped in our laps without a by-your-leave, I've also been forbidden from sending out a team and building an official HQ. The Defense Minister specifically said that I'm only to send in one man. It makes no sense."

"Not in the least."

"So, why that order?"

"What do you want from me? You're the one who spoke to the Minister of Defense. You should ask him."

"I'm serious, Yair, don't be childish. Of course I asked him, and he blew me off completely. It's something with the way the Mossad works. I need you to tell me what's going on behind the smokescreen."

Yair stopped to think for a moment, then asked, "Say, how deeply are the Americans involved?"

"From what I understood, they got Saar's group from Africa to Bucharest with F-18s and they're coordinating everything with the Romanians... keeping them calm. They've also sent out CIA agents."

"That's some serious involvement."

"It would seem so."

"Okay, I think I understand," Yair said and told the commander of the *Sayeret Matcal* why he thought the Minister of Defense decided as he did.

Chen listened, paused to think, then said, "You know who I'm going to send out there, right?"

Yair looked at him and cursed.

"I wasn't Mossad—you were," Chen pressed.

"But I was hardly *Caesarea*."

"True. And neither was I. Who would you have me send, then? Someone from active service? To Europe? What would they even do there? They'd be eaten alive."

Yair glared.

"You were a high-ranking officer in the Unit, and you were in the Mossad, too," the commander continued. "I don't have anyone more suited than you."

Yair remained quiet as he kept watching the man next to him. He hadn't seen this coming. To say that it had come at a bad time was a serious understatement. This wasn't about serving in the reserves, this was a complicated, thoroughly intricate mission—which meant there was a high probability of injury. However, with the American's involvement, that risk may have lessened.

Suddenly a more suitable man for the job popped into his mind. It also came with a wave of crippling guilt and honest anxiety. That man was better for the job, but every time Yair had tried to interfere, the man had only suffered for it. Emotion clogged his throat. He would be sending him to his possible death. On the other hand, every other decision he made that was based on emotion wasn't much better. Perhaps he should think this through like a high-tech executive, instead? Weigh in on the decision only through merit? He'd either gain from this or stop suffering. That thought horrified him, and he tried to shake it firmly *off*.

In a cold, tactical view, Amit was a much better choice than he was. He may not have been Mossad, but he'd been security for a very long time. Besides, Amit was already in Europe, and with Michal's murder quite possibly being connected to this, he may very well want revenge. And further still, this whole situation might clear the air with how he'd left the Unit. With the Americans involved, it severely lowered the risk—he'd thought that before Amit's name even popped into his head.

Yair smothered his emotions and forced himself to overcome

it all. His decision was made. "You do have someone who's more suited than I am," he said.

"Who?"

"Amit."

"Your brother Amit?"

"That's right."

"Are you kidding me?"

"Not at all."

"Look. I appreciate you and your input, but you're hardly objective in this situation. There are things you seem to be forgetting. Even if—and this is a big if—I put the past aside, with his girlfriend just getting murdered, his judgment will be way off. That's completely out of line."

"You're right, I'm not objective, and the last thing I want is to send my brother on a mission like this, but he's more qualified than I am. And he's in Europe as we speak. His girlfriend being murdered could actually be a point of motivation against the Iranians. He's also got a lot more experience protecting people than I have, plus he's younger. Most importantly, you are the one who has forgotten the past—he acted just as you would have expected him to in a situation such as this."

Chen lowered his gaze and stared at the steering wheel for a few moments. Yair let him digest his words. They were both remembering what had happened back then, and they each refused to say any of their thoughts aloud.

It was a good few years ago, about twenty kilometers into Syria which had, at the time, been a sovereign country rather than the battle-filled country it is today. Amit had been lead-ing a force along a mount, which quickly proved to be much steeper than satellite pictures suggested. Half an hour out of position, one of the soldiers stumbled. He fell about four meters down the hill and hit his head. It most likely caused severe brain hemorrhaging. The medic with the team had been unsure how long the soldier would last before the wound took his life. The Unit expected Amit to finish the mission. Amit decided to abort and order a rescue. The chopper, Sikorsky CH-53, that came, though, was unable to land, and the wound-ed man had been unable to be elevated to them. In the end, the pilot managed to come close enough to the ground, supporting its weight on a ledge, that they'd evacuated.

The chopper was detected by the Serian radar, and the strip heated up at record speed. Israel and Syria had been a step away from an all-out war.

The wounded soldier had arrived at a hospital and his life had been saved. Some doctors had insisted that if he had arrived an hour later, he'd have died. Others said that he wouldn't have had his condition worsen even if it had been five more hours. The wrath that had hit Amit had been debilitating—both for ordering a rescue and almost dragging Israel into a war and for not completing his mission. Paradoxically, the fighters in the Unit had been angrier about not completing the mission than they were about the possibility of open warfare.

Nothing official was ever said. The inquiry had been incon-clusive, but the atmosphere in the Unit left no doubt: those who didn't complete missions had no place in the Unit.

But here... with this... no. This was different—and on that both Chen and Yair agreed. Here finding the agent was the top priority, so Amit truly was the man for the job. Despite his past.

"You know I'm right," Yair said.

The commander looked at Yair, and just as he was about to answer, his phone rang. He listened for a long minute, then asked Yair, "Where did you say Amit was heading now?"

28.

One look at the empty reception desk, at the lingering signs of struggle, the bloodstains and the open computer, Shaked realized that they were too late and that all the Israelis in the hotel had been "taken care of." The Iranians had left. There were no guards posted.

He didn't even bother with going into the hotel itself. He saw no reason to. So, he ordered the whole force out at once— before the Romanian police showed up. He updated headquarters and through them the director of Michmoret.

They exited the hotel and turned left, then carried on up Victoreie Avenue and then left again down Banului Street. A few meters later, close to a small park, they found a spot they could stop and talk about their plan of action. One car passed by. The air was cold and the sky dark. The city lights combated the darkness of predawn. The sound of sirens that had dimmed when they'd arrived at the Radisson was growing louder. The Romanian police had been summoned to the hotel.

"What's our next move?" Yoav asked.

"Simple, really. We have two options," Shaked replied. "My

assumption and that of the Iranians', is that Michmoret's agent passed the hard disk to an Israeli businessman. So, that really only leaves the possibility of them finding the Israeli and the hard disk—then this whole mess is over—or that they haven't found him yet."

"Inconceivable," Saar cut in, smiling his famous smile.

"Right." Shaked smiled back. He liked Saar's brand of cynicism. "Let's assume they've yet to find it. So, that leads me to ask, why the hell aren't they in the hotel?"

"What do you mean?" Yoav asked.

"It means," Saar said, "That they're being inconsistent. They came, they searched, they didn't find it... so they left? It doesn't make sense. If they came to the conclusion that the hard disk was in the hotel, they would either stay to find it or leave an ambush. If not for the one who has the hard disk, then an ambush waiting for us. Either way, there's no logic in just walking away. It wouldn't have been my move, at least."

"What *is* the logic in that?" Yoav still wasn't following.

"I'm assuming they interrogated the Israelis here and understood that something with their assumption was incorrect. So, they thought it through and reached a different conclusion. That's where they went," Shaked explained.

"So, you're saying we need to get in their head and figure out where they went," Yoav semi-stated, semi-asked.

"Right," Shaked agreed.

"There's only one small bug in that theory of yours," Yoav continued. "You're assuming they haven't found the hard disk.

But no one told you that was what happened. It very well could have been the first option that was correct—that they found it."

"You do see that that isn't logical, don't you?" Saar turned to him.

"Why?"

"Put yourself in this businessman's shoes. A dying Mossad agent bumps into you and gives you something that has to get to Israel. What's your move?"

"Fly to Israel."

"Okay, but there aren't any flights out now. What do you do in the meantime? Do you stay at the hotel? Wait for the Iranians to come to you? Or do you leave for somewhere else?"

"I guess I'd go somewhere else," Yoav replied.

"So, they didn't find him," Shaked surmised.

"You don't say…"

"But that, of course, isn't the real reason the first option is irrelevant," Saar carried on.

"Huh?" Yoav remained baffled.

"The real reason," Shaked cut in, "is that if the first option was the one that came to be, then the mission is over and there's nothing more to discuss. We can gather our things and go home. But we can only do that if we're one-hundred percent sure that that is what happened. Until then, we have to think positive, and we do what we can with what we can affect."

"Long and the short of it is, we have to figure out what made the Iranians leave this place. We have to think like them," Saar finished.

"I don't think so," Yoav said.

"Meaning?" Shaked's interest piqued.

"Like you said back in the flat—we don't have to think like the Iranians, we have to think like the agent. Until now we figured he'd go to the Israeli businessmen. But the Iranians debunked that theory. What we need to assume is that he discarded the idea of using a businessman, and try and think about what he *would* have done."

"Okay," Shaked muttered, "We're listening."

"I'm assuming he made the decision regarding who to go to before he left the airport."

"Because…?"

"Because he was already wounded. He only had one shot."

"Well then… the rookie *is* awake, after all." For a change, Saar's tone lacked any kind of cynicism whatsoever.

"What we need to do is picture ourselves at the airport—we're wounded badly and know that the place is crawling with enemy agents. What would we do?" Yoav continued.

But Shaked was already a step ahead, well before Yoav had finished his last sentence. He closed his eyes and pictured the arrival hall. One of the things that marked the difference between a "regular" agent and an outstanding one was their ability to remember details. Shaked was as outstanding as they came. He looked back at all the details he'd seen; all the things he'd dismissed. What an idiot he'd been. And kudos to Yoav.

"We didn't land at the airport. I mean, we landed in *an* airport, but not a civilian one," Saar said.

Shaked was looking for something that would stand out to him as an Israeli. The things he'd ignored once he'd landed. It didn't take him long to find it: a huge poster that had ignited a small emblem of national pride. A fashion show starring Roni Carmi.

The same person you would never suspect. And, he remembered, the fashion show had been at the opera house.

"Roni Carmi. The model," Shaked said aloud.

Yoav, Saar, and the others all looked at him.

"I beg your pardon?"

"Roni Carmi. The Model. Her face was plastered on an advert at the airport. It wasn't something you could miss. I'm guessing the agent saw the poster and found her."

"And where is she?"

"If I remember correctly," Shaked said, "then she's at the opera house."

"What's opera got to do with a fashion show?" Saar muttered.

"If you really want to know at some point, I'll tell you," Karen said. "But what is relevant to all this, is that it's really close. It's right around the corner."

They went in the direction of the opera house, leaving the Radisson hotel behind them. As they walked, they came across a group of six drunk teenagers. Shaked worried they might be drawn into a fight that would force them to retaliate, but, luckily, the boys ignored them. Less than ten minutes later, they all stood outside the opera house, around the body of their dead agent. They could see the evidence of the Iranian's left-over investigation on the man's body and the garden itself. No one spoke.

A few minutes passed until Karen moved aside. "Would someone please cover him?"

They stood silent for a little longer, then Saar asked, "If they'd found him here, they must know that the device is with the model. So, what went on in the Radisson?"

They all looked over in the direction of the hotel. From their vantage point, the building wasn't visible, but the noise of the sirens was loud and insistent, and Victoriei Avenue was awake once more. More and more first responders passed by.

"I'm assuming she didn't go back there," Shaked said. "They got to her room, understood she wasn't planning on going back, then started the hunt again."

Shaked contacted Daniel on the secure line.

"Any news?"

"Yes. The agent transferred the device to Roni Carmi, the model. She was here doing a fashion show."

"Have you found her?"

"No. We're assuming she was staying at the Radisson, but the Iranians arrived there before us. She's most likely not there anymore."

"So, where is she?"

"I was hoping you could tell me that. You're Michmoret, aren't you? Did she check out?"

"Got it. Give me five minutes."

"I'm not sure we even have that. This whole place is up in arms."

"Understood."

Three minutes later they found out Roni Carmi hadn't stayed at the Radisson at all, but at the Hilton. That was why the Iranians had missed her. Daniel also told them her room number and that she had, indeed, checked out. They also shared the room numbers for her two associates: Inbar and Sean.

All Shaked needed to do was raise his head a little. The Hilton was right in front of him, not far from the dark garden they were standing in. All that divided them was a parking lot and taxi station.

"The man knows nothing, go for the woman," Keren told Shaked.

"You see," Saar added, "You've still got a lot to learn."

Even Shaked cracked a smile at that.

They all waited in the garden, waiting for Shaked. The taxi station in front of the hotel was also up and running, and some people crossed the large parking lot that separated the garden from the hotel. Luckily for the team members, everyone was busy reaching the Radisson and they remained undetected. It took Shaked fifteen minutes to return and tell them the whole story: the fight Inbar had had with Roni, and how Roni had subsequently left for Barcelona on her own. He called Daniel and updated him on the new information.

At the end of the conversation, Daniel passed the phone to the Director.

"I've given the report to Daniel," Shaked said. "I'm getting everything ready to get to Barcelona."

"NAGI."

"Sorry?"

"NAGI. I believe that's how the younger generation says it."

"And that means…?"

"Not a good idea. You're not going to Barcelona."

"Why?"

"Look, you did a great job, you really did. But we've been pulled."

"*What?* What do you mean we've been pulled? How could we be pulled? The mission isn't finished. The Iranians will reach her. We can't just stop because someone figured giving up would be better!"

"You're right, but we've still been pulled. It's been transferred to the military."

"The *military?* In *Europe?*"

"Orders from high up. Our hands are tied."

"So, what are we supposed to do now?"

"Tell the rest to fold up everything that's ours and come back to Israel. The Romanians will stay out of your way."

"Okay."

"Just a second."

"What?"

"Everyone but you."

"Huh?"

"Tell the rest to follow the orders. You're going to be doing something different."

"Okay, and what will that be?"

"We're not allowed to be involved, so you *can't* go to Barcelona to protect her."

"Then that is what's *not* allowed. What can I do?"

"That's it. That's all. I can't tell you what you can do because it's not allowed. You follow me?"

Shaked did.

29.

"Amit is on his way to Barcelona, but it doesn't matter," Yair answered. "He's got a French mobile phone that works in Spain, too, and more importantly, he's got a scrambler on his phone. I believe he's already landed. I'll call him now and tell him to redirect to Bucharest."

"You won't believe this."

"What?"

"The phone call I just got…" the Commander of *Sayeret Matcal* started.

"Yes…?"

"The mess in Bucharest just moved to Barcelona."

"I don't understand."

"The Mossad agent, the one who took whatever-the-hell-it-is from Iran and got to Bucharest—"

"Yeah?"

"He's dead."

"*Dead?*"

"Dead!"

"Chen, have you noticed the time right now? Can you cut the drama?"

Chen smiled. "Before he died, he transferred the device to someone else. And by someone else, I mean Roni Carmi."

"Roni Carmi? The model?"

"That's the one."

"Fuck you, Chen, I can't be bothered with these games. Do you want to tell me what the hell is really going on?"

"I'm not kidding, man. It sounds just as messed up to me.Roni Carmi has the device now. The model. I'm serious. That's what the defense office just told me. They wouldn't pull my leg."

"What does it mean?"

"Good question. First, it doesn't look like she's allowing reality to interfere with her plans. Rather than return to Israel, she's carrying on with her fashion show schedule. That's why she's on her way to Barcelona. Whatever my thoughts on your brother, he's obviously the man for the job."

"And...?"

"And her phone is off. The guys from 8200[7] can't prepare her."

"So, what now?"

"I think Asaf might be there... but, no. No, that's not a good idea. Never mind."

---

[7]   Unit **8200** is an Israeli Intelligence Corps unit of the Israel Defense Forces responsible for collecting signal intelligence (SIGINT) and code decryption—specializes in cyberwarfare.

"Asaf? Who's Asaf?"

"It wasn't a good idea. Drop it."

"Okay."

"You know Daniel from Michmoret, right?"

Yair knew Daniel well.

"He's the head of this operation," Chen continued. "Contact him, have him bring you up to speed, then activate your brother. Keep me in the loop. All the way through."

"All right. I'll talk to Daniel then I'll talk to my brother."

"Don't forget to keep me updated."

"Of course."

"And two more things," Chen added.

"Hmm?"

"Don't tell Amit that Roni has something. Only tell him that she needs personal protection."

"Okay… but why?"

"Because tactically, the right move would be to take it from her."

"So, maybe it would be a better move, then? Why shouldn't we tell him that?" Yair asked.

"How long do you think she'll last if you take it from her? The Iranians couldn't know she no longer has it, and they *will* get to her. When they don't find it, they'll kill her. And not before they torture her for it."

"I got it. I got it." Yair took a breath. "You said there were two things."

"Right, the second order is for Amit to protect her under the strategy of Orbiting Star."

"Orbiting Star? *Why?* That just complicates things!" Yair exclaimed.

Rather than the normal procedure of protection, where the person being protected is informed of the act, Orbiting Star meant protecting someone without them being aware of it. The main reason for such a strategy would be the inability to predict how the subject might take to being protected. Or to the knowledge that they were in danger.

"Caesarea tried to figure out why she might be going through with her initial plans rather than return to Israel," Chen replied. "They think she was following the agent's advice, otherwise it makes no sense."

"So?"

"So, if she spoke to the agent, what do you think he told her? Why wouldn't she contact the embassy or Israel in another way?"

Yair thought for a moment. "He told her not to trust anyone…"

"Or she figured it out on her own," Chen finished.

"Either way," Yair nodded to himself, "Caesarea is worried that if someone identifies themselves as protection, she'll react badly, maybe throw away the device, disappear, or any other unexpected move."

"Right."

"Then Amit has no idea what he's going to protect, and Roni has no idea she's about to be protected. Perfect."

"Hmm…" Chen looked momentarily embarrassed. "It's not great, I'll give you that."

Yair looked at him for a second but didn't say anything more. He left the Hummer and watched the Commander drive away.

He called Daniel, and after the initial pleasantries, got a fair update and came to some needed conclusions. Now all he needed to do was talk to Amit.

He returned home and sat at the kitchen counter, took three deep breaths, and called.

"Are you calling to ask if I'm sleeping, or can you not fall asleep?" Amit picked up by the first tone.

"Both, I guess."

"I'm okay. I'm sorry for dropping it all on you like that." Amit did sound more put together.

"Don't be sorry. There's nothing to be sorry about. It's good that you called me. Don't be ridiculous."

"You know… rather than only me being awake, it doesn't seem like you've got any sleep either."

"That's the last thing you should be worried about. Besides, my not sleeping isn't your fault at all."

"No? What then?"

"Don't think about that now. Where are you?"

"Barcelona airport. Why?"

"Look, I figured out what happened with Michal. Do you want to hear it?"

"Of course I do!"

"Then turn the scrambler on."

"Okay."

With him working security, Amit always had a scrambler for his phone with him—a device that encrypted the sound before it was sent through. It was illegal in most countries, but it looked like a simple disk-on-key, so getting it through airport security wasn't an issue. Yair held the same kind of device that was keyed to the one that his brother had.

"I'm scrambling," Amit said not half a minute later.

"Right, I don't have a clear connection yet, but there's a suspicious set of coincidences. You know me. I don't believe in coincidences."

"Okay, tell me."

"There is—well, there was—a serious mess beck in Bucharest. It doesn't matter really about what, but it set Caesarea against the Iranians, and it was high level. It seemed to have included the Americans, too. Michal's murder looks to be connected to it somehow, though we're iffy on connecting the dots."

"Okay, thank you. Not that knowing helps much, but... still. Thank you for trying. Truly. I appreciate it."

"There's more."

"Oh? What?"

"Other than what went down in Bucharest, there was also a fashion show there. You know Roni Carmi?"

"Nope. No clue…What do you think?"

"So, she had a show there."

"*No way!*"

"Hold the cynicism. With the whole mess there, it seems like the Iranians are now after her."

"See? And we say the Iranians aren't human. Of course they're after her. What red blooded male wouldn't be?"

"Are you one of those men?"

"Huh? You want me to go after her, too? You're aces at setting me up, man. And you can seriously pull it off."

"Just listen a second, you idiot."

"Go on."

"I'm serious. She met an agent of ours there or something, and now all the Iranians are after her. They're trying to kill her, Amit. I know it sounds a little far-fetched, but it's the truth. The agent is dead. He can't help her anymore. And it doesn't seem like she's particularly aware of what's going on around her. She needs protection. Someone needs to protect her."

"Okay, fine. I still don't see what this has to do with Michal. More importantly, what the hell does it have to do with me?"

"She's on a plane now. Want to guess where she's about to land?"

"Barcelona?"

"Got it in one."

"And you want me to protect her?"

"If you agree."

"What? You mean, it's a mission? You're giving me a mission? I can't believe it. And here I was thinking what an awesome brother I have. Look, I can't figure out what's going through your mind right now—you do remember what just went down a couple of hours ago, right? Michal, I mean? Remember that?"

"Listen, if you don't think you can do it, don't. Forget about it. Truly. I don't want to guilt you into this. But if you really want to clear your head like you said, and in a certain sense that means getting back at the bastards responsible for all this... look, you really don't have to do anything. I wasn't even sure how you'd react. I figured you'd go off on me—more than you did, that's for sure. But the bottom line is that the ball is in your court. I even fought Chen over this."

"Chen? It came from him, then? I suppose everything makes sense now."

"What does? Chen didn't want to give you this mission. I'm the one who insisted."

"Chen was against it? That son of a bitch."

Yair almost reprimanded him for that. You don't call the Commander of *Sayeret Matcal* a son of a bitch, no matter what you think of him. But he figured it was best to keep quiet. He could practically hear the wheels turning in Amit's head.

"Chen was against it?"

Yair didn't answer.

Amit stayed quiet for a moment, and Yair didn't break the silence.

"So, bottom line, you really did get me a date. And some date. And some situation, too. You're such a shit," Amit said, and Yair understood the matter to be closed. Amit paused for a moment before adding, "Well, you are paying, at least, right?"

"Of course."

"So, what's the plan?"

"Let's start with me getting you a room at a modest little hotel. Something along the lines of a shitty youth hostel."

"I really don't care where, as long as it's got eyes."

"Yup. It's got eyes, all right."

"No way! At the Ohla?"

"Ohla Barcelona, the hotel with eyes."

The Ohla hotel in Barcelona, beyond being considered one of the top hotels, was also famous for its eye-like decorations over its entire front. Amit, who'd spent a lot of time in Barcelona, always told Yair that the exterior looked insane with all the eyeballs, so he had to stay there. But he'd never bothered.

"What happened, have you people suddenly become exceptionally generous? Or am I just lucky?"

"Calm down. With all due respect, I do need to put up Roni Carmi in a respectable hotel."

"Oh, so, what, she's staying there?"

"She doesn't know it yet, but she is. Anyway, you'll be getting there before her."

"What do you want me to do, then?"

"One of the guys from Michmoret will be waiting in the court in front of the hotel to give you a gun. You get yourself organized at the hotel and wait for her there. She'll come to you."

"She'll come to *me?*"

"*She'll come to you.*"

"How?"

"We'll get it done."

"How will you get it done?"

"Michmoret. Are you familiar with it?"

"Shut up. I'm serious."

"So am I. They'll take care of it. You don't need to worry about that. She'll get to you."

"Okay. Then?"

"You need to stick right by her until she gets to Israel. No matter what. If you need to open fire and shoot someone, you do it."

"I hope she won't panic with all this," Amit muttered.

"She won't, because you're going to protect her through Orbiting Star."

"*Orbiting Star*? Why?"

"Because the guys up top don't know how she'll react to knowing you're protecting her. Their assumption is that she won't react well."

Amit thought it all through for a moment. She would most likely panic if he came up to her, told her she was in danger, and that he was planning on protecting her. She may even see him as a threat. Yair didn't say it explicitly, but it was clearly implied it was part of the dangerous situation. On the other hand, if he didn't tell her he was there to protect her, his life, and job, would become much harder. *Damnit.* "So… if the procedure is Orbiting Star… it's Roni Carmi: what makes you think she'll let me get anywhere near her? I'm no one!"

"She'll be arriving there alone and exhausted. She needs

someone to lean on. You know, it's hard to notice, but she is human, too. Just be there for her. Hit on her, for all I care."

"*Hit on her?* On Roni Carmi? How would you even go about doing something like *that?* What should I even say?"

"I've no idea. Let's think it through. Maybe tell her this completely bullshit story about how your daughter was a stillborn, your girlfriend—her mother—dumped you, then you went to your previous girlfriend only to find out she was murdered."

"You're such a shit."

"We've already been over this before."

"I don't even know how I tolerate you for more than a minute."

"You don't really have much of a choice about it. I'm your brother and I love you, even if it's hard for you to realize sometimes."

"Or maybe you're just trying to live vicariously through me."

Yair paused. "You know, I never thought about it, but you may be right."

"Right. Fine. Bye." Amit hung up, deciding the conversation was becoming too touchy-feely for his tastes.

He boarded an airbus to Catalonia square, then took the short walk to the hotel. A Michmoret agent was, indeed, waiting for him there, and he passed him a bag. Amit went into the hotel. The receptionist was sleepy, but the check-in was done in a matter of minutes.

He went up to room 604 and threw himself down on the bed. He took out the Glock and fiddled with it for a bit. Then he looked in the bag. There were ten magazines in it. Ten! He'd figured he'd get no more than one or two. But *ten*?

What the hell was coming his way?

He lay down and tried to fall asleep. He was sure he wouldn't manage it, but thirty seconds later, he was already sleeping deeply.

30.

Roni couldn't sleep. That stare from the man who'd chased her back at the airport played over and over in her mind, merging gruesomely with the guard from outside of the Radisson hotel. As her taxi had driven past, she'd convinced herself the man hadn't been able to see her, but now she wasn't so sure. Added to those stares, she now seemed to also be haunted by the thoughts of Inbar and Eran in bed together.

She shook her head, trying in vain to rid herself from the images, but they only seemed to get worse. Pictures became scenes, and suddenly she could see Inbar and Eran—hear her moaning and the way he'd give that muffled shout she'd always loved when he came.

She started crying, wallowing in self-pity. Eran's betrayal and—worse—Inbar's... how could it have happened? How could she not have noticed? *That hypocrite.* She could have him if she wanted him so badly. Who needed him. Who needed them *both.* Let them choke on each other. No-no-no! What was she even *thinking*? Inbar couldn't have him—talk about eating the cake and having it, too.

The dead agent, the man who'd died in her arms, only added to her heartache. And the task he'd set for her made everything so much *worse*. She didn't even have a phone to help her get through it all. *God.* She could be so stupid. Punishing herself for Inbar's actions... and now she was alone. With no help. She'd never felt so alone... so lonely.

An image of Sean popped into her mind, giving her a look that basically said '*no one? Really? Then what am I?*'

Sean... a faint smile slipped through her tears. Yes. That was true. She did have Sean. And parents who were definitely getting up in the years and waiting only for her to get married, and two older brothers who had done as expected and got married and built a family... so no one really cared about her.

Suddenly the plane jerked. She woke from her reveries, panicked and absolutely positive the plane was going to crash. Then she noticed the lights of the runway outside and realized that they'd simply landed. The sky was turning a ruddy red-blue. It would be sunrise in a few minutes.

A new day, she told herself. *Screw the last one, I'm starting over. No one else is going to drag me down.* She sat straight, wiped away the tears, and felt a little better with her new resolve.

It was only while she stood waiting for her luggage that she felt that niggling worry creep up on her again. The discomfort between her legs was more pronounced than before and it made her look around nervously. There was no sign of "them."

For a moment she contemplated simply leaving... but should

she really leave her bags? Wasn't it bad enough that she had no phone? Giving up her luggage seemed like too much. No. She'd wait. She was in Spain now, and it was all well behind her. There was no one here who was a threat. With that positive thought, she noticed her bag.

She picked it up, left the airport, and found a taxi.

"Hotel Sofia, please," she told the driver and leaned back.

"Tell Daniel I'm in," Alex said to his team leader. "Give me a minute and I'll reroute it as he wanted it."

"No problem," the team leader replied. He called Daniel and said, "We're in." Half a minute later, he added. "Reroute complete. Done."

"We're here," the driver said, waking Roni from a fitful sleep. *Barcelona.* Roni got out and looked around. Unlike Bucharest, Barcelona had already greeted spring. It was still cold, but the city was already awash with the first rays of sunlight, and the few people she could see walking around, were smiling. Life went on at a lazy pace, with a Spanish rhythm and a lot of good intentions and honest delight. Even the Catalonian fight for independence didn't seem to change the city's spirits.

Roni looked at the hotel's exterior as the driver passed her luggage to the bellhop. She paid the driver and walked into the lobby. It was the first time she'd decided to stay in this hotel— not because it was common, quite the opposite, the place was rather lavish. The problem she had with it was its location. It was a little far out from the center of town, or if one looked at it differently, closer to Camp Nou, Barcelona's famous football stadium. It was that particular stadium where she would have the fashion show this afternoon.

That gave her a little time to rest, or, more accurately, sleep. She'd probably slept more in the taxi than she had on the plane, and that was still far from enough. She needed sleep.

Roni went to the receptionist and held out her passport. He took it and studied the monitor for what felt like a little too long. "I see here that you canceled your reservation."

"*What?*"

"It says here that you had a room here, but that your reservation was canceled."

"I definitely didn't cancel anything."

"It's what is written here."

Roni could feel the desperation and hopelessness work their way back to the forefront of her mind.

"There were three rooms, not only one. What about the other two."

"Yes, I can see that. All three rooms were canceled."

"But why? Who canceled them?"

"I can't see who called to cancel the reservations, all I can tell you now is that they were. Hang on a moment." The receptionist picked up a phone and spoke to someone for a minute. Soon the head receptionist came up to them, and the two of them looked at the computer monitor together. They argued amongst themselves.

Roni knew a little Spanish, but it seemed to her that they were speaking Catalonian, and that meant she couldn't follow a word. The first receptionist showed the one in charge something, which seemed to convince him of whatever it was. The head receptionist finally gave a nod of agreement.

The head receptionist turned to Roni and said, "I'm truly sorry. This has never happened to me before. We apologize."

"What happened?" Roni asked, the despair growing with each passing moment. "Who canceled the reservations?"

"The system."

"What? Who?"

"Our reservation system. We've had a lot of people arrive, and it seems that due to the influx, the system started canceing upcoming reservations, giving the rooms to whoever arrived."

"What? How can something like that happen? We even paid a deposit!"

"Yes, we'll give you a full refund, how—"

"I don't want the money!" She tried to stop herself from bursting into tears. "I just want a room. I've been up all night, I'm exhausted, I'm tired, I'm hungry, I smell—so I just *want a room!*"

"I understand, and I'm truly sorry, but we don't have one we can give you."

"So the reservation was canceled. So what? Just give me a different room."

"We don't have one. Everything is taken."

"There's no such thing! There's always at least one room

214 | HANDLE WITH FORCE

spare—even when everything is full!"

"You're right, but even those have been taken. The system wouldn't have canceled your reservation if there were any rooms available."

"So, give me someone else's room, who hasn't arrived yet."

"I can't do that."

"Why the hell not? It's what you did to me, isn't it?"

"I'm sorry, it's not me—it's the system. I can't do that."

"Then what am I supposed to do now?" she asked, completely despondent.

"Can I offer a solution?" a guest who was standing behind her cut in. She turned to him, ready to accept practically anything.

"I'm leaving now, and plan to be back in about three hours. You can use my room in the meantime, and they can fix this mess by then. My bed is made, you can even go to sleep."

Okay... maybe not every offer.

The head receptionist looked at her, nodding as though he thought it was a wonderful idea. She looked at them both, quite horrified.

Luckily for the receptionist, he at least came to his senses quickly and changed his tune, telling the man, "Of course not! What on earth are you offering. I must ask you to move along, sir."

The man looked disappointed, but he left nonetheless.

"What am I supposed to do now?" she repeated her earlier question.

"We'll find you a room at another hotel, of the same caliber. Please, don't worry," he tried to calm her. The clerk began dialing.

He spoke to someone for no longer than a few seconds, then hung up. And so it went, over and over. Roni couldn't believe this was happening. It couldn't be possible. Was the whole world conspiring against her?

The head receptionist also didn't seem to find it possible and started getting short with the other man, who only looked at him as if he couldn't understand what he could possibly want from him. Two more conversations went the same way, then the head receptionist himself took the phone and started calling.

It made no difference.

The receptionist took a book out of the desk cabinet and put it in front of them. He opened it and resumed calling.

Roni spoke to the man in charge. "What, do you want to tell me that no hotel has a room free? Anywhere?"

"It seems so," he said, and he seemed relieved to not be the only problematic place around. "We haven't managed yet. We'll have to try hotels of slightly less high-quality."

"How? How could there not be one room in any hotel in this city? Does it seem logical to you?"

"It happens in Barcelona, especially during the Mobile World Congress."

"But there isn't a world congress going on! Of mobile or otherwise!"

She'd almost completely given up, but then the clerk gave a bright smile and started talking quickly, "*Si, si!* Senorita Carmi, *si.*"

Roni smiled.

"There's a room and they're holding it for you. A specific room that's definitely empty, no matter what the computer says." The man was practically glowing. Roni too. So was the head receptionist.

"Where?"

"In the center of town, not far from Catalonia Square. A beautiful place. A beautiful hotel. The Ohla Barcelona."

"Is it far?"

"No more than a ten-minute drive. We've called a taxi for you, we'll pay the fare," the head receptionist said, and added, "as long as we get to see you smile. Welcome to Barcelona."

Roni couldn't help but smile back. And her smile always had the same effect. Especially on men. The two men melted.

She got in the taxi, with the receptionist himself taking her luggage and directing the driver on where to go.

Once they were driving, she decided she'd stay awake the whole drive, this time. And she did. For exactly one street.

31.

This was the third Gaudi building he'd visited. *You have to see the Gaudi houses,* he'd been told, *and don't forget all the cathedrals or churches or whatever they're called.* Very, very interesting.

It wasn't that Barcelona wasn't a beautiful city, and it wasn't that he regretted coming here for his vacation, but Gaudi? Really? He hadn't even managed to see a football game yet.

Asaf put a mental checkmark on seeing the place, then left quickly. He contemplated what to do next. What hadn't he seen yet? His vacation was almost over, and then he'd be back in the army. If he had the choice, he'd ask to be released tomorrow. There was the chance that if he asked, they'd let him leave, too. But he wouldn't dare ask. It wouldn't be an admittance of failure—he'd already failed at that spectacularly—it would simply be too obvious.

He'd needed a year and a half until he'd managed to work up the courage to ask again, and even then his request had been denied. *We need you. You're excellent,* they'd said. They'd even seemed to have meant it. He was, after all, very good at his job, but that hadn't brought the "yes" he'd hoped of hearing.

Asaf had come to *Sayeret Matcal* as a young officer. He started in Shaldag[8] and was exceptional there, but after going through a course in counter-terrorism, he requested to leave Shaldag and remain in a counter-terrorism unit. He grew and shone there. Then he went through officer training, and when he came back, carried on making headway. Sayeret Matcal noticed him and asked him to transfer to their unit and carry on working in the counter-terrorism division. He'd accepted.

In *Sayeret Matcal*, he continued to excel, but he'd wanted more. He wanted to go on missions behind enemy lines. To that, he'd received a hard no. Operations over enemy lines were reserved for fighters who'd started in the Unit. In the past, there had been very few offers to fighters who'd started outside the Unit, and even then, only when they were particularly exceptional.

It all fell apart when one of them, who hadn't even been an officer, fell and hit his head while walking. They'd called in a chopper and almost brought on another war. The criticisms hadn't even been directed at that solider but at the commander of the force, Amit Koren, who'd called the operation off. Still, the attitude of "those who hadn't started as soldiers in the Unit didn't know how to walk in the dark" remained, and those who

---

8   Unit 5101, more commonly known as **Shaldag** (Hebrew: שלדג, Kingfisher), is an elite Israeli Air Force commando unit and one of the main Israeli special forces units.

hadn't started in *Sayeret Matcal*, were no longer offered to join operations that took place over enemy lines. Simple as that.

It drove Asaf mad, and he was far from accepting it. His rage he firmly directed at Amit, who'd been a part of the Unit numerous years ago and whom he didn't even know. It made no sense. It was nothing more than prolonged and ongoing frustration.

I haven't visited the aquarium yet, but that's exactly where I'm heading next.

32.

Amit awoke with a fright. He couldn't figure out where he was or why he was holding a gun. A second later everything came rushing back. Michal was gone. It felt as if a boulder was crushing his chest. He could barely breathe. It took him a good minute to calm down, and he looked at the gun in his hand. He had a mission to do. Grieving would have to wait.

He went into the shower and came out refreshed. How long had he slept for? It couldn't have been long, since it was still early morning.

He got dressed and went down to the breakfast hall. He didn't have much appetite, so he sat in the direction of the concierge desk, watching the people going in and out while he sipped his coffee.

Five minutes later, he almost dropped his mug. Roni Carmi had just walked into the hotel.

33.

Layla shot out orders as fast as an honest bullet, both to those who remained in Bucharest—a force of only a few to keep the basic blocks up in the event she was wrong—and the main force who would go with her to Barcelona. So far, units 2 and 4, who'd remained in the Old City, weren't answering the comms, and she wouldn't wait for them. They would eventually join those who stayed in Bucharest.

She updated Baharam regarding her plans and got the confirmation. He told her he'd track the model's phone so they could catch up with her the moment they landed.

After talking to Baharam, she called the unit in Marseilles. Their orders—the cell that was in charge of the whole south of France region—had been to enact operation Breadcrumbs and wait. At the moment, Layla only had the three members of unit 1 with her and the watchman in the airport. She needed more people with her and didn't have time to wait. The unit that had been busy with Breadcrumbs in Nice would have to be deployed. They'd reach Barcelona before her.

Their weapons would have to remain in Bucharest. The cell from Marseilles will correct that issue. It was good that there wasn't an Israeli consulate in Barcelona—she wouldn't have to waste manpower with blocking avenues of escape.

It took five minutes for the unit to be in a taxi on their way to the airport. They watched the police cars rush past them. They met Abas at the airport, who'd bought them all tickets for the next flight out to Barcelona. It still left them waiting for more than an hour for the flight.

She used that time to question Abas.

"Yes, she looked at me," he said.

"But it was while you were running to the gate. It doesn't mean anything."

"When I got there, I stopped running and looked confused, as though I'd simply mistaken the gate I'd needed. Everyone else merely glanced at me uninterested. She, though… she kept watching me."

"Okay. And what kind of look was it?"

"At first surprise, then fear. Definitely fear. And she didn't break the stare."

"So, it wasn't random. She knew why you were watching her."

"No question."

The conversation affirmed Layla's gut instinct. She was in the right direction.

She wasn't allowed to make any mistakes with this. The smallest miscalculation could mean failure. She asked herself what scared her more: the damage it would bring Iran, or knowing she'd failed her mission? She tried to avoid the answer that unapologetically popped into her mind, but couldn't shut it down completely. She didn't like the truth of it—not even a little. And, to think, she'd lost her Steve over all this. *Her Steve.*

The boarding call brought her back to reality.

The flight was relatively empty, so the seat numbers were nothing more than a suggestion. She decided to sit far away from her unit members. They, on their part, were happy with her decision. They admired her and were willing to do just about everything for her, but they also feared her more than a little.

The plane took off.

She put her head against the headrest and planned on sleeping. It had been a long, tiring day, and the next one wasn't going to be much different. She had to rest. Unlike how most people tried to go to sleep, Layla didn't try. She knew she would succeed. And she did. Moreover, she even knew of whom she'd dream. And that happened too.

She spent the flight sleeping deeply with a smile on her face.

Baharam called her right as they landed before they even left the airport. His news wasn't encouraging. He hadn't been able to track Roni's phone, which made him believe she'd taken out the battery—especially since the last known activity had been in Bucharest at the opera house. Perhaps that meant she wasn't as naive as she seemed. Though, it was more likely that the dead agent had told her to keep it off.

With the way she was behaving, it seemed that the thief hadn't thought she would be a target, so had told her not to change her plans. And he'd been right. They'd only figured it all out because they'd found his body while getting ready to hit the Radisson. If it had gone differently, the thief's plan would have worked.

So, really, not all was bleak.

"Her fashion show is this afternoon. At Camp Nou. She's at the Sofia hotel—right by the stadium."

"Thanks, Baharam. You're sure about the hotel? Because we missed her by a matter of minutes back in Bucharest all because we went to the hotel next to hers."

"It's not a guess, this time. She's got a reservation there."

"Okay. We're on our way."

"The unit from Marseilles is already there. They're waiting on the street, about a hundred meters from the hotel."

"Great. Thank you. I'll keep you updated."

"Good luck to you."

The unit left the airport and got into a taxi. Not long after, they reached the hotel. They stopped a little before and met up with the Marseilles unit.

Layla always felt calmer when she was armed, and it seemed like all the other unit members felt the same. Most of them stayed outside, not far from the entrance to the hotel. Layla and the leader of unit 1 went in and stopped at the front desk.

It was mid-morning, but the hotel didn't have many people around.

Layla smiled at the receptionist and asked for a room for her and her husband. This man also got a clear view of Layla's assets as she leaned forward and smiled.

The receptionist felt inordinately lucky. He didn't know whose idea it had been to organize a fashion show at the Camp Nou stadium, since it seemed like the last place to be connected to fashion of all things, but he was far from complaining about the outcome. How could he, with the number of beautiful women who kept stumbling his way. The system malfunction had been fixed about half an hour after Roni Carmi left. It must have been a computer issue since the hotel wasn't even close to being full. It was a shame, but no big deal. There were plenty of models. And here was another one. Just as beautiful, though not as tall as the ones who'd passed through earlier.

"Passports, please," he requested.

"Yes, of course," she said. "But, just a moment, I'd like to ask something."

"Of course, how can I help?"

"You know us models, we have all sorts of funny requests."

Yes. He *did* know.

"So, I'd really appreciate a room next to my friend's," Layla continued. "Her name is Roni Carmi. She's also a model. You must know her. She checked in earlier this morning. What room is she?"

The request left the clerk speechless. What could he possibly say to that? On the one hand, he wasn't allowed to talk to one customer about another—and definitely not let them know what room they were in—but on the other hand, Roni wasn't even in this hotel, and all because of a stupid computer malfunction. So, with her not being one of the hotel's guests, was he allowed to share what he knew? He wasn't sure.

And anyway, if he told her she wasn't in the hotel, she may choose not to stay here either and join Roni Carmi instead. That meant losing a customer. It was all too complicated for him and he didn't know what to do, which led to him standing in front of Layla looking like a discarded plant.

Layla, understanding what was going on through his mind, decided to help him along. She opened two shirt buttons, showing more skin, and complained about the heat.

He, in response, finally made up his mind. He would do anything she asked. Even drive her to the other hotel, if she wanted.

It was the final decision he made in his short life. The unit leader figured since there had been no response, even with Layla's opening of her buttons, that the receptionist wouldn't be giving them the information they needed. The system was open, so he sent the man off to a world where he could feel no pain. The receptionist looked like he'd simply decided to take a late-morning nap as his head dropped to the desk.

"Patience!" Layla gritted out. "I had him."

"The system is open," the unit commander justified.

She didn't like the way he'd taken matters into his own hands. No one had noticed so far, but it seemed completely redundant. Her intuition had told her the receptionist was about to give up his own parents if she would have asked. Still, she couldn't ask her lieutenants to take initiatives without them doing so—even when she found the timing less than appropriate. She decided to keep her mouth shut.

Layla began thanking the receptionist loudly so as to remove suspicions, and the unit commander slipped behind the desk to check the program.

"She's not in this hotel," he said.

"What? How is that possible?"

"I can see her reservation here, but she canceled it this morning. She never checked in."

"She must have decided to switch hotels. She's not as much of an idiot as I thought."

"What's our next move?"

"First we have to clean up the mess here," she said.

The unit commander held the dead receptionist so that it seemed as though he was doing nothing more than napping on him, then Layla came up to them, thanking him profusely for agreeing to show them something.

They left the hotel together.

It was enough for the security cameras not to pick up on them right away, but she knew that it wouldn't take them too long. She hoped to be in Iran by then.

"What do we do?"

The question hung in the air, the receptionist's body cooling in the bushes beside them. She'd already updated Baharam, who'd told her he'd track Roni once she used her credit card, and would soon tell them which hotel she was staying in.

Layla decided to give up for now. It seemed like a pointless, fruitless chase.

"Now we go to another hotel, rest, and prepare. We'll catch her at the fashion show."

34.

Roni walked into the hotel and hesitantly walked up to the small concierge desk to the right of the main entrance. The man directed her to the floor above—to the hotel's main reception desk—where she was pleasantly surprised to find her name already on the list. The subsequent check-in went fast and smoothly. She went up to the room that had been reserved for her as promised: room 605.

Amit watched Roni Carmi disappear deeper into the hotel. What was he supposed to do now? He had no real answer to that, so he decided to go have breakfast. He needed all the energy he could get. He'd only slept a few hours, but it would tide him by—though he needed food for that to hold up. He walked up to the buffet table and started—unwillingly—piling food onto his place.

Roni walked into her room, locked the door, and lay down on the bed. All she wanted to do was sleep. A minute later, she dragged herself up. She wouldn't let her exhaustion control her life. True, she needed at least a few hours of rest before the show later that day, but she had time, and no one in Barcelona was after her. There was no threat.

A shower was first on her agenda.

She pushed the hot water lever as far as it would go and scrubbed herself roughly. She imagined washing off all the horrors of the previous night. She got out and got ready quickly: deodorant, a little body lotion, and perfume. Nothing more. She hated using makeup and fluffing up in general. It made her think of work, where putting on makeup could take hours. Anyway, she still looked beautiful even without all the trimmings. She looked at her reflection in the hotel mirror and was happy to see that even with the dim hotel-room lighting, she still looked great.

Unlike many of the girls she worked with, Roni was actually very happy with the way she looked. She'd even forgotten the margarine.

Now, to breakfast, she told herself. She refused to skip the meal before a show.

She went downstairs.

Amit watched Roni walk into the dining hall on the hotel's entry floor where they were still serving breakfast. She took some vegetables, crackers, and cheese, then sat down not far from him. He couldn't decide on his next move. Should he approach her? How would he even go about something like that?

What would he say? He suddenly realized he was trembling. His stomach was full of especially aggressive butterflies, too. If before he'd played with his food, now, consuming it seemed like an impossible task.

How long had it been since the last time he'd hit on someone? On the other hand, it was a mission. He had to pull himself together.

Give me an easy job—like going up against terrorists. I'd take that any day over this... he rose and made his way over to her.

From the corner of her eye, Roni could tell someone was walking up to her. She couldn't help the instinctual dread. She pretended not to notice and concentrated on her plate.

"I'm sorry, I don't want to intrude," he said in Hebrew.

What now? She thought. *Who is he and what does he want? He speaks Hebrew!*

"I just... I noticed you were eating alone and thought you might like some company. I'm three tables down if you'd like to join me. Only so as not to eat alone—nothing more. Okay, that's it.... I won't bother you anymore," Amit added awkwardly and went back to his table. His face was burning. God, he was such an idiot. *Is that how you hit on someone? It would have been better to say something like, 'What's a girl like you doing in a place like this?'* No. Instead, he went on about not bothering her while bothering her! He wanted the floor to swallow him whole. At least then he could drop this awful mission.

He sat back down at his table. Unfortunately, he was still facing Roni. He was so embarrassed he could barely lift his head to her even once. He had no choice but to eat then, and he tried to get through this nightmare as fast as he could—which meant *not* playing with his food.

Without having to look in Roni's direction, he could practically feel the weight of her gaze. She was checking him out—though that may have been wishful thinking. It definitely didn't help his ears change back from the reddest they'd ever been.

It was only now that he noticed her smell. It was something that could never be transmitted through pictures or screens, and it was intoxicating. He really wished for that hole to eat him up already.

Roni, on the other hand, was rather shocked. The man had come out of nowhere, speaking Hebrew to her, and walking away seconds later. What even was that? Was he trying to be threatening? It didn't seem so. She tried to judge the event to the best of her ability.

He spoke Hebrew and had no accent, so he was clearly an Israeli. This *was* Barcelona, after all. There had to be at least a couple of Israelis around. *And he was here well before me,* she thought, *so there's no chance of him having followed me.* Her reservation had been for a different hotel, too. So, he clearly didn't pose a threat in the same way as that guard at the Radisson had, or the man at the airport, either. He was probably merely someone trying to hit on her. She suffered through plenty of that—and had no trouble rejecting them, especially not when she was in such a public place as a hotel.

Also, she'd never gotten hit on so clumsily.

She looked at him. If he was anything like the other men, then he'd sneak glances at her; try and see if his *fantastic* opening lines had worked their magic.

But he didn't look at her even once. Instead, he seemed incredibly embarrassed. Roni even noticed his red ears. He was either an incredibly good actor who'd situated himself entirely by accident, or he was a nerdy guy looking for some company.

Intense loneliness suddenly rushed through her. She would have loved some company. And this was public enough... she didn't think it could hurt. If she found him to be some kind of sex freak—sadly, one of many she'd encountered—then she would simply get up and leave. She would only be in this hotel for one night, anyway. He would never bother her again.

She made up her mind, got up, and walked over to him.

"Are you worried about me eating alone, or more worried about yourself?" she asked as she sat at his table. The waiter rushed after her, helping her bring over her things.

"Both, I think," Amit replied. He was surprised she'd come. He couldn't hide it, and she was amused by his expression.

"So, was that you hitting on me?" Roni didn't leave him room to wriggle out of it. She preferred knowing where she stood, and it was better to get it over with sooner rather than later. Worst case, she'd apologize.

"Yeah, huh?" Amit said, looking at her with a certain amount of despair. "There's no way anyone would come up to you for simple company, is there? All the men just want to hit on you... it must be a serious price you have to pay."

She stared. He didn't sound condescending, only accepting. Maybe even a little empathetic. It was surprising.

Amit noticed her reaction to his words and continued. "I can tell it's your automatic response. People are probably either too intimidated by you, or they're looking to screw you. No middle ground. But no, that's really not where I was going with… that. If you knew what I'd been through these last twenty-four hours, that conclusion wouldn't even cross your mind."

"Okay," she said. "I get it. You're the one who wanted company, and your offer was merely an excuse."

"Could be," Amit replied, and for a moment considered the truth of that statement. He couldn't tell her that he was there to keep her safe, but he could unload a little. It even served the mission's purpose. As long as he didn't break down while doing it.

But… he couldn't be that much of an egotistical bastard. He knew she needed help, even if she didn't show a lick of the nervousness and fear he knew she had to be feeling.

"Look, you may be a pretty good actress, and sitting next to you, I feel like some kind of… toad, but…"

"But?" she pressed.

"But even I can tell you're pretty low. You can blame only me for wanting some company, I'm fine with that. But you need it, too. It's possible I can see it because I'm feeling the way I am, but it's still clear enough…" he paused. "And, no. I'm not hitting on you, and not only because it would prove your point. I'm here if you want me to be, and we can keep talking only about me, if you prefer."

"Misery does love company," she said, smiling. His squirming was amusing.

"Sure," he agreed.

Wow, she thought, *he seems in an even worse spot than me.* Surprisingly, that thought actually made her feel better, which only led to her feeling guilty about it.

"So, what's happened these last twenty-four hours?"

"We going to be talking about me?" Amit asked.

"We can start with your story. I'll be kind and let you go first."

"Well... where should I begin...? I suppose the best place is from the end. I just got here from Nice. I was supposed to meet my girlfriend there."

"Supposed to?" she asked.

"We did, I guess... only she was dead. She'd been murdered." He looked down at his plate, breathing heavily.

Roni was shocked. She hadn't seen that coming. Was *everyone* dropping dead?

"She was cold when I touched her," he continued, the tears making his voice thick. He looked away from Roni, trying to hide his eyes.

Roni kept staring at him, shocked. She covered her mouth with her hand. She couldn't think of a thing to say. This seemed as far from a play as it could be. No one had ever taken such a roundabout, twisted way merely to get into her pants. No wonder he offered her company. The man was clearly broken up. He was desperate for some comfort. "I'm so… I'm so sorry," she stuttered. She reached out to take his hand, then paused with her hand hovering. She pulled her hand back to her lap. He didn't even notice.

"You see," he said before Roni could say anything else, "so, I told myself 'Amit, you've got to do something to dull this pain. Go to Barcelona, watch a football game… something.' But even that was canceled because there's some kind of fashion show and the game is an away one."

Whoops, Roni thought. "But, on the plus side, the fashion show made it so you could meet me."

Amit looked at her in disbelief.

"Instead of the football match, I mean," she quickly clarified. "Not instead of… God. I'm so stupid. I'm sorry, that's really not what I meant."

"It's okay," he said, giving her a crooked smile. "It's not your fault. And don't take this the wrong way, you're amazing and all, but over football? Meeting you rather than seeing Messi?"

She huffed a laugh. "Well, coming second to Messi… I think I can live with that." She gave him a cautious smile back, watching him closely to make sure her words weren't offending him.

"It's not all—that was only the final hit… it's less dramatic, but the path to yesterday was far from easy."

"I'm still listening," she said, this time with more empathy than the previous suspicion that had clouded her tone. She'd never met a man who'd opened up to her so quickly.

"It's rather a long story," he said but started telling her about the fall-out of his romantic life.

"Your daughter was stillborn?" She asked, minutes later, utterly horrified.

"Yes. It was a long time ago." The memories of the birth came flooding back, though, as if no time had passed at all. He had to stop talking to make his breathing even out again. When he raised his head, he saw Roni's eyes were red.

"I'm bringing you down."

"No, not at all. I'm sorry, it's just... I'm sorry. I couldn't stop it."

"It's all right, I'm through with the heavy stuff. Now it's only those pesky little things."

Roni wiped at her eyes and tried to smile encouragingly. It was a good thing she'd forgone makeup.

"A few days ago, I got back from a business trip in Europe and had a layover here," Amit said. "I love watching football matches here, and I invited Michal to come along too. Then—"

"Then you lacked the courage to leave your current partner, so you simply cheated on her," Roni stated.

"No! God, of course not! What do you take me for? It's not that I didn't want to, I did, terribly, but that's not the kind of man I am. I wanted to get things straight... to clear the air after the way we ended things." Amit sighed deeply. "My brother's friend took a picture of me—of Michal and I together—and then sent my brother the photo. The idiot then posted it to my Facebook wall."

"What? Why?"

"So that she'd break up with me so I could get back to Michal."
Roni looked at Amit, trying to figure him out. He was busy
playing with his food now that he'd finished talking. "So, she
thought you'd uploaded the picture so she would let you go,"
she stated.

Amit looked back up at her. *Not bad for a model,* the fleeting
thought made him feel guilty for thinking it in the first place.

Roni seemed to read something from his expression, because she said, "Not bad for a dumb blonde, huh?"

"That wasn't what I was thinking," he tried to deny it.

"You're not the first," she said easily.

He was silent for a moment before nodding. "I'm sorry."

"You are the first to have said *that,*" she said, and the last of
her defensive wall crumbled. All she wanted was to give him a
hug. She couldn't tell if what she said affected him. His feelings
seemed too well hidden.

"Well, that's everything," he finished. "My brother was also
the one to buy the plane ticket for Nice, and what happened
after, you already know."

Roni looked at him with pity and reached for his hand once
more, but he didn't react to her touch, fleeting as it was.

"What about you?" he asked.

"Me? After hearing all of that, I really don't have much to
complain about. My boyfriend cheated on me with my makeup
artist, who was closer to me than even my closest friends…
nothing serious, really." Roni didn't mention that she had
cheated on him, too. Nor did she say a word about the Mossad

agent who'd died in her arms.

"A double-cross—and from those who were closest to you," he said.

"Yes." Roni looked up at him, the tears stinging her eyes.

"No one has ever betrayed me. Not ever," he said, searching for every reserve of sympathy and support he had to give. "I've been fought with, dumped... it's definitely not always been easy going, but I've never been cheated on like that. At least not to my knowledge. I'm really sorry to hear you've been through that."

"Don't worry about it. In the end, despite everything you've been through, it looks like I'm the one who's ended up bringing you down."

"It's fine. I did the same to you. It may not be so much misery loves company, but more that company loves making the other miserable."

"That's true. And I really should get going."

"You're right. We really should quit."

She'd meant to simply get up and leave, but then she looked at him and regretted her decision. Her heart went out to him. She wanted to hug him to her. To comfort him. Or, maybe more so, she wanted him to comfort her.

He was attractive, she thought. And he smelled fantastic. Masculine. The thing she wanted most of all at that moment was to fall asleep wrapped up in his arms. She wasn't looking for sex, and it didn't seem as though he was, either. Just to lay cuddled together.

She wanted to invite him to come with her to the fashion show. Maybe he'd also be able to keep her safe. He was an Israeli, after all… and most importantly, she wouldn't be alone. He seemed like the perfect choice. And that was the problem. It was all too perfect. She wasn't so much afraid of there being a catch, she was more worried about her possible loss of control. That it would go too far.

In the end, the loneliness won out. "So, as a way to compensate for your canceled football game, can I invite you to Barcelona's stadium, to the fashion show that ruined your plans in the first place?"

"What, you mean to watch the fashion show? At the stadium?"

"Not only to watch but to come with me—be my escort to the show."

Amit frowned. "What do you mean, escort you?"

Roni felt cornered by his question. Her invitation suddenly felt too intimate, perhaps even an opening for sex. She wanted to take back what she'd said, just a little, but with the pressure of finding the right words, did the exact opposite and said without thinking, "Just to come with me. Nothing more. Don't get any ideas. It's not a date, or anything like that. It's not an opening for you to hit on me." His expression darkened with every word, and she realized how badly it had all sounded. She tried to fix it, but it was too late. "No, I mean like how now you've kept me com—"

"I think I understood you perfectly," he said coldly. "I…

you… I told you how I held the body of my dead girlfriend last night, and you're worried about whether or not I'm trying to hit on you? When you're the one asking me out, besides? Why? Only because you're a model? Did you even listen to a word I said, or was it all just a big show because you were too self-absorbed to notice someone else's issues? You know what, just leave it. Go to your show. I wish you luck and that you find another boyfriend soon. Hell, maybe you'll just forgive the shit who cheated on you and end up marrying him instead. Whatever floats your boat. I'm sorry for disturbing you during your meal. Now, please leave me alone."

He got up and left the table, leaving Roni stunned, with tears welling in her eyes. "Shit," was the only thing she managed to say.

"Shit," Amit muttered to himself, too. But he didn't turn back.

35.

"I don't get you."

"You don't get *me?*" The Director of the Mossad found that hard to believe. "This was *your* initiative."

"Turning to our superiors? Letting them know we've dropped the ball on this? That we need help? That was something we had to do," Daniel said to the Director.

"I agree, and that's exactly the reason I did it. I just don't know what you're complaining about."

"I think bringing in the army instead of having us there is a joke," Daniel said. "And them sending only one man out there?"

"I agree with that, too." The Director nodded. "But the Prime Minister gave his orders. He took into account more aspects than we did—political, other forces being involved rather than just ours... the country's image and reputation. Despite the Americans helping out, and the Romanians being as patient as they were, the showdown in Bucharest was a total disaster. Parts of it are already being leaked to the press. If the Prime Minister wants to lower our profile, then that's what needs to happen."

"But the *army?* And are you truly going to sit back and let the Iranians—and you've seen their capabilities—kick our asses like this?"

"Of course not. But I'm doing all I can within the frame of the new orders. We're working with Yair—his brother is the one out there, isn't he?—and you're behind the cyber division through Michmoret, right? So they're far from being completely alone. But I can't send out Saar and his people, because I was specifically told not to, unfortunate as that is."

"Isn't there more you can do?"

"Like what? Go against the Prime Minister? The same way you did? Have you forgotten where you were twenty-four hours ago?"

But the Director was already thinking it through. Even before his conversation with Daniel. He had some sleeper-agents from Caesarea in Europe he could deploy. The closest one was in Nice. From the moment the CIA representative had warned them on the open clean-up order, they'd tried to warn everyone. Some had received the warning on time, but they were all far from Barcelona. The agent in Nice hadn't been so lucky.

"We don't have to go against the Prime Minister. We can walk that shadowy line—and that's where we excel, isn't it? Can't you order one or two people to support—even from afar… in an Orbiting Star tactic, perhaps? Something that doesn't include Saar?"

"Look, I can't order someone to follow through with his mission, because it's against the Prime Minister's orders. But not *not* ordering someone something like that… that I can do."

"I didn't follow."

"Neither can I explain it, do you understand?"

"I believe so. Who is it?"

"Who?"

"The one who didn't get the order not to do what's not allowed?"

"I've no idea what you're talking about."

36.

Shaked Yossef asked himself how he felt.

He was on a plane from Paris to Barcelona, which was half an hour away from landing.

After talking to the Director of the Mossad, he made sure the operation in Bucharest was shut down. He'd also directed the guys to transfer all the bodies they could find to the Israeli embassy. Most of the casualties were in the hands of the Romanians, but the Americans would help them out in that regard. They will also be sure to transfer the correct bodies over to Iran.

Shaked had warned the group that the Iranians most likely still had agents remaining in Bucharest, and that they had to keep their guard up at all times. Still, the chances were slim that there would be another incident.

When through, he'd told them to head back to Israel.

"Does this make any sense to you?" Yoav had asked.

"Of course it doesn't," Saar had answered, the smile absent from his face.

Shaked had looked at Yoav with an expression of powerlessness that echoed Saar's words.

"And what about you?" Yoav had pressed. "Aren't you coming with us?"

"No. I'm needed in Paris," Shaked had said without elaborating further. It hadn't satisfied Yoav, but he'd dropped the issue. Saar had merely carried on watching Shaked, until finally, Shaked gave him a surreptitious nod. He caught the gesture.

"C'mon, everyone. Get to work," Saar rallied them and led them in the direction of the Old City. On the way, he stopped by Shaked and gave him a tap on his back. A minute later they were gone.

Shaked got rid of his weapon and took a taxi to the airport, where he bought a ticket to Paris. Later on, he'd get the one for Barcelona. He was in no rush. There was no way for him to intercept Roni Carmi in the hotel. He hoped she'd make it. No, he would have to find and meet up with her later on. In the meantime, it was important for him to choose a flight that would take him off a suspect list or potential surveillance of Iranian agents. That meant an indirect flight with two tickets bought separately.

Shaked asked himself how he was feeling—the routine check he gave himself every once in a while. The answer he came back with wasn't one he liked. He asked himself if he'd succeeded or failed.He succeeded, he told himself: first and foremost, the bottom line was that Israel was still in possession of the device. The Iranians hadn't managed to get it, despite pushing out a significant force that was astoundingly well trained. Furthermore, most of the Iranians were now out of the game. And that was his doing.

He failed, he told himself: Bucharest had become a bloody battlefield between different agencies. The Iranians were a step ahead of him the whole way. They definitely knew who had the device, and despite their fumbling around in the dark last night, they were now closing in on her with quick, cruel efficiency.

The success of transferring the device to someone else, someone who'd managed to get out of Bucharest, was solely held to the agent who had come from Iran's credit. Not remotely shared with Shaked or anyone from his team. Yes. His team, together with Saar's guys who'd arrived thanks to the substantial help of the Americans, had been the most deadly foreign force that had acted on European soil in the last decade. Still, that hadn't helped at all. In the end, the Prime Minister had transferred the duty of getting the device to Israel from the Mossad to the IDF. The IDF! That wouldn't have happened if Shaked hadn't failed.

Shaked was, most certainly, unhappy with his analysis. But it had had to be done so he could know exactly where he stood. He had to take the right lessons from all this mess so he could assist in finally finding the device. With the response it seemed to have generated, the device itself was probably of the highest possible priority.

Since the Mossad's Director had pushed Shaked into working

in the shadows, he couldn't use his colleagues in Michmoret or Caesarea. He was entirely alone. Being as such was hardly novel for him, but under the circumstances, it was definitely less effective.

Shaked noted to himself that he was currently the least important line of defense. There was at least one man from the IDF stationed close to Roni and charged with protecting her. Perhaps even more than one. Whoever they were, they weren't agents. He had to mark them to make sure he wouldn't end up hurting them or have them thinking he was the enemy. He had to find a way to help them complete the mission.

He knew how to find Roni Carmi. This time he simply went online: she was going to be in the fashion show scheduled for that afternoon at the Camp Nou. He'd wait for her there. In the meantime, he was going to sleep. The chances of him getting any shut-eye in Barcelona were slim to none. But with him having two flights now… he would sleep through them all.

37.

Avner Nitai stood in front of his bathroom mirror, looking at his reflection. He saw nothing but failure staring back at him—at least, he'd managed to convince himself of the truth of that. Though the reality didn't quite align with that statement, it didn't stop him from mercilessly throwing it at himself over and over. He'd had the possibility of focusing on his family—a loving wife, four wonderful children—a successful military career, at least, according to anyone close to him, which culminated in a highly sought after job as a pilot for El-Al. And yet, Avner Nitai dwelled constantly on the things he'd missed out on, keying in on what he didn't have, and the events he'd deemed as failures.

"What are you doing in there? Can you stop drooling all over her already?" his wife's voice broke through his musings.

"Oh, come on, quit that nonsense," he said back.

"You stop it. Leave her. I sure do hope you're only drooling over her and nothing worse."

"You're insane. I'm not even thinking about her—why is it

the first thing *you* think about?"

"You don't notice you do it, but every time you think about her, you get stuck in front of the mirror."

"Are you KGB?"

"I know you're looking at your passenger list. If you're stuck looking at the mirror, that means she's on that list. Is it to or fro?"

"You're insufferable."

"How do you know who I'm talking about?"

"Because you're obsessed with her. God only knows why."

I sure don't know the answer, he added to himself silently. His wife was clearly correct.

"She's your sister-in-law, for God's sake. Let's put aside the fact that you're married to me—that's it. You're screwed. But do you really want to embarrass yourself during every family gathering? Do you think you can hide your feelings? Just let it go."

"She's not my sister-in-law."

"Not yet, perhaps, but she definitely will be someday."

"I find that hard to believe. I doubt my brother will marry her."

"Why? Is she not good enough for him?"

"The opposite, actually. She'll dump him at some point or another."

"Then will you dump me and sail away with her into the sunset?"

Avner laughed. His wife heard him and came into the

bathroom. She wrapped her arms around him in a hug from behind. "Careful," he told her. His face was already covered in shaving cream. "Your clothes will get all dirty."

"I don't care," she said and kissed his neck. "I don't know what you're thinking about, but I'm quite happy with what I have right here. Your brother is great and all, but he's a brat. And that's not something I have patience for. I'm not jealous, either, for your information."

Avner looked at her questioningly.

"I know you, you wouldn't do anything like that. And I can't control your thoughts. As long as it's only a part of your mind, I have no problem with it. But still, I care, because you're so... transparent. I just don't want you embarrassing yourself."

Avner smiled with pleasure. He spun around to his wife and kissed her. Her face got smeared with shaving cream, but she merely smiled. She pushed him away from the sink and washed her face, dried it quickly, then blew him a kiss and left the bathroom.

Avner told himself he was lucky. He kept on believing it for exactly twenty seconds.

He shaved and thought about his brother. He couldn't smother the feeling of jealousy that came along. "Son of a bitch..." he muttered under his breath. Avner loved his brother, but he envied him more than a little. Envied his life, the choices he made, his irresponsibility and his free spirit. And yes, envied him for his girlfriend, too. Eran was fucking Roni Carmi. That fact never gave him rest; it made him lose his mind.

It's the flight back, he answered his wife's retreating back soundlessly.

Avner saw himself as the black sheep of his family. During every family gathering, his parents always boasted, "Eran got accepted to Nissan Native," "Eran is Roni Carmi's boyfriend! Can you believe it?" and that had made him by far second best in his parents' eyes. He was married to a wonderful woman and had given them four grandchildren. He was a captain in the air force. But, so what? They could just take that for granted.

Who'd even heard of Eran? An actor. *Sure.* And Roni Carmi's boyfriend!

Oh, were you a squadron leader in the air force? No shit. Which one? 114? You mean an F-16? No? F-15? No? Oh... so, helicopters then. Apache? What, no to that, too? Really... Sikorsky CH-53, then? It's not a helicopter gunship, is it? It's a big, clumsy-like transport chopper, right?

No, it hadn't been that, either. It was the best helicopter in the IDF, better than the Blackhawk by far. Ask those Army guys, let them tell you which ones they'd prefer. They'd all say the Sikorsky CH-53. From each rookie soldier to every special forces leader, they'd all prefer the Sikorsky. It beat the Black-hawk, the Bell 212, and any gunship besides.

But no one ever asked the Army, at least not in the air force.

So, when he was discharged after being a squadron com-mander, hoping to become an El-Al pilot, he was told he had to have a minimum of ten-thousand hours of flight experience on a fixed-wing plane. He'd said that he had well over that amount, what with him being a squadron commander in the air force, but when he specified that it was flying the Sikorsky CH-53, he received the same droll answer of, "Oh, so not even a gunship..." that left him aimlessly flying around the Cessna for hours on end to be accepted.

Of his missions, those flights beyond enemy borders, no one counted as extraordinary. Not even about a particularly exceptional mission when he flew in to extract a *Sayeret Matcal* team that had been stuck deep in enemy territory. One of the soldiers had fallen and hit his head. The force had then called in Avner, who'd managed to land in a place where a landing was completely impossible. The mechanic who'd flown in with him had hung out of the plane as if using a trapeze in a 470 sailing boat and had adjusted the rear right wheel. Avner had managed to land that wheel on a small ledge, and the left one on a rock, while leaving the front one above ground, hovering. He kept the craft steady with the help of opening the back hatch, through which the injured soldier and team piled in.

His maneuvering had been exceptional through every standard. His flight back through the steep valleys of the Lebanon Hermon, too. The air force commander at the time had said, "I have never seen someone fly like that." But since the whole ordeal suffered harsh criticisms—through no fault of his own—and a war almost broke out, everything concerning that night became a moot point, not even fitting into different battle legacies.

Avner finished shaving and started pulling on his clothes. In a few hours, he would act as captain for a passenger night-time flight to Barcelona. It would only be a short layover, then he'd be taking the same plane back home again.

38.

Roni watched Amit's back as he walked away and immediately started berating herself. *What am I doing? What could I possibly achieve by insulting him?* Years of cultivating her reflexes to *defend* had her sharpening her claws even when it was least appropriate. She'd clearly hurt him, though what she was unclear about, was why. *Is it all because of the bullshit rushing through my head?*

She kept beating herself up over it, then paused and pulled herself together. *Right,* she told herself. *It happened—now, what do I do about it?* A thoroughly egotistical thought flashed through her mind. She needed him. She wanted… no—it wasn't that she wanted—she *needed* him there with her at the fashion show. It would make her feel safer after the Bucharest fiasco. It would also make her feel desired, though perhaps not sexually so. Since meeting the agent in Bucharest, and then everything that had happened with Eran and Inbar, she kept questioning her ability to give a good show here in Barcelona. If she had Amit by her side, she knew she'd manage. It wouldn't be giving

Barcelona a show, it would be giving one to *Amit*.

Besides, she was lonely. She didn't have Inbar and she wanted company. Amit was everything she needed. Moreover, if she was wrong and he really was trying to hit on her... well, let him. It may not be official, but on a practical level, she was most certainly available, wasn't she? If Amit truly did try something, the thought suddenly didn't disturb her as much as before.

Okay, so, what now?

The logical part of her brain took over and she decided the only thing to do was go to sleep for a while. *If he's still around when I wake up, it'll be a sign I have to grovel and ask forgiveness. And if I don't see him... then no.*

She went back up to her room and went to bed.

Amit was insulted to the core of his soul. He strode away from Roni, still able to feel her eyes boring into his back. He'd noted her reaction to what she'd said a moment before he got up and left. He knew it meant she regretted her words, but her words echoed in his mind. He wasn't capable of pushing the hurt down to muffle the offense.

The feeling of Michal's cold body was still so fresh on his hands, and still, he put everything aside for this mission—all to help that ungrateful bimbo. He'd opened up to her like he'd never done before, not even with Michal, and she... all she cared about was whether he'd hit on her or not. She merely listened to whatever served her own interests, thinking only of herself. She could go screw herself.

He stopped in the hallway, two steps after leaving Roni's line of sight, and took a deep breath. However ungrateful she was, he was still charged with protecting her. He walked into the bar and watched her from the far side of the dining room. His vantage point allowed him to both keep an eye on her and make sure no one suspicious entered. This was an Orbiting Star tactic.

He watched Roni leave and get into the elevator. He kept his focus firmly on the elevator bank, waiting to note any suspicious activity. After five minutes of nothing happening, he went back up to his room, closed the door, and sat on his bed.

He knew it was childish, he thought after calming a little.

He made himself sort out his head for the first time since getting so offended. No, she hadn't meant to hurt him. She *had* been listening to him. That gross comment of hers was most likely made through a reflex she couldn't control, and that had nothing at all to do with him. He got it. She seemed to have said it by accident. Moreover, it looked as if she wanted his company and was, in fact, more worried about *herself,* than him. That was all.

He assumed that if he wasn't mere hours past losing Michal and working on little to no sleep, he wouldn't have been offended in the least. He really should pull himself together. If the problem was lack of sleep, then he should *sleep.* He doubted she was planning on leaving the hotel any time soon—with how tired she looked, he figured she was planning nothing more than hitting the sack, too.

He still had to find another way to escort her to the fashion show… but there was time. He'd find a way. Worst case, he'd apologize to her.

He set an alarm and lay down, though sleep remained out of reach. It took him a good few minutes to understand what it was that was bugging him. Here he was, once again in the midst of a mission—a simple one at that—and he was failing, stopping before it really started.

Shrouded in guilt, he finally fell asleep. Later, the alarm went off and Amit glanced at the clock. It hadn't been the alarm—it was the hotel's phone.

Roni awoke, got dressed, and sat on her bed. *If he's here, the first thing I have to do is apologize. If he isn't, then I won't.*

She called the reception desk and asked to be put through to Amit, though she didn't know his surname. A short moment later, she was put through.

Amit lifted the receiver and listened.

"Amit?" It was Roni's voice. He had more luck than brains.

"Yes," he answered. "Roni?"

"Yes," she said in a rush. "I'm sorry. I'm calling to apologize. Please don't hang up. Will you listen? I didn't mean to hurt or offend you, though I know I did. So, I'm truly sorry. I didn't think all you wanted was to hit on me, honestly, I didn't. And I was listening to you. It's this automatic defense mechanism I have—and I swear I didn't mean it. Please don't be mad—I'm so, so sorry. Will you forgive me."

"I forgave you after the first 'sorry,'" he said.

"And what—did you just want to hear me grovel?"

"I actually thought about stopping you, but I couldn't really get a word in." He laughed. "Besides, I liked your squirming."

"How very unkind."

"Then is it my turn to apologize?"

"Naturally."

"Then, I'm sorry."

"And I forgive you."

There was silence.

"So…" Roni started.

"So, what?"

"So, can I ask you to join me at the show again?"

"And choose you over Messi?"

"Well, we did say I came second, and Messi, I believe, is unavailable… so, will you?"

"And no issues with—"

"Nothing. Of course not. I'll keep my tongue in check. But, come with me. Like a big brother, okay? I want a big brother around me."

"I've got one of those, but I've never had a younger sister."

"I've got two older brothers, but it's been a long time since they've paid any attention to me."

"Maybe they're jealous."

"Maybe. I've no idea. Honestly, though, I am lacking a big

brother. Can I order one?"

"You may."

"Hey…"

"What?"

"It seems a little silly that we're talking on the phone like this. What room are you in?"

"604."

"Really? I'm in 605."

"Ha, get that."

"I'm coming over, then. You decent, big brother?"

"I'm decent. I'll have the door open for you."

"Bye."

"Bye."

He put down the phone and immediately hid his gun.

Roni put down the phone, left her room, and turned to the door next to hers. He opened the door for her and smiled.

She walked into his room, looking embarrassed. He motioned her to come in and watched her.

All she wanted was a hug.

"Can I have a hug?" she asked. "Just a hug?"

Amit looked at her for a moment, trying to decide whether she was playing him… but no. He didn't think she was.

"Sure," he said and pulled her to him.

She put her head on his shoulder and promptly burst into tears. She'd been so alone all this time, and now she finally had someone. Someone she could lean on. The same someone she'd so tactlessly almost pushed away. But now all of that was in the past. His arms wrapped around her, as they were, made everything seem brighter. God, she'd needed that hug. She felt as if she could stay like that for days—surrounded by his embrace, his scent... protected.

"Come on, you're falling asleep on me," he said and pulled away. He'd needed that hug himself, the problem was the smell of her. It drove him crazy. It also made him feel awkward. He was a big brother now, after all.

"Sorry," she said bashfully.

"Again with the apologies?" He shot her an honest, wide smile. "I think we can move on from that."

She nodded. "What now, then?"

"You tell me. When's your fashion show?"

"There's a while yet. Do you want to go downstairs to have something to eat?"

"Food again? What's the time, anyway?" He was hungry though. He hadn't really eaten that morning.

"Noon," she answered.

"Then let's go."

And they went downstairs.

During their meal, they spoke about themselves. Amit told her about his childhood, about how his parents had died in a car accident when he was young, and that his older brother Yair raised him and still worried about him constantly. He told her about Hadas, who, in a sense, helped raise him, too. He shared about his time in the Unit, and about the mission that had ended as it had and had brought on his subsequent discharge.

"With all the death that surrounded you, you still chose life rather than completing your mission," she said. "This may not be worth much, but I'm definitely on your side." She smiled.

She can't smile at me like that, he told himself.

"You know," she continued, "I think you may have chosen a career in security and protection as a way to compensate for the way you had to leave the army."

"Or maybe I'm just good at it," he argued back. "Very, very good at it."

She looked at him with a gentle, forgiving smile.

He looked up at the ceiling for a moment and tried to get his thoughts in order before focusing back on her. "You know, I haven't really thought about that before, but maybe you're right."

Roni loved the way he was looking at her. There was value and appreciation radiating from him, and it felt like an age since someone had looked at her that way—when it had nothing to do with her appearance.

"What did we say before?" he added with a smirk. "Not bad for a dumb blonde."

She laughed loudly and they glanced around to check if they'd disturbed the other diners.

Roni shared stories with him about growing up with two older, successful brothers, about how she always felt part of the background. She'd always been a "pretty girl," but when she was

younger she had been a little chubby—"Fat," she corrected—
and that she'd been teased a lot for it.

Once, in the sixth grade, when she'd started coming into
herself, she went up to a seventh-grader who she'd liked, but
he'd looked at her so disgusted that that had been what had
pushed her to get herself together.

She'd started watching her food and being more physically
active, and a year later, with puberty and the growth spurt she'd
had, she looked like a completely different person. Still, to this
day, she still struggled with her weight.

"Before the show last night, I weighed myself and saw that
I'd gained four-hundred grams. Four-hundred grams! Do you
know what that means?" she asked dramatically.

"The equivalence of a medium steak?" he asked.

"Dumbass. That's two packets of margarine."

"No shit."

"I know!" she said, a moment before she noted the cynicism
in his voice. "Beyond working out and diets, what that git of a
boy taught me was that if I wanted something to happen, I had
to work for it. I had to do it myself. Since then, I've set goals
for myself and I've reached them all. Everyone thinks that I'm
some princess who's had everything handed to her, and who
got everything so easy. But that's really not true. It's all hard
work that I put endless effort into. It only seems like I'm successful merely because of my looks, but there are plenty of girls
far more beautiful than me. Take my breasts and ass as an example. There aren't any models like that because it's considered

to be too "fat." So, I took my natural assets and added them to my famous spin. And that is something everyone goes crazy over—but I worked *hard* to make it happen."

Amit looked at her and couldn't hide his smile.

"I go on and on, and you just sit there smiling at me."

"I wouldn't dare cut in when you're on such a roll."

"Well, say something now."

"It seems that the whole world needs to thank a snot-nosed seventh-grader."

She laughed.

"Luckily, you haven't had to deal with much death," he added.

The image of the agent popped into her mind and Roni's face darkened. "No, not in the way you have, but I have been touched by it once."

"Oh, I'm sorry. I didn't mean to bring up a difficult subject."

"No, don't worry about it. You couldn't have known. It was years ago, when I just got started modeling. He was a young model too, and we hit it off. He wasn't really a close friend... but a friend nonetheless."

"With benefits?"

"A few benefits," she smiled grimly. "Yes. We were together all the time."

"And?" he asked.

"And he died because of an overdose."

"I'm sorry to hear that."

"Well, it was a long time ago."

"Still."

"Yes. It's because of him—or, well, thanks to him, I don't go anywhere near those things. Drugs are rather prevalent with our crowd. I also don't really drink alcohol. When I do, it's very little."

"I know it doesn't comfort much, but it seems that with his death he carried on helping you."

"Yes. He has." She felt her thoughts weigh down on her and it took her noticing the time to pull herself out of it.

"Shit, we're late! No, wait, not quite. But we've only got a few more minutes until we have to leave."

"Say," he started, changing the subject to something not so grim. "I've been thinking about something."

"Hmm?"

"What's the big idea about having a fashion show at a football stadium? And at the Camp Nou, no less? It seems almost sacrilegious."

She laughed. "I agree a hundred percent. I've no idea what they were thinking. We're in the city of Gaudi architecture, and rather than choose one of those buildings, we're having the show at a football stadium. That's a sign of serious lack of taste."

That wasn't quite what he'd meant, but Amit let it go.

"This hotel is rather far from the stadium. We shouldn't be late," Roni said.

"What now, then?"

"Now we go upstairs and get ready quickly. Wait for me here in ten minutes."

Roni went upstairs to get dressed. Amit went back to his room to get his gun. He figured two clips should do. *Show time.* They'd been relatively protected so far because no one knew where she was, but that would all change once the fashion show began. He had to be alert. Luckily he'd managed to stay close to her. Though, it was much more than luck.

They met up downstairs and got into a cab.

Twenty minutes later they arrived at the stadium. To Amit's surprise, the place was already packed, just as if there was an actual football game scheduled. *Perhaps no one told them of the change of plans*, he mused.

He got out of the car first, with Roni following close after. He escorted her through the crowd, one hand firmly on his gun and the other on her shoulder. When they reached the entrance, he heard a bang from behind him. He saw two people bump into each other, and about a meter away from him, he thought he saw a knife. The massive crowd didn't let him be sure.

He pushed Roni in and led her quickly to the dressing rooms.

She looked at him with a quirked eyebrow, confused, but allowed him to maneuver her around.

"Rather excitable fans," he said drily.

She nodded and went to carry on, before she froze in front of a figure blocking their path.

39.

The commander of unit 1 turned to Layla and told her they were ready.

Layla perused the force under her command: three members of unit 1, Abas, who at the start of the mission was stationed at the airport in Bucharest, and six members of the cell from Marseille. The agents from Marseille weren't as well trained as the four members who'd been with her in Bucharest, but they'd do. She'd use them as backup.

Once they found a place to stay at one of the simpler, smaller hotels that were not far from the stadium, Layla ordered everyone to get some rest—to sleep—then eat. They had to have their strength up. Waiting up wouldn't make the fashion show start any sooner. One of the key attributes skilled and well-trained agents had was the ability to rest and build up strength. Luckily for her, the people under her command were sufficiently skilled.

For that reason, when they all left for the stadium, they were alert and prepared for action.

They arrived well before the show was scheduled to begin and spread out. The cell from Marseille was positioned relatively far. unit 1 was stationed in the parking lot close to gate 9, where the pedestrians would come in, while Layla and Abas waited in the passage between the ice-skating rink and Palau Blaugrana that was on the right from the souvenir shop and the actual stadium on the left.

Layla assumed Roni Carmi would go through the passage.

A short time later, the place started to get crowded.

She instructed her people not to hurt the models. They were to kill whoever Roni had with her, but not harm her. That was no act of mercy—it was strategy. This was a fashion show. Roni Carmi would change outfits, and many of those outfits included very little fabric. Hardly the most ideal situation to hide a hard disk or any such device. She likely would have left it somewhere. If she were to die, they might never find it. It was possible that neither would the Israelis, but they could never be too sure. It was best to get it and ensure its destruction.

If they were lucky, they'd get her alive. That would eventually lead them to the device. There was no doubt about that. If they couldn't nab her at the stadium, they'd follow her to her hotel and get her at night.

"They're here," the leader of unit 1 said. "There's one other person with her. No one we know. I'm leaving Razah in the parking lot and following them with Hassain.

"Affirmative," Layla said and signaled Abas. He nodded his confirmation.

"Her escort is holding onto her with one hand. He's got a gun in his other." unit Leader 1 said.

"Take him down," Layla ordered. "But carefully. Don't hit the model!"

"Got it," he said. "Twenty seconds."

Layla and Abas searched for the model and her escort, or at least for the commander of unit 1 and Hassain, but there were simply too many people milling around. Layla ordered the cell from Marseille that was securing the area outside the passage to start closing in on their direction.

She heard a bang. She looked around but couldn't see anything. She saw the model get pushed by someone into the souvenir shop. She knew that from there they'd make their way to the stadium, and Roni Carmi, no doubt, was already out of reach. However, two meters away from her, something had happened. She had to take care of it. She motioned Abas to follow her and started moving to the exit.

One moment she saw Hassain in front of her, looking right into her eyes, and then he was gone.

40.

Shaked took the Airbus from the airport to Catalonia square. He walked around there for a little, then took a taxi to the stadium. He arrived almost four hours before the show. He was quite sure that would suffice. There were clearly Iranian lookouts about, but they wouldn't notice him. All they'd see was a Barcelona club mega-fan.

He walked around the entryway, asking about the show. This passage was, indeed, the way in. The show itself would be in the Colonnade below the seats, in short,where the club's trophies were usually exhibited. The trophies themselves had been removed for the event, an act nothing less than sacrilegious to the fans. Since Shaked had arrived in the guise of a die-hard fan, he protested such action loudly.

The thing that "annoyed" him most was the decision to switch the home game to an away match. The ruse worked and soon another fan joined in, protesting and complaining in fluent Spanish about the decisions the team's sponsors made. He wondered if the fan talking with him could be an Iranian agent, but decided against it. The man had a heavy Catalonian accent, and wouldn't have been enough of a cover... not unless the man was a perfect agent. Shaked decided he was not.

He spent the remaining hours similarly, talking to the Catalonian fan about the team's passes after the end of the era of its last coach. Time flew, and despite the heated debate, Shaked never once stopped examining his surroundings.

He couldn't see the cell from Marseille, but he clocked unit 1. He kept looking for Layla—the commander he'd heard so much about last night—but couldn't identify her.

The passage became more and more crowded, and Shaked finally said farewell to his Catalonian friend, promising to come to visit him at some point.

He settled at the end of the passage, where the Iranians who'd spread out through the parking lot couldn't see him. Half an hour later, Roni Carmi exited a taxi. With her was a tall man. He kept close to her. The man kept his left hand on her shoulder, while his right gripped a concealed weapon. He looked around, but couldn't see anything. *Like a bull in a china shop.* What was the big idea with sending in an army man? The Iranians would take him out with no trouble at all.

One member of the unit stayed behind, while two others followed Roni and the soldier. Shaked followed. They were good, he admitted to himself. Very good, in fact. Both agents closed the gap quickly. He marked the distance between them and the model and soldier, and concluded that the Iranians would gain on them. They'd take out the soldier and take the model. They

272 | HANDLE WITH FORCE

didn't stand a chance.

His dilemma fell on whether he should act or not. Without his intervention, the model's chances of surviving were slim to none. If he did, he would most likely be hurt himself. He could take both of these agents, but he'd be left open for all the others. He'd be exposed.

Just as he was watching this go down, so too were the Iranians, and their commander was still unidentified. The woman was considered their most qualified agent, and he was certain she was here. Interfering meant suicide.

He didn't have much time. The first agent was a meter away from the soldier, a long knife was gripped in his hand. Shaked didn't think—he acted. As he moved, he heard Tzukerman yelling in his mind, *The enemy in the wings! They're in the wings!*

He silenced Tzukerman and moved with surprising speed toward the first agent. He knocked into him, pushing him off course a moment before he stabbed the soldier. Shaked kicked at the surprised agent's hand, and gripped the man's jaw and back of his neck. A split second later, the Iranian agent's neck snapped. Shaked took his weight, carrying him to the side of the passage. He dropped him over a low wall and turned to the agent who'd already marked him. He was close. Too close. Shaked moved fast in the agent's direction, then turned back again. The agent fell for the feint, the movement making him raise his arm, the knife still clutched between his fingers. Shaked grabbed at the man's arm, twisted it, and stabbed him straight in his heart. The whole maneuver took less than a second, an Aikido technique that flowed into one harmonious action. The problem came from the agent's gaze. He wasn't looking at Shaked, but over his shoulder instead. That could mean only one thing. Shaked didn't need Tzukerman screaming in his ear for him to know full well. No. He finished off the agent, and spun. He wondered if he had the time.

He didn't.

He noticed green eyes and black hair, right as Layla's knife cut through to his heart.

She's so beautiful, was the last thought that rushed through his mind.

41.

"Sean!" Roni shouted and jumped on the man standing in front of them.

"There's my perfect girl," Sean said, rocking backward with Roni's weight hitting him so fast. "I was getting worried."

"Why?" Roni asked. Seeing Sean was surprisingly emotional.

"Inbar told me you two got into a little fight, that your phone died, and that you left for Barcelona angry. I don't want to push my nose in where it doesn't belong, but I figured—without her saying anything, mind—that it had something to do with Eran, too? So, yeah. I worried. Besides, you came right to the show rather than getting here in time for rehearsal. You know I don't like that. I've told you before, it's unprofessional. Even if you're only walking the runway once." Sean paused. He couldn't seem to look quite as stern as he seemed to be trying to. "Anyway, it looks as though you got everything sorted, so, I'm glad." He looked over at Amit, sending him a look that clearly said *I don't care who you are or what you're doing with her, but God help you if you fuck up this show.*

Amit stood by silently. This wasn't hurting Roni and was, truly, none of his business.

Roni, on the other hand, laughed heartily. "I've missed your bullshit. Here, meet Amit, my big brother. He's coming along with me instead of Inbar. Don't worry, I'll give a killer show. You'll be well pleased."

Sean's worried expression melted into one of satisfaction. "That's how I like you." He turned to Amit. "I take it you're a master with makeup, yeah? Look, whatever you do with her is none of my business, but it can't hurt her abilities here. If she gives a shit show, I'll kick your ass. If she blows the roof off this place, I'll kiss you." Sean took a step back, giving Amit a thorough once over. "Maybe even more than a kiss."

Amit couldn't hide his smile. "With such a threat I'm not sure what I want more."

Roni laughed and Sean smiled, muttering in Amit's direction, "You don't know your own capabilities." He turned back to Roni and said, "After this show, you're going back to Israel to get all of your things in order, your phone, too. You can't work like this. I'll be going to Paris to finalize the contract we spoke about last week. Don't let your 'big brother' here interfere too much, yeah?"

"Yes, Mom," Roni teased and kissed Sean's cheek. "Have you noticed who is making me late now?"

"Go! Get ready."

Roni took Amit's hand and pulled him toward the dressing rooms.

Amit scanned the area, and quickly figured out where the show would be—it wouldn't be in the actual stadium. The runway had been built in the team's trophy room, where the trophies and the team's history pieces had been removed. *They were insane,* he thought to himself. It wasn't the Iranians Amit would have to protect Roni from. It was the Barcelona fans.

They got to the dressing room where two large guards stood. "He's with me," Roni said to them, and they were allowed in. A moment before entering, Roni turned to Amit.

42.

Layla called Razah, and together with him and Abas, they managed to move the three bodies to the side. The sheer number of people made it impossible for others to pay too much attention to their surroundings. It seemed as if they all were brought down due to pressure and not violent assassinations. The main trouble was that Hassain and the Israeli agent were bleeding quite significantly. That meant that their hearts hadn't completely stopped. However, it will only take minutes, now.

As she'd assumed would happen, they'd missed the opportunity to get the model at the show's entrance. Now they had to stake out the place and trail her back to the hotel. The chances of Roni and the unknown man going straight to the airport from the show were rather slim, she believed. They would need the device. Still, whatever their ultimate decision, Layla was ready.

She called in the Marseille cell and had them go to the cars. They would take two cars, while she, together with Abas and Razah, would take the third. She had planned a three-car tail, and if they did it correctly, there was no chance they'd be found out.

Layla redistributed her force. Now, all that was left, was to wait.

43.

"Listen, this is important," Roni said. "We're about to go behind the scenes of the fashion show. Though there are quite a lot of people around, it's also where models, both the men and the women, get dressed. With all the good intentions of the MeToo movement, it arrived at the fashion industry rather late. So, anyway, the lead models usually have their own stalls while the others get dressed behind curtains—though, not all of them, and they're not always used, sometimes even because of the show's time constraint. So, you're about to see a lot of boobs. Maybe more than that. Some of the models here are famous, too, so, do me a favor, don't stare—not at the girls or their breasts—and definitely don't take out your phone to take any pictures, okay?"

"Okay. And what about you?"

"I always get a stall. Stay close to me. You'll also be coming into the stall with me."

Roni walked in without waiting for his reply and Amit dogged her heels.

They moved through a sea of people, most of whom were women, at various stages of undressing. Amit felt so uncomfortable, all he could do was stare at Roni's back. A few steps in, Roni stopped to talk to someone. *A man,* Amit realized and raised his gaze. It was an older gentleman, with white hair and modest clothing. He seemed familiar to Amit, but he couldn't remember where from.

Roni and the man chatted about the upcoming show, and she requested to have a makeup artist sent her way because hers was ill. The man promised to do so, kissed Roni's cheek, and they continued on their way.

Roni's stall turned out to be not so small. Both of them fit into it and, eventually, someone came, carrying some kind of... clothing. It distantly resembled a dress, though it was mostly put together with straps rather than fabric.

"Okay, listen," she started.

"Again with the listening?"

"I'm serious. Look, I'm going to have to wear this. That means that I'm about to get almost completely naked. I'll only be wearing a nude thong. I don't want to offend you, but..."

"It's fine," he cut in. "I'll turn around."

"Amit, I don't—"

"Don't worry, I'm not offended. What kind of big brother looks at his sister's boobs?"

Roni laughed and Amit turned around. He could hear and feel Roni undress behind him and his stomach swooped. *Roni Carmi is naked behind me.* His breathing quickened and he felt as if he were floating. A minute later he felt a hand on his shoulder that sent chills up his spine.

"You can turn around now."

Amit turned and looked at Roni. The outfit was layered in strips over her mostly exposed body, covering the essentials in the most strategic ways. The vertical lines gave off an illusion of height, and she suddenly seemed incredibly tall. And beautiful. Long and the short of it, she looked incredible. He opened his mouth and couldn't seem to get it to close again.

"You're… you're…" he stuttered. He could barely take in a breath. "You're the most beautiful thing I've ever seen." The words fell from his lips and he instantly wished he could take them back.

Roni didn't. She blushed and averted her eyes.

"Can I come in?" a voice came from outside, and the older man from before came in with a makeup artist. The man looked at Roni who smiled back at him with twinkling eyes. He examined the outfit and adjusted it slightly in a couple of areas, then told the makeup artist what he wanted, gave Roni a quick peck, and left. *The designer,* Amit realized.

The makeup was minimal so as not to take away from the clothing, and ten minutes later, the artist left too.

Amit kept looking at Roni then quickly looking away awkwardly, drinking her in as he could.

"Say something," Roni said.

"I'm finding it hard to speak, to be honest," he replied.

Roni watched him, feeling happy. "You're allowed to stare

at *me,* if you like. You have my permission. I don't find it embarrassing."

"I'm rather embarrassed, though."

"You can go outside and wait at the end of the runway, if you prefer. There's a seat by Sean."

"Yeah, I didn't imagine this being quite so difficult."

"I'm up right at the end, so be patient," she said, stroking his back.

He left the stall and walked through the changing area. The models were all already dressed, but Amit barely noticed them. He walked through them, feeling as though his head was in the clouds. He was a little worried about leaving Roni alone, and before he left, he did a quick calculation. He was supposed to protect her, but there was security all around her now. Besides, she would be walking out on the runway soon. He wouldn't manage to get out in time to protect her there, so he really didn't have much of a choice. Leaving was his best option.

He found the runway, recognized Sean, and went over to sit next to him.

"How does she look?" Sean asked.

"Breathtaking," Amit replied, and Sean seemed satisfied.

The show started and dragged on lazily. Amit kept his focus mostly on the crowd, but nothing stood out as suspicious. Roni finally walked out to the sound of thunderous applause. She glided across the runway, staring straight at Amit. He watched her, hypnotized. He didn't even notice he was holding his breath.

Roni's chest sent warm vibrations throughout her whole body when she noticed Amit. It made her feel so high that she wouldn't have been surprised if her feet weren't touching the ground. She wasn't showcasing for the designer, she was only there for Amit. She reached the end of the runway, kept that heated eye contact with him, then spun. The crowd cheered and the camera flashes sparked across her vision.

Amit stared at her, his eyes shining, and she felt the world fall away. An eternity passed between them, then she smiled widely—just for him. She spun again and made her way back behind the scenes.

Sean stood up beside Amit, clapping wildly, and the whole crowd followed his lead.

A moment after Roni disappeared, she came back arm in arm with the designer, leading all the other models. The crowd lost it; Amit was ecstatic.

When they all went back, Sean turned to Amit and said, "I don't know what you did to her, but I like it!" Then he made true of his promise and kissed Amit. He, in turn, was still so hypnotized, that he didn't even resist.

The kiss pulled him back to reality, and he stared at Sean a moment before making his way through the masses to the changing rooms and to Roni's stall.

"I'm coming in," he said.

"Hang on… okay, come."

She'd just finished clasping her bra when Amit walked in. She stood in front of him in a tiny thong and semi-transparent bra. He looked at her and his breath caught in his chest. His cheeks burned and he covered his mouth with his hand. Roni, seeing his reaction, quickly slipped on a shirt and pants.

She smiled up at him happily. "How was I?"

"Amazing. Crazy sexy. Simply perfect."

"A lot of it is because of you."

"Me? What have I got to do with it?"

"The way I look—it's not only about what I'm wearing. It's also about what I feel." She blushed. Amit did too.

"Well, what's certain, is Sean seemed very happy about the performance. He even kissed me," he decided to change the subject.

"*Really*? He's the best." She laughed. "Okay, come on. I'm dressed. Help me get organized and let's go back to the hotel."

He did, and they soon left. On the way out, Roni said good-bye to the designer, who appeared incredibly pleased. He turned to Amit and thanked him. Amit looked at him, lost.

Sean was waiting for them outside, clearly over the moon. Roni gave him a hug and promised to call once she arrived in Israel. They walked over to the parking lot. Amit looked to the sides but saw nothing. Neither did anything happen. They got a taxi and Amit instructed, "Hotel Ohla," and they were off. He checked to see whether they were being followed but noticed nothing, and twenty minutes later, they were back in the hotel.

A three-car tail meant that every time a different car closed in on the taxi, switching with another after a while. It was extremely difficult to detect, even if you were a pro. "Hotel Ohla," Muhamad, the leader of the cell from Marseille, said. "Layla waited another half hour then made her way to the hotel. An hour later, six of them checked-in to three rooms on the third floor. One unit consisting of three agents from the Marseille cell remained outside.

Roni and Amit went up to their rooms. When they reached their respective doors, Roni took Amit's hand and tugged him across her threshold. "I want a hug," she said and burrowed into him. He hugged her back. She clung to him, her head between his neck and shoulder. She breathed him in.

Amit did the same. He held her tightly, and the image of her, standing in front of him, wearing nothing other than that nude thong and see-through bra, burning behind his eyes. His cock started to harden. He tried to keep her from feeling it, pulling his hips back, but Roni didn't let up. She rubbed her groin against him and in moments he was completely hard. He knew there was no way she wasn't able to feel him.

"I'm releasing you from the role of big brother," she whispered in his ear and came ever closer. To herself, she added that she would likely have to take *it* out and hide it somewhere, and she had no idea where—at least until after Amit…

"Oh, God… Roni," he uttered.

She lessened her hold on him enough to pull back and look in his eyes.

He could feel the warmth of her breaths against his face.

"Don't take this the wrong way," he said quietly, "I want you… but I can't. I need some time. Please be patient with me." He looked at her, finding it close to impossible not to throw her onto the bed and fuck her right now. She seemed to read his mind, because she only widened her stance, pushing herself against him even harder than before, gyrating against him. Her hands worked their way down to his ass and pulled him to her.

"Fuck, Roni…" he moaned.

"I'm not offended." A devilish smile spread across her face. "But neither am I giving up." Then she pulled away completely and took a few steps back, smiling that smile of hers.

For a moment she simply looked at him, then she closed the space between them, kissing him deeply on his lips.

Amit was too surprised to respond.

She released him again and pushed him gently out her doorway. "It's late. I don't fancy eating. I'm going to sleep. See me tomorrow at seven for breakfast?"

"You're not hurt, are you?" Amit was a little unsure of her reaction.

"You're such an idiot," she said fondly, and closed the door in his face.

Amit took that as a "no" and found it difficult to wipe the smile off his face.

He went to his room and got ready for bed. He wasn't hungry either. Tomorrow, they'd be on their way home together. The mere thought made him smile.

Then he remembered Michal. His spirits instantly took a turn.

He sunk into his thoughts. As it was, it didn't seem like anything was happening. Yair's whole mess was more likely nothing more than a false alarm. He found it hard to believe that Yair had made something like that up. Michmoret wouldn't have fixed up the hotel room and acquired his gun if it was *nothing*. But it was probably not as dangerous as he'd assumed. It seemed like Yair had set him up on a date and not a mission in the end. He was such a shit. Even when he screwed up he somehow pulled it off—so how could he stay mad? Anyway, it didn't look like sleeping would be in the books for him tonight.

After a while, he decided to go downstairs for a drink. He didn't notice the time, though it was getting late. He sat at the bar, ordered a beer, and drank it as he snacked on peanuts. At some point, a lone man sat at the bar not far from him.

Amit drank his beer slowly, but something started to niggle at him. He couldn't put his finger on what it was, but the feeling only became stronger. A warning bell started to go off in his head, getting louder with each second. Something was wrong. He couldn't explain it even to himself until it hit him full on. The other man—the man at the bar next to him—hadn't looked at him even once. Not even a nod hello when he'd arrived. If there were only two people at a bar, they each gave a cold, detached hello to each other. That was simply the way it was. And if the other man wasn't paying him any attention, that meant that he was paying him *a lot* of attention. He was being guarded!

Roni!

288 | HANDLE WITH FORCE

He shot up from the bar—which was on the first floor—and ran into the hotel. He thanked God that at least he'd taken his gun with him and that the silencer was still on it too. With all due respect to agents, trained as they were, when it came to urban warfare, an expert at counter-terrorism beat them at every turn. There was no time to wait for the elevator. Amit rushed up the winding staircase at the center of the hotel. It was dark. He took the stairs two at a time, landing on the balls of his feet, going silently and fast, his gun pointed ahead. *What an idiot.* How could he have left her?

On the bend between floors four and five, he found the first lookout. An exact gunshot to the bridge of his nose—the lethal triangle of death on the man's face—and he fell silently to the floor. Amit passed him and paused. He was tempted to go straight up to Roni, but knew that the guard from the bar was hot on his heels. If he pushed forward, Amit was surel to get shot in the back. He went up to the fifth-floor landing and waited. Ten seconds later, there he was. He stopped for a moment to check on his friend, and that was enough for Amit. He shot him straight through the head. He fell in a heap.

He went up and reached the sixth floor. There had to be many Iranian agents around, he realized. If there were only a few, then they would have risked taking him out. If they allowed themselves to leave him alive and merely under watch, it meant they had enough people for them to avoid a kill that could potentially ruin their plans.

He stood at the edge of the staircase, hidden from the

backside of the elevator shaft. He rounded it slowly and looked left into the darkened hallway. He saw, about two meters away, two Iranians breaking into room 605. Roni's room. The Iranians believed the stairwell to be secured, so the two trying to break in didn't even look back. Amit shot a volley of three bullets into each, and they, too, fell. He glanced to the right—to the other side of the hallway—and when he saw no one, he darted toward the two Iranians and shot another bullet into each of their heads.

He looked left and right once again, but the place was empty. He stood over the two people who'd tried to break into Roni's room and pushed back the impulse to open her door or at least talk with her to make sure she was okay.

There was another guard on the floor above—there had to be.

He went back into the stairwell and started taking slow, measured steps. Slow and silent. When he'd run up before, he'd had to move fast, so he'd let the balls of his feet absorb the sound. Now, he took the stairs slowly, so he moved per tai-chi teachings, heel first, then a slow roll of the foot until it reached his toes. It ensured complete silence.

But the guard had heard the shots from before—silenced as they'd been—and he was ready. He took the first shot at Amit, and missed. Amit fell back three stairs, then went back up and shot three times. He didn't hit him, and the guard escaped further up. Amit followed, wary of becoming a target himself. The guard went up to the eighth floor and escaped to the roof area.

290 | H<small>ANDLE WITH</small> F<small>ORCE</small>

Amit did the same and saw the guard's back was to him. He shot another three bullets in his direction, but only two came out. The slide was open. He was out of ammunition. And he didn't have another magazine on him.

The guard heard the click of the end of the magazine, then turned and made his way back. He was unhurt. Without pause, Amit threw the gun at the man. He stopped for a moment and hesitated. That was all Amit needed. He quickly moved towards the guard, kicking him in his abdomen. The guard choked out a muffled groan, but still held up his gun, aimed, and shot. Amit wasn't there anymore. He'd moved left and delivered a kick right to the guard's neck. He lost his balance but kept his feet. Amit grabbed him and smashed his skull against the poolside.

The man's neck pressed against the glass poolside as Amit held his face under the water. Amit's weight prevented the man from moving. After two minutes, the man finally stopped convulsing. Amit didn't move for another three minutes, then finally let him go.

He picked up his discarded gun, even though he had no ammunition. He looked for the Iranian's weapon, but couldn't find it. He decided not to dawdle any longer and made a fast pace back to Roni's room. He saw nothing had changed since he'd left.

He stood in front of her door, wondering his best course of action. He contemplated going back into his room to take another magazine, but in the end, simply decided to take the

Iranians' firearms. He rooted through their gear. He didn't find guns, only break-in tools. Finally, he found a key card. He checked all the doors on the sixth floor, but it didn't open any of them. He planned to go down and check all the hotel rooms—it had to open one, after all. On his way, he intended to take the Iranian who'd guarded him at the bar's gun. However, the second he walked into the stairwell, he noticed there was something wrong. A slight play of light and shadow. He quickly changed direction and sent his leg out in a vicious kick. A gunshot went off at the spot he'd been moments before. That same gun got kicked by Amit's foot, and ended up flying from the Iranian's hand. The Iranian switched from gun to blade in a blink of an eye and came at him.

Amit retreated into the sixth-floor hallway. He couldn't believe it. The Iranian was a woman. She had coal-black hair and green eyes. She moved with astounding agility and speed. Amit figured out quickly that she'd take him down without much effort on her part.

Many years ago, when he was still in the army, an instructor in military strategies gave a lecture on some well-known battles and the lessons you can learn from them. The lecturer asked how Montgomery beat Rommel in the Second World War at the battle of El Alamein. The guys had all raised some suppositions, and the lecturer had refuted each one. "Look," he'd said. "Rommel was the better strategist in every way, surpassing Montgomery in every parameter. And he'd beaten him every time. What tipped the scales in El Alamein was a simple

292 | HANDLE WITH FORCE

fact. The difference in mass. Montgomery used his only advantage—his sheer numbers—and hit Rommel with a full, frontal attack. Montgomery suffered serious losses, but he kept cutting down Rommel at every corner, never stopping, never quitting. Until he won. You're a bunch of schemers," he'd concluded, "but in a fight, it often comes down to a simple question of mass. You take a hit because you can, then you take down the enemy."

Amit knew that the fighter in front of him was much better than he was. He was about to get hit, and badly, but if she failed to kill him with the first shot, Amit would use the advantage he had over her—his mass. Amit was much taller and heavier than she, so all he needed to do was survive her attack.

And Layla attacked. She shot out with her legs and right arm, which held the knife away from him. Amit realized that the knife was aimed at his heart and ducked. Her hits threw him off balance, but he stayed low. Suddenly, in a flash so fast he could barely follow it, her arm with the knife flashed forward, impacting his left in a fraction of a moment when he'd left it unprotected. Rather than block the hit, a move that would have most likely been destined to fail, Amit straightened.

The knife was lodged in his left side, below his ribs, missing his heart by mere centimeters. Amit grabbed the woman's left arm with his right, and tilted his body in her direction, dropping her to her back.

Layla had instantly realized that not only had she missed his heart, but Amit's move, too. She estimated she had approximately a second until she hit the floor. If she waited that long, getting back up would be very difficult. Luckily for her, there was no reason for her to wait. In her world, a second was plenty of time. She could make a quick turn and break free. She could bend her legs to her stomach and kick out. She could also bend one leg, dislodging his arm that still held tight to her arm with the knife, then both arm and knife would be free. Whatever the choice, she would be dealing with an injured man. Taking him down would be of no trouble.

It took her less than half a second to go through her options. She made the decision right away, and all she had to do was wait to hit the floor. It took an age. More than half a second.

Layla fell on her back with Amit on top of her.

He bent her left hand above her head to her right. His right hand that had been busy with her arm, he moved to her neck. Amit bent his right hand a little and pressed down with his elbow on her windpipe.

Layla closed her eyes for a moment. Her right arm was still pinned under Amit's weight, her left arm bent behind her head, and her neck blocked by Amit's elbow. She couldn't go without a struggle, so she fought with the only thing she had that wasn't pinned down—her legs. Amit, in response, pressed his knee with astounding strength to her groin. The pressure was so immense that her pubic bone shattered. The breaks pushed inward, tearing up her womb.

Layla ignored the blinding pain in her pelvis and the fact that she had been unable to breathe for seconds and asked herself what she wanted to do. The answer came immediately, and she let her muscles go limp.

And so, seconds before she lost consciousness, tears filled her eyes and her lips mouthed a single word over and over. She had no air, so the whisper was practically soundless, but Amit, whose face was so close to hers, found he could understand her easily. The word was "Steve."

Amit remained over the Iranian agent for another five minutes before he let himself get off her. He pulled the knife from his body and checked himself. He went into his room and treated himself as best he could. He would live, he figured. He only hoped there weren't any more agents left. There was no way for him to know. Either way, he reloaded his gun with another magazine.

Now for the difficult part. Amit went downstairs and started checking the keycard. In the end, he found the room on the third floor.

Carrying six bodies from the roof and the sixth floor all the way to the third floor was no easy business when uninjured. Hurt as he was, it was herculean. Moreover, despite the late hour, there was still the chance of bumping into guests. Amit assumed most of the hotel guests would use the elevator, so he chose the stairs, which made carrying the bodies all the more difficult. He stopped on every floor to make sure the coast was clear. Fortunately, no one came to floors six or three. One couple came up in the elevator to the fourth floor and went into their room right as Amit was passing their floor. He kept himself hidden in the section of stairs behind the elevator bank, so that event passed without issue, too. An hour later, with no further issues, he finally completed his task. He packed the bodies in the third-floor room, leaving the keycard in one of the bodies' pockets, put up the sign for *Do not Disturb*, slammed the door, and left.

He stood in front of Roni's bedroom, unsure as to what he should do. Eventually, he made a decision.

He went into his room and opened the window, then pulled apart a curtain and used it as a makeshift rope. He wrapped the "rope" around one of the decorative eyes of the building, pleased to finally find some kind of use for them, then swung Tarzan-like to the balcony of the next-room-over's balcony. Roni's room. The small square below was lit with an almost full-moon light, but as late as it was meant there were hardly any people around, and none of them were busy looking up in his direction anyway.

Amit slid the window open and got into Roni's room. She lay in her bed, breathing quietly. *Thank God.* They hadn't managed to get to her.

He decided to stay in her room and guard her from inside the room, close, in case there were more enemy agents around.

He looked at her moon-lit room. There was nothing unusual. Roni was sleeping on her back, the blanket arranged in such a way that one of her breasts was completely exposed. Amit looked at it. The moonlight caressed it, accentuating the simple perfection of her. A pink nipple, hard due to the cool air, left a modest shadow line over her perky mound.

Amit moved silently toward her and reached out. His hand hovered over her breastand pulled the blanket gently, covering her. He went back to sit next to the window. He stayed that way for hours, alternatively watching Roni and the door, fighting pain and exhaustion. A little before dawn he decided nothing more would happen. He left as he'd come in, took a shower, and went to bed.

Some did indeed notice Amit's return from Roni's room. Three of whom were stationed in a room overlooking both Amit and Roni's from the building on the other side of the street.

"What's his status?" the commander asked.

"He seems to be wounded, but he's pulling though. However, we can go in," another voice replied.

"No. The orders were clear. We aren't to interfere so long as the model remains unharmed," the commander insisted.

He looked left and right. He had close to thirty men spread out, ready to intervene. More than the people he'd had around the stadium. But the orders had been clear. They were to stay out of it. "But we did intervene. We shot the three Iranians who were stationed outside when they were about to go into the hotel."

"Yes, but that was from afar."

"We also intervened at the stadium."

"That was also from afar. And only after everyone was

off scene. Also, it was nothing more than an extraction, and because the agent closest was relatively new and didn't fully comprehend the meaning of 'stay out of it.' How's the guy from the stadium holding up?"

"His heart was hit and he's lost a lot of blood. Our rookie reached him rather quickly, but it's still unsure whether or not he'll make it."

"All right. We're keeping positions and not moving as long as the model remains safe."

"And if we're noticed?"

"There's no chance of that. This is a soldier, not an agent, remember? That was the only stipulation from the higher-ups. And that's why we insisted on a soldier rather than an agent as insurance for our noninterference. The Israelis kept their word."

"I remember," the man said and muttered something to a third person close to him. The third man kept mum. He was busy with security. He was lying on a table placed away from the opened window, watching the hotel's area through a sniper's telescope. The muzzle of his gun had already had the time to cool since the previous three shots he'd directed hours ago at the three Iranians. The weapon was a Ruger. A Ruger sniper.

44.

The plane landed perfectly. Avner Nitai was pleased. There wasn't applause—those he'd earn once he touched back on Israeli ground. He maneuvered the plane over to the terminal and left his second to shut everything off.

"A smooth flight," his co-pilot said.

"Yes. The best way to have them."

"When are we taking off back home after all the schedule changes?"

"They returned the time to the original departure hour. Lift-off at 12:05. I think getting to the plane at ten will do."

"You know, that's enough time to sleep for me, but it's hardly following regulations."

"Yeah, they cut where they can. Once upon a time, there were two teams that switched between themselves, but cutbacks and everything… you know what it's like."

Avner chose a hotel at the airport. With so little time between flights, it was best to stay close and sleep as much as possible. He turned on his phone and immediately saw a text

from his wife. *I love you.*
He smiled with satisfaction.

45.

Roni had slept like a baby. It had been ages since she'd slept so well. She woke up with a smile on her face and it didn't fade away through her whole morning routine. Not while she brushed her teeth, showered, or got dressed. One would think she'd got lucky the other night.

He wants me, she knew, but he'd just been through something traumatic, and he needed more time. Eran and Inbar were nothing more than a distant memory. Now she had Amit.

She left her room, contemplating whether or not to knock on his door, but eventually decided not to and simply went downstairs.

Amit slept only a few hours, but he slept deeply. He woke up and immediately felt a stabbing pain in his side. He checked the wound in the shower. He wasn't bleeding, but the area was red and swollen, and overall didn't look too good. He bandaged himself the best he could and got dressed. He was ready before Roni. He listened closely and heard her leave to go downstairs, then he followed, walking into the dining room a mere minute after her.

Roni smiled at him once she caught sight of him walking toward her. Her smile was so wide and genuine that Amit almost didn't feel the pain in his side. He took some toast for himself, cheese, and some cut-up cucumber, and sat next to her. She kept on smiling.

"How did you sleep?" she asked.

"Not bad, I think."

"Not bad? You weren't worried about me, I hope. I'm not planning on letting you get away."

He looked at her and smiled. "I don't see that happening."

Her smile only grew once she heard that answer. That was it, she knew. He was hers. "So, what do you say. Should I let up a little and give you more time, or should I carry on pushing?" She never did enjoy having things hang in the air.

Amit laughed. "What did you say yesterday? That you weren't about to give up?"

"That's right."

"Then just carry on being exactly as you are. It seems to be going well for you."

She couldn't hold back and lunged at him, hugging him tightly.

Amit groaned with pain.

"What happened?" Roni asked, letting go immediately.

"I don't know. My stomach hurts. I think I ate something off yesterday."

Roni watched him, concerned, and suggested he only drink something. Amit was unable to eat, anyway, so he agreed.

"I think we should go to the hospital," she said.

"No way," he said. "It's just a bit of a stomachache. I'm flying back to Israel, and that's final. Hospital... honestly," he muttered.

"Okay, then I suppose I'll have to take care of you." She seemed relieved at his answer.

"Hey," he started, "just so I don't blunder this up, you are flying El-Al 394, right?"

"I can't remember," she replied and reached for her cell-phone—which, of course, wasn't there. Amit watched and huffed in amusement.

"Don't say a word," she warned with a smile, then started rooting through her handbag. She found the paper with the ticket and silently thanked Sean for being more organized than she was. She checked the information and finally nodded in agreement.

"And business, right?"

"I would think first class. I'm not sure. How do you know?"

"There's no first class from Barcelona. It's probably business. Let me see.... Yeah. It's business."

"So?"

"So, that means I bought the right ticket."

"Oh wow, you didn't even have a ticket back, did you? I didn't even think about that."

Amit looked at her with a smile.

Her smile couldn't be smothered even if she were inclined to try.

She trusted him with all her heart. He'd told her he had been in *Sayeret* Matcal, besides. He was going to be her boyfriend. She could probably share her burden with him. Though with all the excitement from yesterday, it had been pushed back a little, the worry about it was still present. Her mission. Having someone die in her arms. And that dull feeling between her legs that wouldn't let her full forget even for a moment.

"Hey?" she started.

"Yeah?"

"There's something I want to tell you."

Amit was just thinking about how he could meet the Michmoret agent without Roni noticing. "Okay, but only if it's quick because I still need to pack and I don't want to be late."

"Pack? How long does that take?" She looked at him amused.

He gave her an embarrassed smile back. "You don't really want to get into that."

She laughed and decided to give up the idea. They'd be in Israel in a matter of hours, anyway.

But she wouldn't give up on everything.

"Well, we can forget about it on one condition."

"Negotiating, are we?"

"Yup."

"Name your condition."

"That you tell me how you feel about me."

"Wow! Extortion!" He started to laugh.

Roni was a little embarrassed, but she didn't want to let it go.

"What I feel about you?" he contemplated his answer. "That you're a pain in the ass."

She grinned.

"Come here," he said. And she did.

He cupped her cheek and pressed his lips to hers, and the two of them kissed for a long minute.

46.

Alex scratched his head and seemed frustrated.

"Can't pull it off, huh?" his team leader stated more than asked.

"No. Not at all. And I've been working on it for a while."

"A while? More like from the moment they checked in to the hotel," the team leader replied.

"Well, the security cameras are a little trickier. It's not merely changing her credit card registry. You want me to be connected to a live stream, and there's nowhere I can connect to," Alex said apologetically.

"What does that mean?" the team leader asked.

"That they probably don't have a security monitor who watches the live feed. It only records."

"And can you delete the recordings?"

"Oh, of course. That's simple."

"Okay, wait a minute." The team leader spoke to Daniel then turned back to Alex. "He said it's already too late for live. They'll be leaving the hotel soon. Just delete it."

306 | HANDLE WITH FORCE

"How far back."

"Take the time from when they came back from the stadium until this morning."

"Done," Alex said. All the security feed recordings from that time frame were deleted.

47.

Amit set to meet Roni back downstairs at nine, with everything packed and ready. He slipped away for a few minutes beforehand and met up with the agent from Michmoret. He gave the gun back and went back to the hotel. Roni was still not down. Amit couldn't fly back with a gun, so the agent took it back at the last minute. He wasn't armed anymore. He felt naked.

He went upstairs to finish the checkout, then Roni joined him and did the same. They got into the taxi they'd ordered and made their way to the airport.

Amit was nervous during the drive, but he tried to hide it. Roni noticed but decided against saying anything. She attributed his behavior to the stress regarding his grief over Michal and his growing feelings toward her. Though she wasn't planning on giving up, there was also no reason to press at the wrong time.

After going through security, Amit's nerves calmed, but the pain from his injury escalated. They took a quick walk around the Duty-Free then, at his request, headed for the plane.

308 | HANDLE WITH FORCE

Asaf was well over being in Barcelona. But he still wasn't ready to head back. He got on the plane unenthusiastically. At least he'd managed to score a seat next to the emergency door, so he had those extra inches for his legs. He allowed the couple sitting in the middle and window seat respectively to pass and leaned back.

No. That was all he needed.

He noticed Amit Koren at the front of the plane. Amit Koren. That scum. And as if to add fuel to his fire, he had Roni Carmi on his arm. Roni Carmi! Amit's hand rested on her back as he led her across the way. That son of a bitch. Asaf glared. Amit turned back and their eyes met. *Let him see exactly what I think about him,* Asaf said to himself. *Let him choke on it.* Amit looked away.

Roni and Amit went into the front part of the plane. The plane itself was small and relatively old, and as he'd expected, there was no first class section. The business area wasn't particularly lavish, either, but at least it included only two seats on each side instead of the standard three. Such is the life when you have to escort a supermodel—the government assures you only the best. He smiled to himself at "screwing the system" so nicely… at least a little. Then his smile disappeared. He scanned the passengers and his gaze fixed on one man who was glaring at him. There was no doubt as to his intentions. *Inside the actual plane…* he said to himself. After the fight last night, the Iranians had given up on gunfights and settled for hand-to-hand combat. They were on the plane. And there was at least one of them. His injury throbbed in reaction and Amit groaned with pain. His vision whited out for a moment before he managed to steady himself again. "Sorry to be graphic, but shouldn't you go for a shit?" Roni asked.

"No, don't worry. I'll be fine."

"What's up with all of you?"

"Who?"

"Men," she answered simply. "Who are you trying to impress, exactly. You don't need to worry about that with me, I promise. When you come out of there, I'll still be right here waiting."

Roni smiled.

So did Amit, though it was more of a grimace.

"Drop it. It's got nothing to do with it, anyway. It won't help. I tried. Do you want the details?"

"All right, all right, I believe you."

Amit shifted in his seat, and the pressure on his wound lessened. He would be fine. It was lucky they were in business class.

"*Welcome to El-Al flight number 394 from Barcelona to Ben Gurion Air Port,*" the captain's voice came over the speakers. "This is your captain, Avner Nitai—"

"Yes! Excellent!" Amit said, just as Roni groaned, "Oh no."

"What? What do you mean oh no? It's Avner Nitai!"

"I'm not deaf, I heard that bit."

"So, what's the problem? Do you know him?"

"The real question is where do you know him from?"

"Don't ask. He saved me. Without sharing too many details, we were once on a mission deep in enemy territory and someone of ours was badly hurt. I've told you all about that part—but Avner was the one to make an impossible landing with the Sikorsky and save us all. He's the best pilot in the world. He's amazing."

"Good for you."

"Wow, such excitement. Where do you know him from?"

"Oh, nothing, he's just my wonderful ex-boyfriend's brother."

"Really? No shit. Avner is your boyfriend's brother? Small world, huh?"

"Welcome to Israel."

"We're not there yet. Besides, just because your boyfriend was a bastard and cheated on you, doesn't mean his brother is the same."

"True, but the fact that every time I see him you'd need a saw to get his eyes away from my tits kind of proves he is."

"Well, that just makes him normal."

"Spare me the male solidarity, it does nothing for me. You're not like that."

"Oh well, the question is whether or not I should go say hello to him."

"Please don't, that's all I need."

"Let's see… okay. I prefer you, anyway." Amit gave her a wide grin. Her frown melted away in a moment.

"So, I'm rated under Leo Messi, but above Avner Nitai. Not bad for a dumb blonde."

"Yup. All we need is a bit of work on your actual IQ, but other than that, you're pretty okay." Amit smiled even wider and Roni sprawled all over him.

The plane took off and the time passed. Roni napped on Amit's shoulder, but he couldn't sleep. He was getting worse. He was starting to sweat and hallucinate. He carefully moved Roni off him and got up, swaying on his feet.

He was minutes away from falling on his face. He couldn't leave Roni unprotected. They'd attack her. *What do I do?* He couldn't think clearly enough to sort out his options. The only thing he could think of was to talk to Avner. He didn't know if it would work, but it was his only choice.

He turned to the flight attendant and told her he wanted to talk to the captain.

"Sure," she said. "Like that is going to happen."

"Look, you don't understand. This is an emergency. I need to talk to him."

"No, you listen. If this is a real emergency, you better tell me what's wrong immediately. If it isn't, go back to your seat, because what you're doing right now is a felony."

"Okay, I'm sorry, but please tell him Amit Koren wants to speak to him."

"Does he know you?"

"Yes, from the army. And it's essential I talk to him. It's really important. Please tell him Amit Koren wants to talk to him and that it's an emergency."

The flight attendant looked him up and down for a moment

before holding out her hand and saying sharply, "Passport."

He held it out to her. She opened it, examined it closely, then gave it back. "You don't look so good," she said.

She picked up the internal phone and spoke to the captain, then turned back to Amit and told him to look to his left. He did, and saw a camera there.

"Okay, take the phone," she said and held out the receiver.

"Amit?" Avner asked through the phone.

"Hi, how are you?"

"It's so good to hear from you, man. How's it going? Are you back from vacation in Barcelona?"

"Not exactly. Listen, I need your help. I'm on duty and I need someone I can trust."

"Oh, okay. What kind of duty? What do you need?"

"I'm doing something for the Mossad. And I'm injured. What I'm doing is a matter of national security and I'm about to be out of the game."

"Wait, what do you mean injured? I need to land the plane."

"No, no. Absolutely not. You have to—no matter what—land in Israel."

"Amit, you're freaking me out. What's going on?"

"I'm escorting Roni Carmi. She's in danger and she has to get to Israel."

"Roni Carmi the model? What's this got to do with her?"

"I don't know, but the whole world is trying to kill her. The Mossad is trying to keep her safe and bring her back home. That's my mission. They managed to injure me badly and I'm about to be out for the count. I need you to keep her safe."

"Shit, you know I'm—"

"Her boyfriend's brother, yeah, I know. She told me."

"Okay, well, we're on the plane, what can happen?"

"There's one of them here. At least one guy. I'm about to lose consciousness and then he'll strike. I need you to protect her."

"You're fucking kidding me."

"I wish I was. Look." He flashed his wound at the camera.

Avner's copilot asked him what was going on and he said nothing. It wasn't a satisfactory answer—he'd only heard Avner's side of the conversation, but what disturbed him was Avner's expression.

Avner was very worried. He rarely trusted people, but if there was one person he did put his trust in, it was Amit Koren. He was one of the few who saw him as a great pilot and was genuinely grateful for the extraction he'd done back then.

"You sound paranoid," he told Amit. "I don't know how you were hurt, but it has to be affecting your thinking."

"Could be, Avner, but a while back I killed six people, and one of them injured me. I'd rather be paranoid and wrong than assume everything is okay and have Roni get hurt."

"Look, if there's really a hostile on the plane, then I have to call for an emergency landing. I also need to get security involved."

"No, no, that won't help."

"Won't help? He can blow up the plane!"

"That won't happen. I'm assuming they couldn't get any

explosives on here, and if they had, then they would have done it already. No. It will be hand-to-hand, and they'll take down the security guard, too. I've seen how they fight, and I know all security procedures. Trust me, it will only make this worse. It's better they don't know who the security guard is."

"So, bottom line, what do you want me to do?"

Amit didn't answer. A sharp pain in his abdomen made him sway in place.

"Amit?"

"Yeah, I'm here. Have her come into the cockpit. Lock her in there. That's all I'm asking."

"Are you insane? There's no way she'll agree to that. And if she will, she'll accuse me of harassment. Then I'm in trouble not only with her and El-Al, but with my brother and wife, too. No way."

"Deal with it! I don't have a choice. I'm about to pass out and there's someone here that's going to attack her!"

"Listen, I'll have her come in here, but let's have you be the one to convince her to come in. I can't even begin to think of how."

"Okay," Amit said. "There's one more thing."

"Something *else*? What?"

"Don't worry about me. I'll manage. Don't send anyone for me."

"What the hell?" Avner barked. "Of course after she's in the cockpit we'll take care of you!"

"No, you won't. I don't want to show them any weakness.

This way it'll look like I'm only sleeping. When we get there, wake me up. There's not too much for you to do, anyway."

"Amit, this seems like a really bad idea."

"Trust me," Amit said and hung up. He hobbled over to Roni and woke her up.

"Hey, wake up."

"Huh? What? I fell asleep. How are you feeling?"

"Fine. Listen, I want you to go into the cockpit."

"What? No way, I told you that already. What's going on, Amit?"

"Look, I—"

"Roni Carmi?" a flight attendant came up to them and interrupted. "The captain has asked for you to come up to the cockpit."

"What? What do you mean? There's no way I'm going in there!"

The woman said something about not being a kindergarten teacher and walked off.

"Amit, what's going on? Did you speak to Avner? Where's all this coming from?"

"Roni, do you trust me?"

"Of course, but what's that got to do with anything? I'm not going in there."

"Roni, if you trust me, please, just go into the cockpit. I get that it's not something you want to do, but you really don't have much of a choice."

"Amit, there's no way I'm going in there, and it has nothing

316 | Handle with Force

to do with whether or not I trust you or not. I've got a choice, which I can make up on my own, and my choice is not to go."

"So, you don't trust me."

"What's that got to do with anything? Stop it!"

With all due respect for Orbiting Star, Amit felt as if he was seconds away from losing it. He had to get Roni into the cockpit, even if it meant going against an order. Even if it meant hurting her. He looked her straight in the eyes and said, "When you were in Bucharest, you met a Mossad agent and he died in your arms."

Roni looked at him aghast. How could he know that? She'd wanted to tell him about it, but hadn't found the time. And anyway, had he just found out, or had he known this whole time? Had he been conning her? Was it all a lie? Up until then, she'd trusted him one-hundred percent. Suddenly she wasn't so sure.

"You're being chased," Amit continued. "They've been trying to kill you this whole time." There was no extra drama to his words. Nothing but him stating simple facts. "You simply haven't noticed. One of them is on the plane now, and he's going to attack you, so you *have* to go into the cockpit."

Goosebumps spread out all over her body. She could barely breathe. The image of that guard at the Radisson and the way he'd watched her popped into her mind. She stared at Amit and didn't know what to do or whom to trust. "Who are you?" she asked, her fear evident.

Amit saw her terror and confusion and wondered about his

best course of action. Yair was right about Orbiting Star. So, what should he do now? He didn't have the time to tell her everything. He could lose consciousness at any moment. He would have to count on her knowing Avner. However much she may dislike him, she still knew the man and trusted him. All he could do was alienate her from himself so that she'd run to Avner. "I'm Yaron," he said.

Roni was shocked. Fear choked her throat. *Yaron?* The man she'd spent all this time with the last couple of days wasn't Amit but *Yaron?* And to think that she'd been moments away from taking out the device so that Amit—Yaron—could take its place. She was terrified.

She didn't know what to do. Her trust in Amit shattered. If he was telling the truth, then he wasn't even Amit, but if he was lying, then why? And where did it come from? And how long had he been lying? From whichever angle she looked at it, the man who she had just been leaning against—the man she thought would be her boyfriend—was no more. Nothing more than a conman and a liar.

Here, again, she was confronted with the person closest to her betraying her. Betraying her trust. Roni was scared to stay beside him. Worse, if he was right, then there was an Iranian on the plane planning to attack her. It was better to have someone "just" stare at her tits. At least she knew who he was and that she could trust him.

Amit-Yaron's look seemed menacing. She was too frightened to cry. She took slow steps away from him, away, and looked for the flight attendant from before. The woman was busy readying a newspaper in the small kitchenette.

"So, changed your mind?" she asked.

"Yes," Roni answered, still too upset.

The woman picked up a phone, closed the curtain between the kitchenette and the rest of the plane, and knocked on the door. It opened and Roni walked in. The airhostess closed the door behind her, and Roni found herself standing half a meter away from Avner.

"Hi, Avner," she said drily.

"You can sit on the seat to the side, there. That's the navigator's chair. It's unmanned now." Avner shot Roni a quick glance, then looked ahead, turning his back. He wouldn't dare look at her. He couldn't meet her eyes properly, anyway.

"Thank you."

"Hi, I'm Amir," the co-pilot said with a wide smile and held out his hand. He had no idea what was going on, but he had no trouble with agreeing for Roni Carmi to sit two meters away from him.

"Hi, Amir," she said.

"You know, this is rather against protocol," Amir said to Avner.

"Yes, I know," Avner replied.

"And...?"

"Those are the orders, Amir. You don't know everything."

"Orders? What orders? What's this nonsense?"

"Again, you don't know everything. I received orders to allow

Roni into the cockpit. It came from up high. I don't know what she did, but those are the orders. It wasn't my call." Avner kept his gaze firmly ahead even while speaking to Amir. It seemed a little ridiculous.

"Come on. Seriously."

"Go ahead, then. Ask her," Avner said.

Amir shot a questioning look in Roni's direction.

"He's right," she said then remained quiet. Amir was more than a little in shock.

Roni remained closed up. It took a supreme effort not to cry. Not in front of Avner, who seemed rather okay here. What had happened here, she asked herself. What was going on? She'd barely woken up and Amit had done a 180. If he even was Amit.

On the other side of the cockpit door, Amit tried with all his might to hold on a few more seconds. He wrote a Whatsapp message to Yair and hoped to manage to press send before he lost consciousness. He wrote, *we're on the plane El-Al 394 I'm seriously wounded and it looks like there's at least one Iranian who'll try and attack Roni she's in—* He wanted to write that she was in the cockpit, but didn't think he could. He hoped the Iranian wouldn't manage to get into the cockpit after her, but he couldn't count on it. Yair would have to handle it. He pressed Send then lost consciousness.

The phone didn't have reception, so it didn't send. Only a little less than an hour later as the plane flew over Cyprus, reception was strong enough for the message to go through. Yair got the message a minute after. Five minutes later the whole top echelon of Israel's security received the same message and Ben Gurion Airport followed emergency protocols.

A call from the watchtower at Ben Gurion broke the tense silence in the cockpit. It requested Avner change to an alternate channel. Once done, Watchtower continued and asked for him to transfer to encrypted transmission. Avner gave his confirmation and did so.

In each of the Israeli passenger planes, there was the option to have encrypted conversations. It was one of the Israeli security protocols.

Watchtower then requested Avner identify himself, and once that was done, said, "I have here people from high up. Very high."

"I see," Avner said. "Take into account that everyone in the cockpit can hear you."

"And who does that include?"

"Amir, my second, and the model, Roni Carmi."

"Oh, Roni Carmi is in the cockpit? That's great. I just wanted to ask you to let her in. Have her stay inside, and don't allow her out under any circumstances. She's in danger. There's a high possibility of someone outside planning to attack her."

"Yes, I came in before he did," Roni said.

"You can hear him because he's on loudspeaker, but he can't hear you," Avner told her, still without turning around.

"So, you tell him."

"She says that she came in before he attacked."

"She did? And what's her status?"

Avner looked at Roni before immediately looking back.

"I'm fine."

"She says she's okay."

Amir looked at her, horrified.

"Thank God for that. Another question for Roni... do you still have it?"

Amir and Avner both looked at her again.

She looked back at them and said quietly, "Yes, I do."

Avner was so surprised that he could barely drag his gaze away from her. "She does," he said mechanically.

"Wonderful! Good. Stay in the cockpit. We know Avner and trust him. He's all right. He'll take care of you."

"She knows me too," Avner said, pulling himself together. "She's my brother's girlfriend. I'll keep her safe. Don't worry."

"That's for the best. Oh... and, yes. Heads up, in about five minutes you'll be getting an escort from the air force until you land. We'll have all passengers extracted for questioning once you land. The regular security protocols."

"Of course," Avner replied, then turned to Roni. "God, Roni, why didn't you say anything?"

Roni preferred to hold her tongue.

"What the hell? Are you Mossad or something?" Amir was stunned.

"Shut up, Amir, what are you, a child?" Avner snapped at him.

Two minutes later they were joined by two F-15 warplanes, one on each side. Avner waited for the passengers to be able to notice the planes before saying on the speaker, "Hello, this is your captain speaking. We'll be starting our descent in a few minutes. In the meantime, I want to update you on there being a state of emergency at Ben Gurion right now. It has nothing to do with us, but it does mean that we cannot land in Terminal Three, but instead need to stop at the sidelines. From there, you'll be safely escorted by security to passport control. For extra safety, we'll be having an air force escort, too, so you can remain calm. Please listen to the staff's instructions. Thank you."

Avner called a flight attendant and spoke to her through the phone. He instructed her to find the man who'd spoken to him before and make sure he was strapped in.

Then he called the watchtower. "Tower, this is Avner."

"Copy."

"I have a severely wounded passenger. Assure medical transport."

"We're aware. It's being handled."

Roni listened to what he said and asked Avner, "Who? Amit?" Avner kept quiet.

"Yaron?" she tried.

Avner glanced at her. "Who?"

"Nothing," Roni said, and went back to her thoughts.

48.

Just as they'd announced, the plane landed and stopped at a side hangar.

"We'll be getting off last," Avner told Roni.

Security came in first and stood guard at the cockpit door. Then, medical personnel came in and took Amit. Only then were the other passengers allowed off to congregate close to the plane.

Finally, the cockpit door opened and they went out. A large security force guarded them—Roni most of all—and led them to a faraway building at the edge of the airport grounds.

Roni was taken to a small, dimly lit room. There were three people waiting in there. One of them was holding a briefcase.

"Hello, Roni," the oldest man said. "First, I'd like to assure you that you are safe and that nothing will harm you. Secondly, I want to thank you, personally and in the name of the state of Israel, for everything that you've done."

He seemed familiar, though she couldn't put her finger on where she'd seen him before.

"And after pointing out those two important details," the old man continued, "We would be eternally grateful if you handed over the device our agent left in your care."

Roni scrutinized them with interest. "And how can I know that it's okay to give it to you?"

"I apologize," the man said. "How rude of me. I'm the Director of the Mossad. And this dear man," he pointed at Daniel at his side, "Is the head of the cyber division in the Mossad. The agent who gave you the device worked under his command. And the man with the briefcase works for him, too. He's about to check its authenticity."

"Alex," the Director of the Mossad said to the man with the briefcase. "Please go and get the Minister of Defense."

"That's not necessary," Roni told the Director of the Mossad. "I recognize you. I just couldn't remember from where. I saw you at some ceremony about a year ago."

"I see, but I would like for you to be sure."

"It's fine," Roni reiterated. "Okay, so, what now? Can I have some privacy or do I have to take it out in front of you?"

"Of course not," the Director said, understanding instantly. "There's a bathroom down the hall and to the left."

"Hang on," Daniel said. "Do you want her to go there on her ow—"

"Come now," the Director snapped. "She's been walking around with it for two days all around Europe. She hardly needs an escort to go to the bathroom."

"I'm sorry."

Roni gave them a tense smile and left the room.

She went to the toilet, took out the condom, ripped it, extracted the tampon and SIM card, and cleaned it to the best of her ability. It felt awkward giving it to them like this, but that was the best she could do.

They'd have to deal with it.

She returned and handed over the SIM. Alex opened the briefcase and put it somewhere inside it. He and Daniel both looked and smiled at the results like two small children.

"Everything is here," Alex said. "I'm duplicating it now. It will take twenty-seven minutes."

"All right. Either way, we can let Roni go," Daniel said.

"What about Yaron?" she asked. "What about him? How is he?"

"Yaron? Who's Yaron?" the Director asked.

He's an excellent actor, Roni admitted to herself. *He honestly looks as if he has no idea who I'm talking about.* "The one wounded," she added.

"Amit?" Daniel asked.

"Whatever," she allowed.

"He's been taken to the hospital. We still don't know his status. We hope he'll pull through."

"Why did you call him Yaron?" the Director asked.

"Good question," Roni replied. "That's how he introduced himself."

The Director watched her for a long moment. He didn't like this. "Are you sure that whoever was hurt was Yaron and not Amit?"

"No, I'm not sure," she answered. "What I am sure is that like some idiot I allowed him to stick by me almost constantly for two days."

The Director looked at Daniel, who looked back at him.

"Avner can positively identify Amit," Daniel told him.

"Do you mind staying here for a moment? We'll be right back," the Director requested, then he and Daniel left.

Alex was rather nervous about being in the same room, alone with Roni Carmi.

Roni noticed and started some small talk to put him at ease. "So, are you one of the hackers who works for the Mossad?"

"Yes," Alex said proudly. "I'm the one who canceled your original hotel reservation in Barcelona and set you up in a room at the Ohla. How was it? Good, right?"

Roni looked at him pensively and started to wonder.

Daniel and the Director entered the room next door, where Avner Nitai was busy giving his report regarding the flight.

"Tell me," Daniel said to Avner, "The man who was with Roni, the one who was injured, was he Amit Koren?"

"Yes, why? Avner asked. "What happened? Is he *dead*?" he asked, horrified at the thought.

"No, no. God forbid. We merely wanted to be sure of his identity. You're familiar with him, right?"

"Yes, of course. It was definitely him. I saw him through the cameras, not only heard his voice through the phone. He even showed me his wound. There's no doubt it was him."

"Good. Then who is Yaron?"

"Yaron? Who is that?" He looked at them, confused.

"That's what we just asked you."

"I've no idea. Why?"

"Roni Carmi thought whoever had introduced himself as Amit was actually a… Yaron. That's what she told us," the Director told him.

"She did ask me something about a Yaron, but I didn't give it much weight. I've no idea why she would think Amit's name is Yaron, all I can say is, it most assuredly is *Amit*. Actually…" he paused and thought for a moment. "I actually think I might have an idea."

"What do you mean?"

"Look, what happened was that Amit told me he was about to pass out and that there was someone on board who he suspected was about to attack Roni, so he needed me to allow her into the cockpit to keep her safe."

"Yes?"

"I offered to deploy the security guard on flight, but he was worried that the guard wasn't trained well enough."

"An apt observation."

"So, I told him there was no way Roni would go in the cockpit after finding out I was the pilot. She isn't exactly on speaking terms with me. A family issue that has nothing to do with this."

"So?"

"So, I told him he would have to think of a way to get her to agree to come in. Maybe he told her something about someone called Yaron."

"All right, that's less important right now. As long as we can confirm that the man who'd been with her these past two days was in fact Amit and no one else," the Director stated.

"Still, if we go according to what Amit told Avner," Daniel added in, "then there's someone on the plane who Amit suspected."

"That's true, but Roni is okay. The mission is complete. Don't forget he was wounded. If there really was someone on board, then we will dig him out eventually. I'm not going to hold back a full plane over it. It's already going to be on the news," the Director surmised. Then said, "Thank you, Avner. You performed exemplarily. Clearly, everything that went on is highly classified, correct?"

"Correct, sir," he said, adding in his mind, *Getting praised from the head of the Mossad. Another thing I have to keep to myself and keep anyone from knowing.*

"We believe everything is in order. You're safe now, so you have nothing to worry about," the director said to Roni when they returned.

"Why did you transfer me from the Princess to the Ohla?" she asked.

Daniel shot a fierce glare at Alex who winced.

"Not everything we can share with you, and I'm going to have to ask you to accept that."

"But you guarded and watched me from afar," she stated. "Or maybe not far at all."

"We did, yes." The Director nodded.

"Is there anything you can tell me?"

"We spoke before all this…" Daniel said. "If you'd like, you can come to the agent who gave you the device's funeral."

"You got his body back? Good. I mean, not good, of course, but good to know that… I'm getting all muddled up."

"It's good to know that he will get a proper burial here in Israel and wasn't left to rot in a foreign country," Daniel surmised.

"Exactly. That really bothered me."

"We owe him so much, it's the very least we can do for him."

"I think I won't attend," she said. "I prefer not to go to the funeral. I'm sorry."

"No apologies necessary, it's perfectly understandable."

"But I would like to know his name."

"Eliad Marom," Daniel said.

"May he rest in peace," Roni said.

"Amen."

"Then, am I free to go?"

"Of course. Only one last thing," the Director said. "I don't believe I have to tell you this, but talking about everything that went on is strictly forbidden."

"Yes, clearly."

"And I'll allow myself to say this again—we and the whole state of Israel owe you a massive debt. It is hard to find the words to describe the importance of what you did."

"But I didn't do anything," she said, and meant it.

"You did very much indeed," the Director said. "We'll start with the fact that you said 'yes.' That's not a given. Most wouldn't have. You took up the task and saw it through. It had been given to you by a dying agent—which in itself showed how dangerous it could be, but you still agreed. That isn't "nothing." That is *everything*. It's a massive responsibility."

Roni smiled at him shyly.

"So, thank you. And… slowly please."

"What do you mean slowly?"

"We won't get in your way, but be gentle. Slowly."

"What are you talking about?" Though she was quite sure she'd figured it out.

"I know what you're planning to do now. You're not someone who gives up. Again, we won't stand in your way, just take it easy."

For a moment Roni looked at the Director of the Mossad, then she gave him a quick hug and stepped out the room.

49.

Two days later, Yair and the *Sayeret Matcal* Commander stood over Amit's hospital bed. The doctors had just woken him up from the long surgery he'd had to undergo.

Amit opened his eyes and saw Yair. "Hey." Yair couldn't even respond. Amit looked right, then left, and asked, "What's this? Where am I? *Chen*? What are you doing here? Yair, what's going on?"

"Slow down," Yair said. "You're post-surgery, but you're recovering well."

"Surgery? What? What do you mean? What happened to me? *Yair*?"

"You were amazing. What do you remember?"

"I went to the airport to go to Michal—you bought me a ticket."

"And…?" Yair pressed.

"That's it. That's the last thing I remember."

Yair looked at the Unit Commander, who looked back at him. Then the Commander decided to take advantage of the situation. "You don't remember the terrorist ambush?"

Yair looked at Chen disbelievingly, but Amit paid him no mind. His whole attention was on Chen as he tried to remember but couldn't. Chen carried on. "On the way to the airport, you were shot at by terrorists. You crashed and got hurt badly, but you still managed to take control of the situation and take them all out. Like Yair said, you were amazing. It's a pity you can't remember."

"Really? Is that why you're here? Because I can't remember a thing."

"Well, you need your rest. Hadas will be by soon. Then we'll tell you everything," Yair said and he and Chen left the room.

"What the hell?" Yair practically yelled at Chen.

"What do you want from me? He can't remember. I gave him a different story."

"You've lost your mind. Where's the doctor? I don't understand why he can't remember anything."

Ten minutes later they found the doctor.

"No, nothing about his injury would suggest memory loss," the doctor said.

"Could something have happened to his head before he lost consciousness?"

"Nothing happened to him. The wound wasn't serious, he simply neglected it, so it got infected. Before he lost consciousness, his fever spiked. What we did in the surgery was fix the surrounding tissue, and painstakingly clean the infection without harming any vital organs. That was the complication.

Besides, we drowned him in antibiotics, but that only weakens the body. not mess with the memory."

"So, why can't he remember?"

"Because he went through a traumatic event. That's the way his brain chose to handle the situation—by not remembering. He's completely unaware of it."

"See?" Chen told Yair. "I did what was best for him. What's the last thing he remembers? Going to see his girlfriend. That's exactly what he wants to forget.

Yair remembered how Amit described Michal's cold dead body. Chen was probably right.

Chen left and Yair stayed with Amit.

A short time later, he spoke to Hadas about Amit's memory problems. Hadas was furious with Yair over the decision he made but decided to accept it nonetheless. No one told him anything other than the cover story the Unit Commander had shared.

50.

Three days later, Yair and Hadas came by for a visit.

"The doctor said they're releasing me," Amit said.

"That's wonderful!" Hadas rejoiced and kissed his cheek. "You'll be coming to stay with us for a while until you recover."

"You think? The monsters will tear him to pieces."

"Call your own children monsters, not mine," Hadas told Yair.

"Ah, that's nothing. I can take them. Thanks, Hadas, I'd love to. At least until I'm done with the antibiotics."

"All right, so do you have clothes? Are they releasing you now?"

"Yes, I'm actually already released. But I knew you were coming so I waited around for you."

"Excellent. I'll step out—get dressed and we can go," Hadas said and left the room.

While getting dressed, Amit asked Yair, "Hey, do you know what's going on with Michal? I've been trying to reach her for days. Her cell's off and no one has picked up at her house. Have you heard anything?"

Yair watched him and remained silent. All he did was shrug.

"I'm decent!" Amit yelled to Hadas, and she came back in.

"The funny thing is that I keep dreaming about her, and in the dream, she's dead. Then I wake up terrified and I remember I still haven't got through to her. It's kind of stressing me out."

Both Hadas and Yair said nothing. Hadas pinned Yair with a glare that clearly said, *Just you wait,* but still, neither said a word.

"What's going on with you two? You aren't going to start fighting here, are you?"

"No, but your brother will be having a time out later tonight with all the bullshit he's been pulling."

"Okay, I'm staying out of it. But, hey, I've also been having some good dreams. Want to hear about those?"

"Of course. We much prefer to hear about something good," Hadas said as they walked out of the hospital.

"You know that model—Roni Carmi—right?"

Hadas and Yair glanced at each other.

"Sure you do—anyway, I've been dreaming about her these past few nights. I know I sound like some lovestruck teenager, but it's not like that. You know, she's hot and everything, but she's never been someone I fantasize about. I've never thought much about her. Now, suddenly I can't stop. It's really weird. Especially since I'm not even dreaming about her in a sexual way. Like, she's hot, of course, but I dream that we're friends. And it's not only that she's beautiful, she's also really funny and

336 | Handle with Force

smart, and she's really great to talk to. And her smell... it's to die for.

"A complete delusion of grandeur, I know, but it's so real. And it balances out the dreams of Michal with how good they are. What do you think? Have I officially lost it?"

Yair and Hadas stopped and looked at each other.

"You have to tell him!" Hadas growled.

"Tell me what?" Amit asked.

51.

The next morning, not far from there, Roni sat in front of Eyal at a coffee shop.

"That's impossible," Roni said.

"That's what I thought as soon as you told me. It's completely insane. But we checked it out and checked it thoroughly. It's all true, down to the Facebook page."

She looked at Eyal. She wasn't quick with trusting people, but she'd been working with Eyal for ages, and he'd never let her down. Whenever she felt like something needed digging into, she called him up. His services didn't come cheap—not nearly—but he was trustworthy and discrete. She couldn't say she was familiar with many private investigators, but, as she said, Eyal had never let her down before.

"So there really is someone named Amit Koren, and everything he told me—as crazy as it sounded—really did happen? Did you confirm it?"

"Yes. He had a relationship with a daughter of a couple who'd left Israel named Michal. She's also in that post on Facebook you mentioned, and—"

"Wait, he's supposed to be this big security hot-shot. How did you hack his page?"

"We didn't. He really is a security expert, and it so happened that one of the guys from our office is a friend of his. The post is still on his wall, just as you said *having the time of our lives in Nice.*"

"Okay."

"And she was murdered in a robbery gone wrong about a week ago. At least according to the papers. His military history has also been confirmed. Even the mission that got cut short, and Avner Nitai—your boyfriend's brother—"

"My ex."

"Your ex's brother—he was the one to come with the Sikorsky CH-53 to extract them. From what we figured out, that was one of the most difficult landings the air force had ever seen done."

"And who is Yaron?"

"I've no idea."

"That's it?"

"There's no one named Yaron who is a part of his life. And we looked. No family, no friends, no army guys. And no—not even in the medical files." Eyal laughed. "It seems to me like the name was a simple heat-of-the-moment misdirection,"

"Okay, and the last thing."

"Yeah?"

"Where can I find him?"

"He was at his brother's yesterday. Today he spent most of

his time in a café right below their apartment in the north of Tel Aviv, reading a book. I'm sending you the Waze directions to the cafe now."

Amit ordered a double macchiato and carried on reading his book.

Immersed as he was, he didn't notice someone sit across the table from him.

"Hey, Amit, how are you?"

Amit raised his eyes and saw the model Roni Carmi.

He stared at her disbelievingly, then started pinching himself.

"What are you doing? Idiot." Roni looked at his pathetic attempts at pinching himself and laughed.

"I'm dreaming," he said.

"About me?"

"Yes."

She laughed. "You're sweet." Her face hardened. "Why didn't you call me?" her expression softened again. "Well, I suppose you didn't have my phone number and you were in the hospital... but you lied about eating something bad. It was so much more serious than that. I forgive you, though, because I know what happened."

Amit may have stopped pinching himself, but he couldn't stop staring at Roni with genuine shock. *What did she want?*

"So, nothing to say?" she asked.

"Have we met before? Have we ever spoken?" he looked at her, confused.

She stared back at him, unable to figure out if he was playing her or being honest. A heavy feeling crept into her heart. "Yaron?"

"Who's Yaron?"

"You tell me."

"You are Roni Carmi, the model, right?"

"Like you don't know."

"Okay, I'm sorry to ask this, but what do you want from me?" She looked at him in despair.

"Could you be confusing me with someone else?" he offered.

"You're Amit Koren, aren't you? And you don't remember me at all?"

"Should I?"

"Unbelievable. What happened to you?"

"I got into a terrorist ambush, but I got out of it okay. I even took them out. But I was still hurt, and I must have lost my memory."

"*What*? When was this?"

"About a week ago."

"*What*? *Where*?"

"On the way to the airport."

"And then what?"

"I've been in hospital since. They only released me yesterday." She couldn't believe it. "And you remember all that?"

"No, they told me about it."

"Ahh… and it's in the papers too, right? Because I can't remember reading that nonsense."

"No, they kept it silent."

"Bullshit. More like they kept *you* silent."

He couldn't follow.

"Okay, look, you've been played. There was no ambush on the way to the airport. You weren't even in the country then. Someone has really done a number on you. I don't know why you can't remember, but whatever they told you is *wrong*."

He looked at her and thought back to the conversation he had yesterday with Hadas and Yair. Hadas had insisted Yair tell him everything, and Yair insisted the opposite. When Amit pushed, Yair evaded him and Hadas ended up close to throttling him. Did that have anything to do with whatever it was that Roni Carmi was telling him now?

He looked at her and seemed lost. Roni wanted nothing more than to pounce on him and hug him tight.

"I can't believe you lost your memory. You really can't remember a thing about me, huh?"

"I dream about you. I never had before."

"Good. That's progress then. What do you dream about?"

"Don't get angry—but that we're friends."

She smiled a smile that melted his insides. "How can I be angry at that?" she asked.

"I keep picturing you in this strappy dress thing."

"You do? That of all things?" Then she moved closer as she pulled out her phone, and showed him a video clip from the fashion show in Barcelona.

"Exactly."

342 | HANDLE WITH FORCE

"It was in Barcelona a week ago. Look," she said and pointed to him in the video. "Who am I looking at?" Amit peered at the screen. She froze the video and enlarged the screen. "That's Sean, my agent, but it's not him I'm looking at. I'm looking at the man next to him. Recognize him?"

He looked, but he couldn't believe his eyes. Still, there really was no mistaking it.

"Son of a bitch," he growled.

"Who?"

"My brother."

"Your brother? A son of a bitch?"

"It's just an expression."

Her heart really went out to him. She couldn't hide her pity from her eyes.

"So, what now?" he asked her. "Are we friends?"

"That's up to you."

"But I have a girlfriend."

"Who? Michal? Or the one you've been living with for years who you're not in love with—and who dumped you after the post your brother wrote on Facebook?"

"What? How do you know all of that?"

"How do you think? You told me."

"Whoa, hang on. You're going too fast. Try and see this from my point of view."

"I've never met Roni Carmi in my life," Roni listed his thoughts, "I have been dreaming about her every night lately, then suddenly she sits down in front of me while I'm at a coffee shop, claiming to be my friend."

"Yeah, something like that," Amit laughed.

"Not bad for a dumb blonde," she said.

"That sounds familiar."

"It does, huh?"

"Hang on, but the bottom line is I do have a girlfriend—Michal, I mean."

Roni kept looking at him with pity-filled eyes.

"Since you lost your memory and your spineless brother is pulling your leg, that leaves me the dirty work."

"What happened to Michal?" Amit asked, panicked.

"I'm sorry," she said. And she was.

"Is she alive?" he whispered. "I keep dreaming she's dead—is that true too?"

She kept eye contact with him and didn't need to say anything more.

He put his head in his hands. "I had a feeling... but I can't remember."

Roni held his hand and stroked his shoulder. "Maybe it's better this way. That you don't remember. Keep the memories you had of her from before. The beautiful ones."

"But how can I be sure she isn't alive?" Amit looked lost.

"Your brother will confirm it, once I have a word with him.

He raised an eyebrow at her in silent question.

"I have to talk to him. I have to understand how we met. I think he knows a lot more than you think. I think he sent you to protect me."

"Protect you? From what?"

"It doesn't matter now, and I think that's the main reason they're not being honest with you now. But I will tell you something I've already told you before. You don't remember this, but I never give up. I won't quit on you, and I won't give up on you. I'll let you not remember Michal, but I won't let you forget about me."

"How long were we together?"

"Two days. Intensely."

"Really?"

"Yeah."

"You know what, there's something…"

"Yes?"

"I dream about your smell."

Roni smiled at him questioningly.

"Can I…"

"Can you what?"

"Smell—I mean, smell you?"

Roni burst out laughing. "Sure," she said, and hugged him.

Amit buried his face in her neck and luxuriated in the smell of her. That's what he remembered. That's what he had been dreaming about.

"Hey… were we…. That… I mean, you know?"

"Fucking?" she asked, laughing, and Amit blushed furiously. "No, but because you didn't want to, not because of me. It was too close to when you…"

"To Michal."

"Look, I hope I'm not going to make you lose it here. You may not remember anything, but your reactions are exactly the same. I'm in love with you, and I'm not planning on letting you go until you remember me. The most you missed out on was a week. Two of those days you spent with me. I'll be staying with you, making you fall in love with me like you did before you lost your memory."

He watched her and laughed.

Then she added, "Come on. I've got an idea on how to help you remember. Does your injury prevent you from doing physical activity?"

"That depends. What did you have in mind?"

"Screwing," she said and pulled him away from the table.

52.

At the same time, in the cafeteria of one of the hostels in the center of Israel, a man sat next to a window and asked himself how he was feeling. He was hooked up to oxygen, and though he could barely move, and despite being after one heart surgery and in need of at least one more, despite him being on the threshold of death—he felt wonderful.

In front of him sat an excitable CIA agent who hadn't fully comprehended the orders he'd been given at the time, so he'd run to save a fallen agent with a stab wound in his heart. The agent hadn't truly comprehended who he'd saved until after the hospital in Barcelona managed to stabilize his condition.

Shaked Yossef was officially part of Caesarea, but the whispers about him carried not only throughout the Mossad, but outside of it, too. Other agencies included.

Shaked always told himself that his career would probably end with him in a coffin. That reckless, inexperienced agent screwed up that plan, as well.

An hour ago, Shaked received an update from Daniel

regarding the quality of information brought in. The young agent told him about the fight scene from outside the stadium.

He succeeded after all, Shaked surmised this last week to himself. He was content.

53.

"They say lightning never strikes twice," NATO commander Robert Skin muttered to himself, about a month afterwards. "So they say."

"And maybe they're right," he added. "It strikes three times."

The NATO Commander looked at the monitors in the command station and watched as the planes reached their destination. It would be an Israeli attack only—but for the first time in history, it would be sanctioned by the United Nations, as a direct result of the Security Council.

About a month and a half ago, a Mossad agent managed to extract a massive amount of intelligence from Iran regarding their nuclear plan. The information undeniably proved that Iran was not only breaking the agreed-upon deal but was incredibly close to creating a nuclear weapon. Closer than any had imagined.

The Americans pressured, the Brits and French supported it, and even the Chinese agreed. The Russians were left without a choice, and the UN's Security Council declared war on Iran.

But that was only the transparent part of the decision. The confidential part stated that those who'd enact the attack would be Israel, assisted by the United States with its military support. The Israelis weren't the assailants merely because they'd brought in the information or because they were the ones under the most significant threat by the Iranians. No, that wasn't the reason. The Israelis had been chosen because of one simple fact: they were the only ones with a coherent plan of how to completely destroy the Iranian nuclear bomb activities.

54.

Ten more minutes.

It was according to plan. In the meantime, there was no talking. Everyone to himself. Each deep their own thoughts before the storm hit. Shaul was focused, but he still couldn't stop the rushing of his mind. He made his way to the most sophisticated war machine there was—the most expensive, too—traveling to a target in Iran. The mission was originally designed for an F-16-I, but instead, now the entire F-35 fleet of the Israeli air force was making its way to the targets in Iran, with him among them.

He would be attacking in the second wave: "The Crushers." The formidable bomb strapped to his plane's underbelly was waiting to be deployed. The first wave—"The Penetrators"—as well as the second wave—"The Crushers"—all had conventional explosives. Yet still, at the end of the attack, the Iranians would be in for a surprise.

He remembered how mid-course, when in the air force, he'd insisted on being assigned to the helicopter unit. Remembered how when he was still a boy in the Kibbutz, all everyone would talk about was how one of the Kibbutzniks, Avner, had made an impossible landing on the side of the Syrian side of Mount Hermon. He'd wanted to fly a Sikorsky CH-53, and it was only pressure from his commanders who'd insisted on him joining a fighters' division that changed his mind. He wasn't sorry for that choice. They were probably right. Simply being one of the first pilots of the F-35s, being part of this strike, and, moreover, being the youngest pilot there by at least five years, were all testaments to it.

The first blink of his mission board. The unmanned aircraft was locked in. Their laser signature lit up on the target. They would stay in position throughout the strike waves—later, too, to give an assessment of the damage wrought.

As if that wasn't sufficient, they would incorporate it in the second wave. The first wave would be going in without disturbance. The Iranians wouldn't be able to locate the unmanned aircrafts or the elusive F-35s. But it was impossible to hide the actual attack. After it, the whole world would wake up—and that made the second wave a lot more dangerous.

Another blink on his mission control. The first wave of the attack was starting. Dozens of "Penetrators" were sent to their destination.

It was starting. In three minutes, he was up. He was cruising at 40,000 feet. His thoughts made space for complete concentration. He watched the radar screen, noting that the area was starting to awaken. *Two minutes.* He started to organize himself. There wasn't much for him to do during the actual bombing. The main part would come after. *One minute.* There was no navigator with him. He was alone. He armed the automatic release mechanism and waited. The weapon system gave its alert, and the plane jolted as the bomb dropped.

The eight-tons of explosives and metal made its way downwards at increasing speed. The aerodynamics and its specialized pointed tip would ensure it would reach dozens of meters below ground before exploding. The bomb was directed by the unmanned aircraft. It would hit no more than a meter away from where one of the "Penetrators" did.

There was nothing more for him to do here. His role was complete. He made a left turn and made his way back.

A dull sound alerting that he'd been locked down by an S-300 missile sounded. He wasn't bothered about that. Three missiles were sent in his direction. Their locking system was weak. So it was when you flew F-35s. He didn't even need to deploy missile evasion tactics.

No, that wasn't the thing that he was bothered by. The real danger was enemy planes. He was still deep in Iranian territory, and his system alerted to the fact that four planes were deployed in his direction. With all due respect to the plane's radar evasion abilities, if an enemy plane was on your tail, they weren't particularly helpful.

Shaul looked at the radar. Four planes were rapidly closing the distance between them. They didn't know exactly where he was, so they weren't flying right at him, but they'd arrive soon, and then he'd be visible to the naked eye. He looked at their heat signatures. They all had their afterburners active. They didn't have a fuel issue. They were gaining height and closing the distance.

Shaul made a simple calculation and concluded that they were about to gain on him. The only option he had was to open his afterburner. It would expose him and leave him without fuel, but he had no choice.

He fired the afterburner and gained speed. His heat signature was instantly discovered, and the four planes corrected their course. He saw eight American F-18s in front of him. Unlike the Iranians, he showed up on the Americans' radar. A little further and they would fall into action. The four Iranian planes kept closing in, but slower now. On the other side, the Americans kept closing the distance, too, though at a much faster pace. He was out of Iranian territory, and was now over the Persian Gulf.

The Americans hadn't yet fired, despite them being close. He was probably still too conspicuous and they were worried about hitting him. In ten seconds they would pass him and break a combined speed of more than 4 Mach.

Shaul saw the Iranians turn back on his radar screen, and right then the F-18s shot past him at a dizzying speed.

He had very little fuel left. He could see on the radar the refueling aircraft coming his way. They must have seen his maneuver and shortened the distance between them.

354 | Handle with Force

55.

Erwin finished deploying his last F-18. He moved aside and smiled, pleased with himself. He had a few minutes until the first planes would arrive and then subsequently land. He looked left at the destroyer vessel floating about half a mile away from them. A little close, he thought to himself. He took the few steps to the edge of the runway and looked down at the sea below.

The waters at the Persian Gulf were quiet and relatively clear. Suddenly, he saw a gray whale three hundred yards from the aircraft carrier he stood on. *Wow. That's really, really close.* The whale almost broke water, then Erwin saw a flash, and a rocket was shot from the whale and out of the water. There was an explosion in the back, then a pillar of fire, and the rocket made its fast ascent skyward.

More rockets followed, one after the other. Erwin watched them for a few more seconds, then went back to his position. They called that "whale" *Dolphin*.[9]

---

9   This Israeli submarine model is called "Dolphin."

56.

Robert Skin saw the "Shalhevet" rocket launch from the submarine. *The third stage.* He found the Israelis' plan ingenious. Devious and contemptible but ingenious.

After the Americans hadn't agreed to supply Israel with GBU-57 bunker penetrating bombs, and after the lessons learned from the Lebanon War in 2006, the Israelis developed a different approach: a sequence of bombs. The first two bombs were almost identical. They both weighed 7.8 tons, had a 2.5 ton pointed, reinforced steel tip, and had approximately 5 tons of especially powerful explosives in them. They were both laser-guided, and were deployed from 40,000 feet.

The first was called "The Penetrator." Its explosives were orchestrated as a hollow-shaped charge bomb. Meaning that the explosives were designed in a concave arrangement that created an explosion inwards, similar to the rockets designed to penetrate tanks. It penetrated about fifty meters into the ground and exploded in the depths. The damage to its surroundings was negligible, but its penetration course became a fine film.

The second was called "The Crusher." It hits the ground at almost the exact same spot, its build adjusted so it would follow "The Penetrator's" penetration path into the ground. It can go deeper than one hundred meters before exploding. Its explosion was like an earthquake, and the damage done spread to more than 3 kilometers, which is massive. More devastating than the GBU-43/B, or the MOAB, the Americans' Doom's Day bomb.

But that wasn't the main part. That had been right when it came to Lebanon, and it had been in use when destroying the Syrian reactor in Deir a-Zor. For the Iranians, the Israelis prepared something a little different. One whispered about in secret only to a few in the upper echelons of the US government.

The main part was the third stage—the Shalhevet rockets fired from the Dolphin submarine. Those rockets had three key characteristics: the first of which was that they held tactical nuclear explosives of the smallest scale possible to still create a nuclear explosion. The second characteristic was a pointed, hardened tip, whose explosive head floated in a special gel that allowed it to receive severe impact and still detonate the nuclear explosion with the right timing sequence. The third was the designed nuclear bomb—it too was shaped in the form of a hollow charge.

The rocket would hit in the exact same spot as "The Penetrator." It penetrates almost 150 meters underground before the explosion occurs. The explosion creates a nuclear jet aimed deep underground. Most of the explosion gets sucked in. The damage to the environment is severe but contained. So, it made it possible to deploy a nuclear bomb five kilometers from a populated area without it being hit. Still, everything within a three-kilometer radius, especially everything underground, wasn't only destroyed, but suffered radioactive contamination to the point where it was impossible to rebuild.

The only residual damage was the possible contamination of groundwater or the danger of creating a new volcano—as occurred in the experiment the Israelis did in the unpopulated island I-752 in the Pacific ocean.

When the Americans asked the Israelis if they were serious, and if they didn't have a problem with being the aggressors in unconventional warfare, the Israelis merely replied that their warhead explosives *were* conventional and that they were planning on attacking Iranian nuclear sites. If the consequences of that brought on a nuclear reaction, that was highly unfortunate, but not Israel's responsibility or initiative.

Robert watched the Shalhevet missiles hit—each in the precise spot, each occurring exactly according to plan. And since the information Israel extracted from Iran included all nuclear plants, Robert Skin was watching nothing less than the end of the Iranian nuclear project. Nothing was left.

57.

Shaul connected to the fueling aircraft a mere minute before his fuel was out. As he restocked, he watched the American armada floating far below in the Persian Gulf. The yellow dots, he knew, were Shalhevet missiles.

A few minutes later, Shaul saw that all targets were destroyed. A one hundred percent success rate. One pilot who'd had to eject himself in the Gulf waters was saved by the British, and two American pilots didn't come back. All in all, however, it was a massive success.

With the refueling complete, Shaul disconnected from the line.

There were more air-fights going on behind him. But this wasn't his fight any longer.

Shaul pointed his plane westward and started making his way home, back to Israel.

URI YAHALOM | 359

58.

At the same time, thousands of kilometers away, a girl watched the man sleeping beside her with hooded eyes. Her man. She leaned toward him, careful not to touch his abdomen, and brought her face close to his so she could feel the heat of his breath on her cheek. She paused, allowing the magic of the moment to fully resonate and settle. She shifted a little and pressed her lips to her beloved's.

59.

Civil defense sirens were sounded throughout Israel.

To read more of Uri Yahalom's stories,
please subscribe to Uri's Short Stories at:

https://uriyahalom.substack.com

Printed in Great Britain
by Amazon